HIDDEN VIEW

T0159426

# Hidden View

*a novel*

Brett Ann Stanciu

GREEN WRITERS PRESS *Brattleboro, Vermont*

Printed in the United States

10 9 8 7 6 5 4 3 2 1

The author gratefully acknowledges permission to quote lines from the following poems:
"One Heart," by Franz Wright in *Walking to Martha's Vineyard*, published by Penguin Random House.
"Wintering" by Sylvia Plath in *Ariel*, published by HarperCollins.
"February: Thinking of Flowers" and "Finding a Gray Hair" by Jane Kenyon in *Collected Poems*, published by Graywolf Press.
"The Pasture" by Robert Frost in *The Poetry of Robert Frost: the Collected Poems, Complete and Unabridged*, published by Henry Holt and Company.

Green Writers Press is a Vermont-based publisher whose mission is to spread a message of hope and renewal through the words and images we publish. Throughout we will adhere to our commitment to preserving and protecting the natural resources of the earth. To that end, a percentage of our proceeds will be donated to environmental activist groups. Green Writers Press gratefully acknowledges support from individual donors, friends, and readers to help support the environment and our publishing initiative.

*Giving Voice to Writers & Artists Who Will Make the World a Better Place*
Green Writers Press | Brattleboro, Vermont
www.greenwriterspress.com

ISBN: 978-0-9961357-0-2

Printed on paper with pulp that comes from FSC-certified forests, managed forests that guarantee responsible environmental, social, and economic practices by Lightning Source. All wood product components used in black & white, standard color, or select color paperback books, utilizing either cream or white bookblock paper, that are manufactured in the LaVergne, Tennessee Production Center are Sustainable Forestry Initiative® (SFI®) Certified Sourcing.

*This book is for my father.*

*"Every human being has been brought into the world according to the will of God. And God created us in such a way that every human being can either save his own soul or destroy it."*

—Tolstoy, *Confession*

# Part One

## CHAPTER 1

THE DAY my husband Hal burned his foot began promisingly enough, late winter with sunlight brilliant over the fields, that particular Vermont glint of light at once harsh on eyes accustomed to winter's dark, and unspeakably beautiful. Last night's new-fallen snowflakes scattered over a gnarled, icy crust winked minutely. Baby on my back, I followed the trodden path from the house, the day gloriously warming and alive, chickadees and sparrows calling to each other, sunlight cart-wheeling over the sparkling snow, Tansy babbling her echolalia part in this wide chorus. At the barn, Hal's cowshit smeared boot prints joined the path, the raised treads filthy bars cutting through the snow where mud bled up, sullying the snow.

Tansy jerked my braid. Above me on the hill, the old farmhouse's crumbling paint held a tainted hue against new snow. In that slant of light, a gibbous moon hung palely reflected in the bedroom's single window. Even from here, I saw I had left the sash slightly lifted, the storm pushed out at the bottom from the latch I had begged Hal to loosen. He wouldn't be pleased to see I was carelessly releasing the house's heat, although I had merely wanted to sweep fresh air through our cloistered domesticity.

"Fern!" Hal called within the sugarhouse. Steam ebbed from the cupola, trickling between the closed doors' slats, the day's boiling work just begun.

"Coming, coming," I murmured. Tansy bleated her mingle of laughter and uncertainty. At the field's lower edge crouched a snowshoe hare, its ears flickering apprehensively, whiskered nose up and sniffing the breeze. I nodded once and whispered to Tansy, "Yes, yes," and then the hare, a large one with oversized back feet, dashed across the field's center, scurrying for its life, and disappeared down the enormous rock pile, hand-created over generations from the harrowed field each spring.

My husband shouted, "Are you coming or what? Jesus, what are you doing? I need your help!"

"Rabbit," I whispered, "bunny."

Tansy's mittened hand, knitted red yarn, caressed my neck.

I hurried down the path. Hal's sloppy prints had widened, as if trying to catch each other, obliterating the clean snow. In the dazzling light, I squinted to see if I could distinguish my prints among his greater ones. My lesser marks hadn't pierced the crust; nor had I tracked manure from the barn and ground it into the earth.

Tansy's eyes yet swept that mound of rocks, gray-black glacial debris with patches of snow. Likely, she had been watching the wild creature in her own quiet way before she jostled my attention.

My lungs pulled deeply at the farm's clear air, as if I

could not get enough. All around me was the dazzling radiance of this hillside, these two hundred acres of pure potential of a rundown farm Hal had inherited from his father. After my narrow childhood as a single child, in my very early twenties I found myself suddenly married and unexpectedly a mother, as alive and quick as the grosbeaks nesting in the farm's two dying maple trees flanking the old house. I believed, richly full as I was of breastmilk, with a gorgeously plump and giggling baby, a marriage, and land around us, *land* deeded to us, that the two of us could make of the world what we desired.

As we approached, steam billowed from the opened cupola doors, enormous clouds of moisture rolling up above the forest into the sky. The firebox's door clanged shut. "Fern! Jesus, I can't do this all by myself!" Hal's voice shattered at the end, like a drinking glass hurled in rage against a wall. I ran through the door and stepped right into work, thrusting a pail and wool filter beneath the spigot and filling the four-gallon bucket with blisteringly hot syrup.

Filtering sweetly steaming syrup into buckets, I chattered over my shoulder, "Dear darling baby girl, what a beautiful day, are you looking for the robin redbreast's return?" then poured those buckets into a barrel. Baby Tansy's eyes, more oval than round, darted like squirrels, flashing and nimble. As the day moved along, baby slept for a bit with her cheek on my shoulder, drooling.

Built in a hollow at the bottom of the farm fields, the sugarhouse, board and batten with battens never nailed on, reigned as an entity unto itself. The building's interior was dominated by the fourteen-foot long arch, its tarnished silver syrup pans higher than my forehead. Hal's father had built the sugarhouse years ago, and by now it was crammed higher than our heads with equipment, barrels, stacked firewood, farm odds and ends. The space was unlike any I had known before. When we boiled, the arch hummed with roiling syrup, clouds of steam winding silently through every bit of that sugarhouse, sweet and wild simultaneously. The year before we had managed to make a good amount of maple syrup. Cash crop.

Hal shouted behind me. The air cloudy with steam and drifting ash, I didn't know at first what he was screaming about or even where he might be. I hurried around the tall arch. He was in the far corner against barrels stacked three high, shaking his foot, his mouth wide open. "Get it off! Get it off!" I knelt with the baby howling lustily in my ear. The laces were glued fast with syrup. I ran around the arch, his screams following me, grabbed a knife from the windowsill, and then returned, bent, and cut the laces. I pulled off his boot, and he hobbled across the cracked cement floor, flung open the door, and thrust his foot in the snow.

My husband glared at me, his eyes outraged, unfamiliar. The syrup boiled over, hit the metal arch with a splattering hiss, and instantly suffused the sugarhouse with coiled smoke and the acrid smell of burnt sugar. Through the hiss and clouded air, I was vaguely aware of Hal yelling. I flooded the pans with sap, but it was no use. The syrup had gotten the upper hand and was determined to escape the pans and scorch. The pans blackened; our day filled with charred carbon and dark smoke. The baby cried and cried, hurting my ears. Missing that one boot, Hal limped around in his wet sock with a twisted mouth. "The day's fucked," he said.

I opened the thermos and poured coffee. My hand trembled and spilled coffee on my jeans. Tiny fingers wormed into my ear.

☾

The next morning, both of us milked. Generally, Hal did the milking alone, but with his upper foot injured and bandaged, the laces split wide on the over-stretched wool sock, I slipped the baby in the backpack, bow-tied her hat under her chin, and walked to the barn, too. A cold front had settled in during the night, and for that I was grateful, as the sap could not run that day. The night before, I had soaked the burned pans with sap and baking soda. After milking and breakfast, my husband limped his way down the icy path to the sugarhouse while I finished the dishes and washed the sheets on Tansy's crib, pee-soaked where her diaper had leaked through in the night. She lay on a folded quilt on the living room floor, chewing a doll's plastic head and babbling to herself. Her little song warbled *aw-rah, aw-rah,* a minute soloist in a footed onesie. Sweeping the kitchen floor, I glanced out the window at snow lightly drifting like decorations on a greeting card. In his black coat and hat, Hal painstakingly pushed his way up the path, stepping gingerly on his burned foot as he used no crutch, grimacing, his face locked in an angry sneer. I didn't linger on his face; even limping, he was a mighty man, a black-clothed figure against the stillness of those white fields and gray and white dappled sky. His wide shoulders, whose strength I knew under my hands, dipped and rose in the black padded canvas coat with his uneven walk.

My husband's anger was new for me, or perhaps newly

emerging from the murkier recesses of our marriage. Our beginning had seemed like an endless perennial garden. Behind the daffodils I found tulips, then gladiolas sprinkled with baby's breath, perfect lilies of the valley, hip-high ferns no wider than my palm. I had never had a boyfriend before, and certainly never wound my body through a man's, our skin slicking sweatily together. My tongue met his; I felt myself suffused not just with my own stale familiar scent but with the spiciness of his breath and the reassuring way my hand folded into the bent crook of his elbow, his body clasping mine. He located a small place on the back of my thigh that could make me scream with joy. Now, my fingers brushed over spiders that might be poisonous, grazed winged insects that could bite.

The baby chirped. I lifted the reassuring fullness of her weight, her breath fragrant with unsoured breast-milk, and circled the kitchen, nuzzling her miniature ear, nibbling her pink earlobe.

Hal hoisted himself up the back steps, and with a wind, the kitchen door banged shut behind him. He sat down in his snow-melting boots and tugged free his leather work gloves, dirt and grease stained, and tossed them on table. "I'll never get those pans clean."

"They could soak another day. The sap's not going to run anytime soon." I rubbed the baby against my husband's upper arm, murmuring sweet syllables of affection, kissing his cold curls.

With his fist, he rubbed his nose brusquely. "Jesus, I've got soot in my nose." He snorted an exhale, a rumble of mucus and noise, and I pulled the baby away. "The wind feels like the weather's going to change on a dime.

It's got that scent of coming heat in it. Pour me some of that coffee, will you? This damn foot's a hindrance."

I handed him a full cup and sat down with the baby in my lap. "I'll scrub the pans, too. I'm sure we can get them clean."

"With that baby on your back? How long you think you could do that?"

I whispered against her neck, "You're a good baby, a sweet one, aren't you?"

"We need that syrup, Fern. There's no ifs or buts about it. We need every syrup dollar to keep us going." He swallowed coffee. "Anything we boil in those pans is going to taste burnt. You have any idea how much less we're going to get for crappy, burned syrup? There's no way now this year I can go find some other pans." He looked out the window. I noticed his chest heaving, rising and falling jerkily with emotion beneath his plaid shirt. "What a fucking waste of a season."

"It won't be. I know we can clean those pans." I leaned forward a little to say something else, but the baby grabbed my arm and bit, pulling my attention.

Hal jammed his hat on his head and stood up. "You know, I'd earmarked that money for the bank."

Tansy gnawed my shirt, wetting over my breastbone. Gently, I tried to pry her jaws with my pinkie.

"I don't mean savings, Fern. I mean mortgage. We owe for the past two months, and I thought we could pay a few ahead. That's what I told them down there, when I couldn't pay it. That the syrup would float us out."

Baby's miniature plump lips pressed against my pinkie tip. "Why are we behind anyway?"

"It's not hard to figure out." He wobbled, awkward

on his foot, and squinted his right eye at me. "The milk checks are shit."

I said, "It's going to work out."

He gazed around the tight kitchen, over the grimy cabinets, the old maple floorboards worn gray and lusterless in curves. "Maybe." He opened the door, and the wind banged it against the house as he limped out.

☾

We had to remedy the pans. Unheated, the sugarhouse was cold and drafty. The floor had been poured decades ago, and, done incorrectly, the cement heaved in slabs, with cracks deeper than the length of my hand. As the spring season progressed, the slabs shifted like tectonic plates, so we often tripped or stumbled over their changing geography. While I tried to keep the old farmhouse marginally passable, the sugarhouse was irredeemably filthy. Rodents and squirrels lived in the bark-filled woodshed. Robins nested above the windows, and swallows every year re-mudded their home along the stack. Spiders claimed the few windows, and everything was smeared with a dried crust of syrup, dust and ash, crumbled leaves blown in through chinks in the walls. I swept out a square between syrup drums, spread it with blankets from the attic, and tried to leave the bundled baby there while I attacked the pans. She cried, so young yet she couldn't crawl or stand. Crouched on my knees, jacket sleeves shoved above my elbows, I scrubbed mightily. All along the bottoms of the two three-foot-long front pans, the maple sugar had caramelized into a coating that could have withstood a decade out in the Vermont elements.

Hal chucked his steel wool at the wall. "This fucking shit. These goddamn pans will never get clean. It's stupid to boil like this. It's stupid to cobble everything together. Everything on this farm is just held together with another piece of broken shit. What am I doing here anyway? Just repeating my dad's goddamn life. This is exactly the broke-dick way he ran this farm, cobbling every fucking thing together." He lurched to his feet and dragged his wounded foot to the open woodshed door. There, over the baby's escalating *aw-aw-aw*, he tipped back his head and shouted, "I hate this shit!"

I wiped my hands on my jeans and pressed my daughter against my shoulder. When I turned around, he was gone.

☾

Out of desperation, I chipped at some of that black with a chisel, fearful I might puncture the pans, and yet feeling that pressure of time. I spent three days, off and on, at those pans. The weather had been cold in the beginning, deep down in the twenties, lower at night, rising nowhere near freezing during the day. But each of those days was a little warmer, a tad less wintry, and I could feel the sap run returning. To make syrup, we would need the pans. Hal came and went in those days, muttering about the pans, limping with a furious jerk. On the third day, we hooked the pans together on the arch, the temperature shot up un-forecast to the fifties, and sap poured in.

Very early the next morning, in the dark that had barely begun to lessen, I made oatmeal and coffee. Hal ate quickly, milked, and limped down to the sugarhouse. Not long after, I followed, the baby bundled in her snowsuit on my back. Later in the morning, when I carried in firewood from the open-sided woodshed, I realized sun and warmth had swept into the day. Redwing blackbirds trilled in a clump of cedars behind the woodshed, so beautiful in song I fancied I could hold their melody in the cupped palm of my hand: a sunbeam in November or a Johnny-Jump-Up uprooted from beneath curled dead leaves in the December garden.

With the baby on my back, I poured bucket after cumbersome bucket of syrup down the big funnel into barrels. All day and night, we worked as hard as we could, the gravity-fed sap dumping regularly with a loud *splash* from the release into the holding tank.

Late that night, on my tired walk from the sugarhouse up the bent path, icy snow crunching under my boot treads, I tipped my head back at the moon, a gibbous, heading-full-moonness glowing like a spill of fresh cream in the dark sky. Tansy yanked my braid. Laughing, I was happy with the freshly made syrup accumulating in barrels—liquid Vermont gold—and the radiance around me, over the sprawling fields of white brilliant with moonlight on snow. Hal had kissed me firmly on the lips before I left the sugarhouse, his *good work!* lingering melodiously in my ears, an erasure of the past few days' misery: a mere hitch, perhaps, that had been. As I ascended the hill, the cows in their old barn were quiet for the night. A little higher up the hill, the porch light I had left on burned beside the kitchen door. Baby giggled on my back, her squeaking of happy sounds. Inside, I knew I would stir the woodstove's coals and stoke the fire, nestle on the couch, worn but satisfied with work, my little daughter in my arms. Already, walking up the hill, I could anticipate my hands caressing her round legs and arms; how her bare feet felt in my hands, squirming and warm, her skin emanating that baby aroma. Her plump ruby lips would take my crimson nipples, one by one, her throat gustily swallowing milk, until her eyelids gave relievedly into sleep, her lashes long and curled at the tips, dark against her pale skin. Those moonlit nights exuded sheer loveliness. My childhood village home had banished the night's mystery and the intensity of moonlight with amber streetlamps, neighbors' houses, television lights, the town itself. In these very earliest of spring nights, as I walked away from the sugarhouse, I listened to my boots trod through the diminishing snow while barred owls called in a stand of white pine, claiming their territory.

That night, after I had laid sleeping Tansy in her teddy bear pajama suit in her crib, covered her and kissed her curled fists goodnight, I slipped into our bed and joined Hal. Moonlight lay in our room like spilled water. We reached for each other with our hands and lips. Wood smoke wreathed our hair. In the midst of movement, my foot knocked his injury. He shouted loudly, "Watch out, girl! Watch out!" He had never called me girl before, although I was nine years younger than him.

Startled, I huddled on my side of the bed. "All right," I murmured, "all right." Where I lay, legs curled, I saw the moon hung in the bedroom window, a chipped teardrop, pale white, a grub unearthed, a piece severed off, by a shovel's blade. Lady Moon, as a child I had secretly named her, gazing at her mysterious, ever-changing orb on my knees from my bedroom window, sailing so incomprehensibly distant through that expanse of night sky. Lovely Lady Moon. When my husband's breath wound into the ease of sleep, I heaved myself up and she disappeared from view. I searched for the stars, but clouds had crept in, and any starlight was obscured by darkness.

## CHAPTER 2

MY SEEDLINGS sprouted on the windowsills, and plant-by-plant, I nestled their thread-like roots in the garden. With the tractor, Hal tilled a wider patch for the garden, and I planted more onions, beets, carrots, broccoli, cauliflower, a lengthy row of kale, and two buckets of seed potatoes. Row after row I planted, the baby cooing from a folded blanket on the grass, her moving fingers spread before her face, weaving her own baby tales. The scent of the warming, turned-over earth rose, desirable as my baby's skin, a richness like nothing else I had experienced. Overhead domed an azure sky. The craven maple tree shook its tender furls of leaves like countless little fluttering fingers. All along the driveway, a great bank of lilacs planted ages ago bloomed. For most of the year, we hardly glanced at those tree-sized bushes, either leafy green or winter's bare sticks, but the spring was effusive with their ivory and lavender. At dawn, we woke with their scent leaching over open windowsills. All around the house the slightest breeze lifted and carried that heavenly perfume. It was the sweeter for being so brief.

That was my second spring on the farm. Hal had grown up on Hidden View Farm with a brother I hadn't met. His mother had died when he was a boy, and his father suffered a brain aneurysm the summer I met Hal, when I was interning at Growing Seed Farm where Hal was the crew leader. After the aneurysm, Hal resigned and went back to his dad's dairy farm, but the two farms were not far apart, and he often visited me. At the summer's very end, when I was about to return to the state university, Hal called one night with the news his father had died. I offered to attend the funeral, but he said there wouldn't be one. Then he said the farm was his, now—*mine,* he said, *mine*—and asked if I would marry him. He asked me this over the phone line, nothing tangible to me but his words in my ear and the images I had in my head of how our lives might mesh together, on what I envisioned as the grassy pastures of the farm.

I said yes.

My mother, a widow, reacted angrily. She wanted me, her only child, to stay in college. You might need this degree, she told me, you might need a way out. But I loved Hal. I wanted to begin our life together. I did not believe I needed a way out. I saw our marriage as a way in. My mother had always cautioned me to be careful. Watch out! Look sharp! She was fearful of so many things: speeding ambulances, unwashed hands, a man walking down a street with a German shepherd. To her, the world was a landscape fraught with perils and unforeseen dangers, but I longed to push beyond the confines of her well-kept boxy house, sleep on the dewy grass at night, thrust my hands among the soil's stones and centipedes and ant eggs. I wanted to fill my own yearning soul with rainy sky and roaming wildlife. As if we had entered a half-coma of our own, my father's death had silenced our house. A great flat stone had shoved over our breathing hole. I saw a way out for myself, an elbowing away of this confinement, a channel to life, and I seized it.

We were married in Montpelier's City Hall, and I brought my few things to the farm in September. The millennium was about to turn over, and, to me, the time seemed right to sink my future into a small farm. The farmhouse, built nearly two hundred years ago, wasn't much more than the kitchen and bath and living room downstairs, two bedrooms at the top of the narrow stairs, and the closet-like room with Tansy's crib and narrow bureau. No female had lived in this house for almost two decades. Hal's mother had died when he was a child, and his father never remarried. A younger brother, Lucien, moved out of state. To my way of thinking, it appeared Hidden View was all ours, woven, perhaps, with the absence of these vanished people, but ours, nonetheless. The appeal of putting our hands and backs to work as hard as we could endure was overwhelming. Tansy was a seed we had not expected to sow, but the baby became part of what we were doing. We simply began.

The first spring I had been in the early months of pregnancy, my belly a burlap sack of rocks rolling around miserably, a constant tumble. This second spring, my baby's eyes reflected the world, staring up at the shifting weather in the sky and the leaves jingling overhead, studying a slender bit of grass her miniature fingers turned around before delicately placing the green blade on her tongue. Along the steps leading into the kitchen, I dug for the better part of two days in the old herb garden, prolific with wildflowers and weeds. I wheel-barrowed loads of rotted manure, forking them into the soil. By fat handfuls, I separated weeds, trying to determine what was edible and what was not. I knew little; my parents had dutifully put in a few tomato and marigold plants by the front porch each year, and occasionally separated some lilies in an overgrown bed. That was all. These weeds and herbs mystified me. What had thrived before was largely lost to me. Pulled greens wilted and curled in my earth-stained hands. I believed I myself had been turned over living on Hidden View Farm, like spadefuls of raw dirt unearthed in a garden. At the library, I checked out gardening and wildflower books, and while I nursed Tansy I read with a book propped in one hand, whispering *purslane, lavender, wormwood, sage.*

Those spring days with the earth rapidly greening, the songbirds at their mating and nesting work even before Hal and I were up, the world at Hidden View seemed almost unbearably alive. I hated to leave the farm in those days. I wanted to garden as much as I could, nurse my baby under the blooming lilacs, listen to tree frogs peeping in the nights while lying beside my husband. During the days, our work was instinctively split: Hal to the barn and the fields, I at the house and the garden and always with the child. Meals and nights, we joined. After the dinner dishes were washed, I often put Tansy on my back and walked down to the barn as Hal finished the evening milking. The baby and I waved *night-night* to the cows, and then the three of us strolled down the road.

Hidden View lay at the end of a dirt road, an old hill

farm that had managed to hang on, despite just about every odd against it, when most other hill farms had long since yielded their fields back to forest, concealing their stone walls and rusting strands of barbed wire. We walked along the steep road, where the sugarbush was to our left, woody acres of it spreading down the hill to the sugarhouse. Up to our right, the mountain rose steeply, with more mixed hardwoods Hal planned to string with blue plastic sapline. As we kept walking, the sugarbush ended at the hayfields Hal cut three times a year. These fields were not part of Hidden View's holdings. Bill and Mary Atkins, who lived in a little square house a quarter mile down the road from us—our only neighbors—had farmed here until he sold the cows and his one horse a few years back. "I got old," he told me. They seemed very old, both bent at their shoulders, wrinkled and wizened, her hands trembling through her forearms with palsy. Some evenings we walked down to their house and sat in their living room for a bit, visiting. Mary said her hands were too unreliable to hold the baby, but her eyes in those brief visits lay only on Tansy, on the baby's skin that was milky white and yet also glowing, with an internal sheen like candlelight through pumpkin skin.

Other evenings, Hal and I simply walked to the hayfields' edge and paused, admiring the sprawl of sky as the sun drew down for the night to the west, a burning disk as the summer's humidity settled in. But whether we went down to Atkins' or not, on our return we always stopped at the place in the dirt road where the steep road leveled out and the road cut a bend, and the farmhouse and Hidden View's fields and the weathered barn were abruptly visible. Hal taught me the names of the mountains in the distant ridge. From there, he pointed out where his grandfather's sugarhouse had been, in a fold of valley, before it burned, and his father rebuilt the sugarhouse, not so deep down in the woods. With his arm spread, he pointed out where he intended to expand the saplines, and pontificated on what sugaring might do for Hidden View. "There's nothing in milk. The future's not there."

I asked, "What are you saying? Where's the future for this farm?"

His black beard was thickening, untended, curling up over his cheeks toward his eyes. In the dusk, his eyes were particularly dark, gleaming circles into deeper recesses. "Fern, you know what the farm is, now. You see the way my father ran it into the ground."

I nodded. "Yes, but . . . It's a hill farm, Hal. Hidden View's never going to be a lush Midwestern farm. It's not meant to be that way. Geography works against that vision."

He was nodding, too, but his eyes were no longer on mine, roaming instead over the fields and woods merging into the night. "That doesn't mean this farm can't thrive. The sugarhouse down there." His arm stretched out, pointing. "That place is held together with duct tape and rusting clamps. This whole damn farm is that way, cobbled together. That's how my father was. That's who he was. A broken down, busted up old man, who ran this farm into the ground as hard as he could. Can we do better? You bet we can." He laced his fingers through mine, joining our fists. "Isn't that why you came? For the farm?"

The night was coming quickly around us, as it did

in the summer. I squeezed his hand, too, tightly, the baby twirling my hair in her fingers. Suddenly, I laughed aloud for nothing but the pure joy of laughing: of being a young mother and woman, in love with her husband, a farm spread out around us with a thousand different potentials.

He bent toward me and kissed my lips, his mouth laced with coffee. "Ah," he whispered. Then he drew back and with his free hand waved grandiosely. "Look."

The dusk was still thin enough that I could see. My eyes went to my garden, where the beds were fattening with leafing beets and carrots. In the warm weather, the fields sprouted green corn and alfalfa. A bat swooped over the garden's center, a dark darting blur, feeding, and then vanished. Tree frogs chorused, alive. I found myself nodding, *yes, yes*, my daughter's minute hand tugging at my shirt collar.

Perhaps that *yes* was simply the song that carried me along through those early days of our marriage. All around me I saw nothing but possibility, never a hand held up to *stop, stop*. That night, I nursed Tansy and laid her to sleep in the crib, then Hal and I undressed in our moonlit bedroom and lay on top of the sheets, the air not yet cooling from the day. He was talking about saplines again, and maple, and goodbye to milk, and I was laughing and not listening, and we were all hands and skin and limbs. But that night, it was different. We had been together for nearly two years by then, but that night the sex rippled through me like green bursts of electricity, giant waves that turned me inside out, and then flowed back through again, like unstoppable water rushing over a mountain's rocky stream. Limb twined through limb, we went to that place devoid of language, of sound or sense, consumed as we were by the electricity roaring through our veins.

Afterwards, I lay sprawled on my back, a sweaty ankle over Hal's slick thigh, my heart pounding, my blood yammering through my head and behind my eyes like a crazed storm. Gradually, I stilled under the moonlight puddling in the room. "Hal," I whispered, light as the lift of a fledging robin's wing, "tell me we'll be this way when we're old and wrinkled. That we'll still have . . . *this* between us."

Disarranged as we were in the bed, with only that singular place of contact, I couldn't see Hal's face, no shimmer of teeth or eyes in the dark, and when he didn't answer, I guessed he slept, and my words had not woken him. I closed my eyes, too, falling into the heaviness of my body, but eventually his words washed to me. "We'll only have maple then. No cows."

I murmured a laugh deep in my throat, still feeling as fine as I could. "But we'll have us, right?"

We lay so still I heard the breath whoosh from his body, a gush of life, and I lay waiting for the suck of air back into his lungs, but that pull of air didn't come, and at first I thought my own coursing blood, my body's throbbing thirst for oxygen, dampened his sound, swallowing up his breath in my beating sex; but as my body's needs dwindled, I realized he held himself rigid as iron beneath my ankle. I sat up and laid my hand on him in the dark. I touched his abdomen, where his muscles were bound hard as chainmail. "Hal?" I whispered.

Quicksilver, he was out of bed and at the window where he was a dark silhouette, his wide shoulders dominating his body and the curl-softened outline of his head. Leaning forward, I spread my hand on the warm and sweat-dampened sheet. “Hal, come back to bed.”

“You know what?” He spoke so quietly I had to rise on my knees and bend even further toward him to catch his low words. “My dad and Ma had this room. I took this room when I moved back here. After Dad died. After I'd asked you to come. Where are they now? Dad's gone, thank Jesus, and Ma, too. Forever ago.” He didn't turn to look at me, and I pictured his words floating from his mouth, breaking down into mere molecules and escaping through the screen's mesh into the summer night air. “I'm not going to promise you, ever, something I can't give you, Fern.”

“I'm not asking for that. I'm not asking for a promise.” I tried to ripple a laugh, tried to make my words into a murmuring chuckle, but instead I choked on a cough, as if dust had caught in my throat. “Hal, just be with me. Come on now. Come back to bed.”

His head tipped down so I couldn't see his face, he moved away from the window and lay on the bed again. A rogue breeze blew in, lifting the curtains high before dropping them abruptly and moving on. Hal pulled me down to him, his words trickling into my hair. “It's land,” he murmured, “land that endures.”

Our hands rubbed over the other's back. We must have yielded to exhaustion, given up to pure tiredness, and slept.

☾

Late the next morning, Tansy gnawed a wooden clothespin on my back while I hung laundry on the line strung from the back porch. I hung our bed sheets, pale blue with pink roses embroidered along the top hem. I held the damp cotton to my face, inhaling laundry soap, brushing those slender threads against my lips. I had found these sheets on a lower shelf in the hall closet, unused for years. What female hands had worked this colored thread so painstakingly? A twisting green vine connected the roses and their diminutive petals delicately, a somewhat uneven curve between blooms.

*Awww!* Teething, Tansy's drool dripped on my shoulder, skin bared around my tank top. Stretching steeply down below me, Hidden View's farm fields were greening in the spring warmth and wet, at an incline most Vermont farmers would decline to till. Below and all around was the forest, pushing from brown to pale green. Baby and I watched Hal walk the bent path from sugarhouse to barn to farmhouse. When he saw us, he waved, striding quickly in his dark green work shirt and pants. As he came nearer, I particularly admired his open hands swinging by his sides: broad palms and long clever fingers. His mid-finger knuckles were what I loved most, reassuringly wide enough to circle my own fingers around. I lifted my hand and waved back. Right then, with my arm crooked over my head, fingers spread wide in the sunny spring day, I had an abrupt realization that I had the pieces of the life I'd always wanted: myself a young woman, a cherry-cheeked baby on my back, my strong husband coming up the path to us, and all around the farm fields, the two immense maples before the old house, my garden with all its mysteries and joys, the barn and sugarhouse, all strung together with the rutted path, in varying months icy or mucky or dusty dry. *I'm going out to fetch the little calf /That's standing by the mother. It's so young, /It totters when she licks it with her tongue./ I shan't be gone long—You come too.* He stopped abruptly, knelt on one knee, and plucked something from the young weeds along the path. He finished the few steps to me, that thing cupped in his hand, then kissed the top of my head and unfurled his fingers.

The tiniest flower imaginable lay in the center of his hand: four-petaled, with a gold sunshiny middle, its petals at their center white, bleeding into a violet blue. A flower so tiny it might have been hardly anything at all. We stood there admiring the blossom. I asked its name.

"A bluet."

In the house, he filled a blue jam jar I never used with water, laid the flower to float, and set it in the table's center.

## CHAPTER 3

In June, when the black flies were at their biting worst, I woke one morning with an upset stomach, and was sick before breakfast. Hal appeared in the bathroom doorway while I huddled on the floor, leaning against the wall. "What is it?" he asked.

"Some bug. Or something bad I ate."

I spent the day on the couch, nursing Tansy and trying to sleep. Hal had fixed his own breakfast and hurried out the door. He didn't appear until late in the afternoon, when the sun filled the living room. I sprawled on the couch, sweaty in just my t-shirt and underwear, Tansy tucked between me and the back of the couch. I heard him moving around the kitchen and called, "Can I have some water?"

He brought me a glass. "You feeling any better?"

I pushed myself sitting to sip the water. "Sure."

He disappeared into the kitchen and returned with a jam jar of bourbon, then pulled up a chair beside me, and sat down.

Hal drank. I knew he drank in the barn. I could smell it on him sometimes when he came up from the evening milking. I smelled it especially in sugaring season. My parents hadn't drunk, and I didn't know much about it.

We spoke a little about rain clouds that had blown over that day and hadn't shed any water on the dry cornfields, and Hal offered to water my garden transplants that evening when the sun began to cool. I sipped the water. I wore only underwear and an old plaid shirt, unbuttoned as I had been nursing the baby. Still talking about the stream through the hayfield and how low it was, Hal reached out and rubbed my middle. His hand was heavy and warm, and I leaned back, closing my eyes, listening to my husband talk. I relaxed into the warm afternoon, my exhaustion, and the comfort of his kneading hand. When my eyes fluttered open, I saw my milk swollen breasts with nipples poking out, sunlight catching in the hairs around my aureole, and my belly rounded with the softness remaining from pregnancy. My baby slept, her lips parted so briefly I couldn't see the tiny shining tooth recently erupted. In my vague tiredness, I marveled at how I could lie so exposed, all skin and sick and slackness.

With the water, my stomach caterwauled, a yowl as though coming to a life of its own, a distinctly unfeminine sound.

Hal laughed. "Here I'd been looking at you, wondering if you were trying to pull one over on me. If you had another baby in that belly of yours."

Again, my stomach lurched noisily. "Not yet."

"What do you mean, not yet?" He swallowed the

bourbon down. "We don't need another baby. We have one."

"But we'll want another."

Hal shook his head. "We didn't intend for this one to come. Look, we have a farm to save here."

"But Hal–"

"We're not talking about this." He drained the jelly jar and held it against his knee. "You have enough to do without another baby."

"I'm holding my own. More than holding my own. This isn't just your decision."

"Nor yours. We're going to make this farm thrive. That's what we're doing now. Let's not get sidetracked in the world of small children."

"But Hal!"

He went into the kitchen. I sat up and laid my bare feet on the floor. The room was very hot, and I felt overwhelmed with my own greasy sweat and the bands of sunlight where dust motes swirled, rising. Beside my naked thigh, Tansy slept, a little hot box of an infant. He returned with the jam jar full. From the couch, I smelled the liquor's bitter harshness.

"Fern, I've got this farm now. It's mine, since my dad's death. And I'll be damned if I'm going to stand by and let it fall apart. That's what he did, all those goddamn years, just let the place fall apart. But now it's mine." He leaned over his hands clenching that jar, his eyes narrowed. "Mine. And I'm going to make this farm thrive, come hell or high water. So you have to go with me on this one." He shook his head. "No baby now. Farm. You got me? Farm. Again: you got me? Farm."

Gently, to not wake my sleeping infant, I laid my hand

along Tansy's thigh. "Hal, this doesn't have to be one or the other. The farm or a family."

He swallowed another mouthful of the syrup, hard. "Who are you in love with here, girl? That baby. Not me anymore, not this farm–"

"That's not true. Hal, love isn't a finite thing. Tansy needs me now, sure, but–"

"Aw, I don't want to argue."

Sickness stomped through me. "Hal," I said, weakly.

He drank down the bourbon in one last great swallow and smacked the glass on the table. "Farm. Thrive. Let's keep to that plan, okay? You got your baby. That's enough for now." He went out.

My head looping with exhaustion, I lay back on the couch. There was nothing else I could do. In both palms, I cupped my slack belly, scarred with pregnancy marks, the tightness of my girlhood given over to a messy, stretched-out drape of skin. My insides churned and kneaded, as though by enduring pregnancy and childbirth I had stretched myself out to accommodate more misery. Feverish, I curled around my sleeping baby and shut my eyes. In a half-sleep, strangely, I thought of my mother and her black paten-leather purse. She had been a missionary's daughter, traveling around, not to exotic experience-enriching places like the Congo or the Far East, but to rundown city storefronts, where the gray streets were lined with blown trash, mothers and fathers struggled with drug addiction and general misery, and Jesus appeared as the most unappealing and tasteless of wafers. She ran away from that to a New England village life of shady streets, a PTO concerned with kool-aid and cookie signups, and a steady albeit small salary in the back office of the Stratfield Water & Light Department. That purse she carried with her was proof she had done well. It was a well-seamed purse, packed with a meticulously kept checkbook, plastic-wrapped Kleenex, a perpetual tube of lipstick, and a pack of Wrigley's for breath freshening. On that stained couch, vaguely redolent of mice, I lay with my foul digestion, my breasts carelessly strewing milk, thinking of that awkward shiny-leather baggage my mother had carried with her, all the days of my childhood, and how here I was, flat on my back, running away from my mother's life.

Without waking the baby, I stretched one arm into that shifting sea of sunlight, sheer loveliness suffused with common house and farm dirt, the mingling blood-red and gold heightened by my fever into a rarefied realm, transforming that everyday living room into a sultan's lair, where a tarnished discarded lamp with a bit of rubbing and polish could produce a translucent genie and three miraculous wishes. I had hated my mother's purse, filled with dullness she believed was required; I had scorned its middle-class squareness. But, at least, she had filled her purse with what she wanted. Or what she believed she wanted, which maybe was all the same thing. Since I was in middle school, my mother had bought me purses of all sizes and colors and materials: the tan canvas shoulder bag, a little red leather box with the very long strap, a white wicker basket, the black tube-shaped item designed to hang down my back. For all I knew, these yet hung on a closet hook in my childhood room, their zippers neatly closed, hanging slack, empty of the jumble of everyday living. Then, and now, I used the pockets of my jeans instead, shoving in crumpled dollar bills, stretched-out hair ties, the pebbles I persistently gathered.

I lay miserably, with my empty hand pushing through dusty sunlight. Perhaps it was simply the sickness and exhaustion, but thinking of my mother saddened me in a way that brought me near to tears, to something that might crack unpleasantly in my chest. I crooked an elbow over my face, and hoped for a better day tomorrow.

## CHAPTER 4

THAT SUMMER, Hal spent more days off the farm. He and Nat Gilchrist drove around visiting other sugarmakers, sometimes at far edges of the state. Nat was building his business, and Hal said he was along for the free advice. As we lay in bed at night, sprawled in the dark, exhaustion chewing at my limbs like an infestation of persistent mosquitoes, Hal talked maple, maple, maple. "Syrup's always been cash, yeah, but hardly worth squat. You know how damn hard it is to make syrup, burning all that firewood I cut and split, piece by piece. But it's going up, see." In the darkness, he described the curve of bulk prices, how maple was becoming a sought-after commodity, its barrel price rocketing in value. Conversely, milk had ebbed up, ebbed down, but its steadiness was down. "Milk's always going to go down, always, while everything else—feed, fuel, seed, property tax, every damn thing on this farm—is going up. Where's the gold, girl? Maple."

On his side, his hand squeezed my shoulder. "Muscles," he said.

I rolled over to him. "Maple?"

"Maple and muscles." His hands rubbed over me.

In the dark, I squeezed his bicep. "Muscles," I whispered and put my lips to his skin. "Muscles."

☾

All through that summer, Hal talked maple at meals or on our less-frequent evening walks, but mainly in bed. With the windows open, the nightsongs of tree frogs and owls wound in. Hal expounded on maple, myself drifting in and out of sleep, my face hot with the day's sun and exertion, the summer's unusual heat a persistence I was gradually beginning to accept.

Nat was aggressively expanding his maple equipment business, and Hal often drove with him to other sugaring operations, returning after I had eaten my share of dinner, and Tansy and I were lingering at the table, her fingers smushing bits of steamed crooked neck squash or green bean on the wooden highchair tray. Hal and Nat drank together. The aroma of beer hung around my spouse like spores when he returned. Crumpled Budweiser cans littered the pickup's floor. Those evenings, he was jolly, long legs sprawled under the kitchen table, smiling. As I watched him, my thumbnail picking at dried and crusted vegetable matter on the table, I realized he was habitually tense as a sapling, furiously alive. Yet, after his trips with Nat Gilchrist, he tipped his head back, laughing, his hands rising in the air, describing what he envisioned maple-wise for Hidden View.

On the pantry counter, under the upper beadboard cabinets, he kept a bottle of bourbon. One evening, after I nursed Tansy and laid the sleeping girl in her crib for the night, I came downstairs to the kitchen to finish what remained of the day's dishes. There he was, drinking at the table, pondering the day, his spiral-bound notebook open on the table. "Peas are about gone by," I remarked. My back to him, I bent over the sink, running hot water.

"How many taps you think we can do?" he asked. "Just how many maples can we press into service?"

I glanced over my shoulder. He was figuring with his pencil in the notebook, and his question was not meant for me.

"Dad was at a thousand. What's that? A paltry thousand. I was thinking three thousand, triple what he did. But then Nat and I were walking through that upper part, between us and Atkins' field, and I think we could do five or six."

"Thousand?" I swished out the dishpan and set it upside down on the drainboard. "You think five or six thousand taps?"

"Yeah." With his head bent like that, I saw a hazy oblong on the crest of his head where his dark hair was thinning, like a lighter section of a storm cloud. As he was taller than me, I rarely saw that view of him.

"Hal, we can barely handle the sap we have now. How are we going to boil so much more? You know how hard it is for me with a little kid? It's nerve-wracking down there. There's that huge firebox, and all that hot syrup. It's so dangerous. And then I have to work so hard, and so much. I can't walk away from there when we're boiling. You don't want that."

"Complain, complain, complain! I'm not going to listen to that."

"But how is this going to work? And then when we have another baby–"

"We talked about that. You're not getting pregnant now. Look, girl, I spent a lot of time in that sugarhouse when I was a kid. Tansy lives on a farm. She's going to have to work."

"She's not even two yet."

"Farm kids start young. She can't be playing all day."

"Hal, she's a baby!"

He refilled his glass in the pantry then leafed through the notebook again. "I have a plan. Nat and I have a plan. Maple is going to pull Hidden View from red to black. We'll update the equipment. We'll get more efficient in one way or another."

"I don't understand."

"Nat and I are figuring it out still. We're going over different options."

I pulled out a chair and sat opposite him at the narrow table. "I don't know how much of this sugaring I can do, Hal. I mean, it's such hard work, and it's not like the meals and the house, not to mention mothering, are going to stop for it."

"But if this is the solution?"

"Is it the only solution?"

"It's a solution. That I know. You want some of this?" He lifted his glass to me. "Go on, try a little."

I shook my head.

"Your parents were teetotalers, weren't they?"

I shrugged. I took his glass, the solid jelly jar, and held it beneath my nose. The scent came into my nostrils like dust-choked sandpaper.

"Try it," he urged. "Don't be such a prude."

I took a sip, a swallow that seared down my throat. *Firewater* the natives called it. We handed the jar back and forth between us. Hal shoved the candlesticks to one side of the table and spread his notebook open. In block letters at the top of each page he had printed MAPLE. Over the lined pages, he had diagrammed how the current sugarbush was currently strung with saplines, and then two proposed variations of restringing it. On other pages were sections of forest he hadn't yet tapped, and plans for most efficiently using those maples. Then he pulled out that stack of sugaring catalogs Nat had given him, and he described different arches, better pans, why we didn't want reverse osmosis, and a preheater he believed he could copy from a magazine design and weld himself. If he had a welder. He refilled the jelly jar.

The evening had swung in without me realizing it, tree frogs peeping through the window screens. Out of my ears came the stuffing of bourbon.

"See?" he said. "See?" His hands waved at the spread magazines and his notebook.

I shook my head, but the booze was stuck, and even my mouth was cottoned. I thought of all that syrup he planned to make, drum after drum of it. "I don't think I can. Hal, I don't think I can."

"Bullshit!" The flat of his hand slapped on the table, hard, rattling the glass. "Who said *can* and *can't* were options? There is no *can* or *can't* at Hidden View. We're just going to goddamn well do it! When the hell was *can't* an option on this farm? There's no possibility of weakness here. You think my mother ever said to my Dad, *no, I can't?* You think she ever had that option, that luxury, of saying no? She did not. And, I'll tell you what, Fern, you don't, either."

In my woolly state, I drew back, pulled my legs up on the chair and wrapped my arms around my knees. "Hal, we both need to decide this."

He set his fist on the table between us, a clenched knot of bone and sinew, flesh wrapped tight. His breath labored in an odd way, as though hauling a significant weight, his face flushed a mottled maroon, veins along his neck cords pulsing.

"Hal." I hugged my knees tight.

His breathing rasped over the glossy slick magazine, his cramped pencil scrawls.

Abruptly, I realized it was not just me and Hal in the kitchen, the drainboard stacked with clean and drying dishes, the overhead fixture burning steadily an ugly yellow, the black-marked scarred table, surrounded by walls that had gone years too numerous without fresh paint or even washing. Through the fog of what I had consumed that evening, I realized the drinking was a live presence in Hal, a turning and a shifting in his personhood, a pulling out not of fresh soil or weed-free earth but of his own clandestine demons of anger and quick fury and unmet desire. Without thinking, I said, "This is a bad idea, Hal, this drinking, this bourbon. We have a child. This is a bad idea. I mean–"

"Goddammit," he drawled, as if in boredom, then stood up and took his glass through the half-open pantry door. Although his shoulder brushed the light's pull-chain, he didn't turn it on. In the near dark, his arm was a sweeping shadow as he poured, lifted as he drank, and then refilled the glass. Watching him from my own liquor-strewn mind, I had a flash of my dead father, a merchant marine, in those slits of time when he returned from the Great Lakes. Through the half-cracked garage door, I spied into his workshop where he labored over birdhouses, increasingly elaborate, always gifted away. My father had been burly where Hal was slim, but they both exuded an inner force I connected to *glowering*. Hal's hands fumbled at something I couldn't see, and he muttered indecipherably. I crouched further over my knees, the bourbon beating like a jackbooted thug in my head. His mumbling rose, fuming, arguing, but the quarrel wasn't with me, alone as he was in the pantry. And then he said aloud, "Goddammit!" with such vehemence the house held not just my husband and I with our baby sleeping upstairs in the crib with the pink sheets sprinkled with crimson couplings of green-stemmed cherries. In my own whirling head was the bourbon skulking through with a presence all its own, and in the pantry Hal was not alone; he was there with his drinking.

The glass slipped from his hand, crashed on the floor but did not break, and spilled. "Jesus," he swore and lifted his work boot.

I pressed the heel of one hand to my forehead, determined to cast out the booze from me.

"Jesus," he said again, "the goddamn fucking bitch." His voice mumbled again, rolling gracelessly, his words rocks tumbling down a muddy incline, gathering a layer of repulsive sludge.

I pressed my fists against my teeth. When I glanced up over my hands, I saw my husband in the pantry door. I wasn't sure how much time had passed. I studied him, looking up over my knuckles. He stood in the doorway, the small dark room behind him, one hand wrapped around that whiskey glass. His hand swirled the glass, very slowly and gently, meditatively, as if liquid and solid were separating in the glass, and he was undertaking an experiment of creation. Then I looked from his precisely moving hand to his face, and I saw his mouth bent up at the ends, curling into a kind of Hal smile. He was smiling at the whiskey, as if it were something especially fine.

That double fluorescent ring over my head knocked into my vision. I squeezed my eyes shut and pressed my forehead to my knees. I remembered that early July at Growing Seed Farm. I had been hoeing in a field far from the farm buildings when an afternoon thunderstorm whipped in. Running wildly, we had taken shelter against an old stone wall along the field, while the storm tore through, sweeping away the afternoon's humidity and sweat. Hal, older than us, was the season's manager, and I was just beginning to know him. He had been working in a field even further, beyond a hedgerow, and as my crew abandoned the stone wall, shaking the rain from our hair and t-shirts and exclaiming about the storm's brevity, Hal appeared on a tractor. He stopped beside us and swung open the cab door. Even now I saw his wide smile, arm outstretched in an invitation only for me, and I remembered glancing back at laughter and teasing and hoes slung over tanned shoulders, and then I climbed up to his lap in the small cab, his breath a whorl in my hair. Although I had been fresh-scrubbed in the downpour, my hands immediately flushed sweat. His chest pushed against my back, and he steered with one hand, the other arm wrapped around my abdomen as I curled into his embrace, all without speaking, as if some other, more primal force pushed us together. The draw between us had nothing to do with rationality, with decision or spoken language, or any kind of asking or telling: our joining was hands together, clasping.

High up in the cab, we sped along that muddy tractor road, the windows clipped open and the cooling breeze streaming in, the air scented marvelously with opened up earth, fresh rain, and the growing crops rising around us. In that rumbling, clattering diesel-fed box, we sailed through that summer world, flesh and bone and sweat conjoined, desire circling us in that container like a snake charmer's steady incantation. With my fuzzy head on my knees now, I couldn't remember getting out; I couldn't recall in the faintest stepping down from that high perch, peeling free from his sweaty and hairy arm, but I was certain I had. Indeed, I absolutely had to have stepped free.

## CHAPTER 5

GRADUALLY, a year and a half into living on the farm, I began to realize the baby diverged us, Hal and I. Like a fist clearing a frosted window, patterns rubbed into view. In summer's onset, light spread mellifluously in the mornings. The rising sun edged its way seasonally, in mathematical regularity along the horizon, to the valley in the line of mountains where it appeared just briefly in the truncated days of December. When there was no moonlight, night in the country was an impermeable stew. By late summer, the sunflowers in my garden soared ten feet tall. The garden burgeoned. From the flat earth, my vision had blossomed and borne fruit. By then, Tansy was crawling, making her way in denim overalls through a baby's forest of leeks. My child navigated her first walking as the apple tree dropped its leaves. Kneeling as she tottered away from me, the thinning autumn sunlight warm on my face, I glanced up at the tree where hard knots of crabapple clung stubbornly to the branches. The blossom season would return after the winter, then fruit, then fall. But in our house I was not so certain of patterns.

Hal cut silage corn. Winter rye sprouted for a cover crop.

Snow piled against the house, over the road, even prettied up the weather-beat barn. I didn't care; in winter I didn't go anywhere but those few rooms and out to the woodshed once a day, to restock my woodbox. Tansy toddled around the house, pulling the kitchen cabinets apart, burrowing through boxes of toys and clothes we had been given. She was still so young, she napped all afternoon. She and I often cuddled on the couch, my finger rubbing her miniature cardinal-red lips. Sometimes we just lay together, snow drifting down outside, warm under our blankets, her tiny body in the crook of my arm, her eyes merry rounds of brown flecked with gold.

I had this picture in my head of a father and a mother and a child, a portrait of a family at the kitchen table every night, cloth napkins on laps, knives and forks in hands, cutting lamb chops smeared with mint jelly, sipping ice water, faces washed and shiny, serenely talking in turns. Where on God's green earth did I dredge up that view? My own parents bickered and sniped like blue jays at the compost heap. But that wasn't entirely true, either. Between my parents dwelt a coldness, an impasse. A place of emptiness where I rattled around like a pea withered before its time.

At Hidden View, the kitchen windows crusted over on the insides with frost. The woodstove was in the living room, and although we left the door to the kitchen open and shut the door at the staircase bottom, only the living room in those coldest days kept any warmth. Wind knifed through that plank house. The back right burner of the range refused to light. The range was an ancient affair I had scrubbed assiduously upon my arrival. The range was designed long before automatic igniters, so we always used wooden matches. Maybe the jets were clogged. Maybe the stove was cursed. I just cooked around that missing burner.

Shortly thereafter, the front right burner fizzled and then gave up its ghost. I picked at the jets with a toothpick, sucked at them with the vacuum, banged my fist to loosen any debris, but neither burner would light again.

I complained one night at dinner.

Hal said, "I don't care."

"I do care. I do the cooking. Let's get another stove."

"What are you? Crazy? We're not getting another stove. That was good enough for my mother, and it's good enough for you."

"Good enough for your mother how many years ago? How many meals ago? Would it be good enough for her now?"

"It would have to be. There's no money in this house for another stove, and that's that."

"This doesn't have enough heat to can. What am I going to do next fall?"

"We'll handle next fall when next fall comes. Maybe the Bomb will have fallen by then, and the point will be moot."

"Hal . . ."

"I don't want to talk about stoves."

"But I do!"

"But I don't."

He forked meat from the stew into his mouth rapidly, then wiped his lips with the back of his fork-holding hand. Oily drops of brown stew clung to the beard hairs under his lower lip.

Tansy chirped and held up a soft cube of potato with glee.

I mashed a buttery Brussels sprout on her tray, peeling the miniature cabbage leaves apart with the tines of my fork, leaf by little leaf.

With one hand, my husband lifted the stew bowl and drank down the floury meat broth, clattered the empty bowl on the table, and leaned back in his chair. He glanced out the window at the early darkness pressing against the window. November now, the night had entirely arrived.

I laid my fork beside my uneaten stew bowl. "Why are you in such a terrible mood tonight?"

"Why not be in a terrible mood?" He shoved his chair back against the wall with a bang and went into the pantry. Without turning to look, I heard a cabinet door squeak open, and a moment later the narrow-mouth bottle *glug-glugged*. He emerged with his hand wrapped around the jelly glass. There were four of those glasses, fancy glass dyed turquoise, with a rippled shell pattern pressed into the glass, a novelty item. I never used them. He stood at the door, looking at what I didn't know: in the pitch darkness I guessed he could see his reflection if he chose, or Tansy and me in a lower corner of the glass, or else something entirely, maybe figments of his imagination. "What I hate is cows. I hate the bitches. Fucking cows, cows, cows. My dad was in love with them. You know that?" He didn't turn around to face me, and I wasn't sure if he was talking to me, or not. "I'd walk into that barn sometimes, and he'd be there, his eyes closed and his face tipped up, and you know what he was doing? You know, Fern?"

"No," I answered quietly.

A bark of a laugh cut from him. "He was smelling. He was smelling that disgusting old barn. And then he was listening. He was actually *listening* to the goddamn cows. He said they spoke to him. Did that old man ever listen to me? Huh? You think he ever would have stopped working and just stood there, listening to me? Fuck no. Oh, fuck no."

"Hal, he's dead. Let it lie. We need to move on. This is our farm now, Hal."

"Simple as that, huh? Just move on, move on."

Tansy held a potato cube toward me, a strip of brown skin curling from one edge. She smiled, her front teeth tiny quartz squares. "Yes, yes," I cooed at her.

My husband made that snorting laugh again, a mirthless sound. At the back of his knee was a tear about an inch long in his workpants, navy-blue long underwear visible. I knew under my hand his thigh would be tensile with muscle and hamstring, with warmth and movement. Yet I could only look at it with that small slit. Even if I were standing beside him, there was no way I could slip my hand into that tender place. The kitchen door's glass was such that I couldn't see his reflected face. I opened my mouth to speak, and then I stopped. I could feel myself doing that: ceasing to speak. As if I had been laughing and abruptly stopped, because whatever I was laughing at was no longer comic. I had been going to say he shouldn't turn into his father. Somehow I had this vision in my head that a son grew taller than his father, but Hal, although strong and broad across the shoulders, chest, and hands, was not a large man. I had never seen a photo of his father, but I wondered if his father, standing beside Hal, would dwarf him. Hal hadn't cut his hair in a good long while, and its brushy black curls, rather than lengthening like Tansy's, had spun tighter and closer.

"You know how many times I've walked through those nasty barn doors to milk? Way more than thousands. I bet it's been a million times. He loved those goddamn beasts. I hate them. I hate milk. I hate the smell of rotten milk. You know, I'll never get that smell out of me, ever, even after I ditch those cows."

"Are we going to get rid of the cows? Is that what this is about? You want to get rid of them?"

He lifted his glass and drank.

Tansy squawked *cah-cah-CAH*, and I glanced at her, unexpectedly wondering if *cah* was cow. Was cow her second word, right after that ma*ma* she had sung to me the other night? She tossed her spoon on the floor with a clatter. Distracted, I bent down and swooped my hand under the table for her spoon. In that brief moment I was beneath the table, I heard Hal's glass strike the table, a knock that threatened breaking but didn't. By the time I jerked up, he was in the pantry, *glug-glugging*, refilling.

*Cah-cah!* Tansy chortled.

I sat at the table, darkness pressing against the windows like wolves. Hal emerged wiping his mouth with the back of his hand and thrust his arms into his coat. I said, "What is it, Hal?"

"I paid half the property taxes today. Half! You know what kind of penalty we're going to get for handing over a mere half? Eight percent. The greedy town. It's obscene, it's just obscene to take that kind of money from farmers. What's the point of farming, anyway? We should just pour the milk on the goddamn ground." He glared at me. "I told my dad this years ago. That milk was nothing but a black hole we were pissing in. You have any idea the amount of debt he put on this farm to keep that milk flowing? And now exactly that—the goddamn cows—are doing in this farm. We're doing the wrong thing here. We're going to lose the farm if we don't shut off those cows."

"What's going on?" I asked, panicky. "I don't understand."

He shook his head and grabbed his hat. "I hate the damn cows." He went out.

## CHAPTER 6

LATE IN THE NIGHT, I woke.

Tansy cried.

I lifted my sobbing child from her crib and pressed her against my shoulder, humming a tuneless, wordless ditty. Her body shook fiercely with distress. Hal's feet clumped down the stairs. A light glowed from the living room below, and, caressing my daughter's silky head, I thought of the heat from the woodstove whooshing up the staircase, fleeing into the frozen night through the ceiling of this plank-built uninsulated second floor. Through the window, stars hung in the night sky, forever distant.

The little girl calmed, wrapped in a blanket and my arms, her shuddering, gasping breath gradually quieting into sleep. I heard a sound I thought at first was an orchestra broadcast from outdoor speakers, as if a DJ had arrived: a trumpeting I mistook on this Christmas morning for Handel's religious music. Perhaps it was the ancient sea, dolphins or whales, their voices raised in holy harmony. None of this was so: coyotes howled down the hill, somewhere near the sugarhouse. In the great ocean of night, I couldn't see them, but I sensed their muzzles were raised to the cold sky, howling in long chimes, one into another and another, and another. With only the little bit of light trickling up the stairs and the stars icy bits, my slumbering child growing heavy in my tired arms, I leaned our weight back on my heels, entranced by the loveliness of this Christmas morning wild serenade. And like that, the coyotes ceased, and the farmhouse was mute again.

## CHAPTER 7

THE BRUNT of cold for that year passed. Nights no longer plummeted to twenty, thirty below zero. With the cold weather, it took me forever to bundle Tansy in her snowsuit and jerk on her boots. I had a diaper to change first, and she tore off her mittens and hat. I could no longer simply open the door and walk out. She was running then, and I could not leave her alone in the house. The broken stove wore into me. I crabbed at Hal. Hal crabbed back at me. I retaliated by cooking stew, stew, and stew: one-pot meals. He said nothing. I wondered if he even noticed. Confined, I turned to the house. I swept and mopped the upstairs. Now that it wasn't so cold upstairs, in that house with no central heating, I spent days in the second bedroom, tucked at the north side of the house. The room had a single window, with a view over the garden. The evening moon hung in an upper pane, glistening.

In the closet's back loomed a tall pair of crutches, concealed behind men's plaid work shirts, washed and worn to fraying white at the cuffs and hems. Beside the single bed stood a tiny table with stacks of books. *Great Expectations, Moby-Dick, Franny and Zooey, Walden, Gravity's Rainbow, The Scarlet Letter*. While Tansy slept, I read. I read with a ferocity I had for nothing else besides my child. Her little face I adored at length, my fingerpads caressing the plushness of her cheek, the indescribable beauty of the bones about her eyes, her plumpy lips redder than any wild raspberry. She was flesh made more lovely than imaginable.

With the babe tucked slumbering in the bend of my elbow, I read. I held the cheap paperbacks in my free hand, turning the pages with thumb and forefinger so as not to wake her. The books kaleidoscoped my life. Reading had always been a place of pleasure for me, ever since those childhood days with Ramona and Beezus, when I imagined a life for myself comprised of siblings, attentive parents, sidewalks leading to quirky friends' houses. Now, I read with a craving bordering obsession. Through the long days filled with stretches of emptiness, broken intermittently by the baby's cry, the heft of wood in the stove, the caw of a wayward crow scissoring the sky, I pondered Natasha knocking at her bedroom window, or lines of poetry I savored like the creamiest of Swiss chocolates sweetening my tongue.

*Will the hive survive, will the gladiolas*
*Succeed in banking their fires*
*To enter another year?*
*What will they taste of, the Christmas roses?*
*The bees are flying. They taste the spring.*

In those lengthening winter days with my little child, I longed for sunlight. I had the curious impression at times I was waiting for something or someone; I didn't know what or whom. I didn't consider myself unhappy: dormant, perhaps, more than anything else. In those long winter nights, I often lay awake, staring out that uncurtained window at the stars in the distant heavens.

# CHAPTER 8

HAL UNCLAMPED his snowshoes, knocked loose clots of ice, and set them behind the woodstove to thaw. I fried pork chops and onions on the woodstove. "It's all tapped. Two thousand, nine hundred, and eighty-three taps this year, that's up from my dad's paltry thousand."

"My god. We're going to be able to handle all that sap?"

Tansy banged a wooden spoon on the floor.

"Guess we'll have to."

## CHAPTER 9

WINTER YIELDED to the urgency of spring. Our road turned to a sludgy mud. That sugaring season, we trudged up and down the path from the house to the sugarhouse, Tansy on my back a significant weight now. Record snow fell in March that year, and when we began sugaring, only minor patches in the fields had melted clear back. The path was a mountainous snowy trek. This year, Tansy had solidity and bulk; she kicked to get off my back. There was no way I could keep the toddler from the roaring arch, from the high pans that splattered and spewed boiling syrup, from the buckets of steaming maple we left on barrels in our rushing need to do something else: keep the syrup from foaming up and boiling over, the fire crazy hot, the spigot open when the syrup was ready to draw off. Fearful for her, I kept her on my back, and yet I needed to work. With that volume of sap, Hal could not run the sugarhouse single-handedly.

Tansy screamed. She yowled. She twisted and fought to get down.

I hated the season.

By Easter, the season was nearing its end, the sap slowing. We didn't boil that day, and I baked a ham. In her wooden highchair, Tansy drank from her small cup, lifting it and saying, "Tea, tea," in her tiny voice. A little girl in a quintessential way, with her skinny legs and knobby knees, silky curls the color of dusk, her quartz-toothed smile too large for her face, my child was bursting suddenly from babyness to her own little personhood.

Finished eating, Hal shoved his plate to the center of the table and went into the pantry. He stood in the doorway, his wrist propped on the doorjamb above his head, holding his glass. "We're fucked, syrup-wise, you know."

"I don't know. There's all those full barrels."

"You don't know shit, really, about syrup, do you? We had a piss-poor yield, girl. We're not going to make much more." His glass and hand lifted and gestured at the sunny afternoon through the windows.

"It looks like a lot to me."

"Yeah, from what dad did. You know how much money I sunk in that sugarbush this winter? I guessed we'd get three times as much, conservative, as we did. That, girl, is piss-poor."

In her singing voice, Tansy said, "Tea."

"That's about all you're going to be living on, girl child. Tea and milk."

"And my garden."

"Whoop-de-fucking-do." His voice cut at me like an ax chopping through wood.

"Hal," I began. I could feel a fearful panic edging into my voice, chewing up my words. "What are we going to do? How are we going to make this farm work?"

"As it always has. One cobbled together piece of shit at a time. Rubber band this. Rubber band that. Outlay the cash for another roll of duct tape. Hope's free."

The hacked apart ham lay on the table's center on an old bone-china platter I had found in the pantry's lower cabinet. I picked a bit of shiny fat from its edge, then dropped it on the greasy china. Without raising my eyes and looking at my husband, I asked, "You really—really and truly—think this farm can keep going, Hal?"

His hand and its glass appeared beside me on the table, a clink of glass to wood, his hand so near me I saw dark hairs sprouting from the backs of his fingers.

"Of course," he said. "Anything's possible."

I dipped a fingertip in the white grease. *I'm going out to fetch the little calf /That's standing by the mother. It's so young, /It totters when she licks it with her tongue.* "You don't think, Hal, we'll destroy ourselves trying to make this farm work?"

"No."

"What about your father? Didn't he do himself in on this farm? Really?"

"Fern, it was just him. There's the two of us. I know we can do this. Will it be easy? No. Of course not. You knew that when you signed on. But can we make this farm thrive? Of course. Don't give up, Fern. Don't give up."

"Tea," Tansy said quietly, "tea."

Hal pushed away the glass. His hand circled my wrist, and he lifted my greasy finger to his lips. His breath came in hot moist blows against my fingers. "We raised this meat. We grew these potatoes. This is our dominion, Fern. Ours. Right?"

I raised my eyes to look at him, but I didn't quite get to his face. Somehow, my eyes stuck on his shoulders, his great broad shoulders in the gray-and-white flannel shirt, unbuttoned partly down his chest, where his t-shirt appeared, a frayed thumbnail-sized hole visible, where his black chest hair sprung through, unruly. Through the hole, I saw more hair, pressing to get out. "How long?" I asked. "I mean, how long can this farm keep going, stumbling along from year to year?"

"The farm is not stumbling. It did, yeah, under my father. And sure, this is not a great syrup year."

"A piss-poor yield, you said."

"Yeah, all right, I did. But we're going to pay that equipment off. And we're not going to have a bad year next year. The good years are going to tide us over during the bad years."

"You don't know that."

"It's the law of averages."

I pulled my hand down from his mouth and laid my palms flat on the table. Tansy was chit-chattering to herself, one word over and over, its small-voiced tune winding into my head. "Rages, rages."

"Averages," I inserted quietly.

Hal pressed his hand over my own. "The law of averages," he said, "should be on our side. My father destroyed himself here, so doesn't that tip something in our favor?"

It was just then, as he said this, that Tansy hurled her spoon and miraculously managed to hit the steel sink with a clang, and Nat Gilchrist appeared at the door, holding out a handful of pastel-colored foiled-wrapped chocolate eggs. "Look what the Bunny brought."

We stood up, both Hal and I, scraping back our chairs. I lifted Tansy into my arms, and Hal stretched out his hand for the sweet. When I thought back, though, I realized I hadn't answered Hal at all. Quite possibly, he hadn't expected an answer at all. But, later, I wasn't sure how that math worked out, whether that law of averages had much to do with me, and if that way of looking at the farm and us was, perhaps, tinged with craziness.

My life immediately went on with its pieces of farm and little kid life. We unwrapped the chocolate eggs and ate them at the table, while Nat helped himself to a plate of ham and potatoes. We talked about sugaring, about the roads breaking up and the muddiest hole in the flat stretch just past Atkins', and laughed at Tansy licking her Easter chocolate. Then the men went outside, and I cleared the table and washed the dishes.

☾

Sugaring season melded into full-blown spring. Bluets bloomed in the fields, miniature beauties deep in the weeds. I walked over those gems in my bare feet.

☾

In May, Nat Gilchrist bought our syrup. Or, as I heard when he came in for coffee and to write a check at the kitchen table, bought some of the drums and took the remainder. Months ago, Hal had promised syrup in exchange for equipment. I set Tansy in the highchair and poured her a mug of milk from the ceramic pitcher.

Nat smiled at the pitcher in my hand. "Hey, I remember that."

"The pitcher?" I asked. I set it on the table.

"Yeah. Your mom always used that for milk, didn't she?" he asked Hal. They sat opposite each other at the table, their legs sprawled beneath, Tansy in her chair between them. I poured myself coffee and sat, too. Nat sported a long mustache he rubbed with his index finger and thumb, draping down the sides of his mouth. He had no beard and was clean-shaven, with a ruddy complexion burnished as if he slapped his cheeks after shaving. In the driveway, his truck, with its humped fenders over the double back wheels, gleaming like an enormous metallic toad, was hitched to a flat trailer where our barrels of syrup were strapped tight. Beside his coffee cup holding hand, a slick maple equipment catalog lay on the table, with his orange *Gilchrist's* sticker on the front, his phone number in bold black print. He said, "Those were the days, weren't they? We used to hunt, all over this mountain. You hunt anymore?"

Hal shook his head. "No time. I get a deer for the freezer every fall, but that's it."

"We ought to do it again, Hal, you and me. We could hike up and camp out like we used to. We should do it." Under his hand working at that mustache, he smiled. Beside Hal in his work clothes with his cuffs frayed and splatters of caulk and oil stains, Nat's clothes were noticeably nice, his shirt ironed with his cuffs rolled up just so on his forearms. "Remember how your brother used to get so mad?" Nat glanced at me, with that easy salesman smile he had. "We'd go hunting, and Lucien would get stuck with the farm chores."

"Yeah, he was always whiny about things like that, wasn't he?"

"I heard Jorgensen is still looking for him. You hear anything about that?"

"Nothing."

I asked, "Who's Jorgensen?"

Nat's eyes slid between Hal and me.

I asked, "Where is your brother? I never hear anything about him."

Hal dipped one shoulder in a shrug. "Looks like no one knows."

Tansy knocked over her milk, spilling it. "Argh!" she wailed in surprise.

"That's my cue." Nat set down his cup. "Thanks again, all the way around. I'm out of here."

While I mopped milk with a rag, the men went out.

"*Aw-rah!*"

"Baby coyote?"

With Tansy walking beside me, the teeny-tininess of her around my knees, I went looking for my husband. "Hal!" I called, "Hal!" my voice rising above the chickens scattering in the pecked dirt around the barn. With the baby, I didn't often head down to the barn, with its decades' accrual of tools and odd debris and the lowing, stamping cows. From the very beginning, I was afraid of the cows, and I feared now, too, Tansy would wander down that way when I was busy, and my back was turned, and the barn with all its dangers would become an attraction for her. He was in the maw of the barn. That little back room was lit only through a four-paned window above his head, the glass so clouded with years of dirt the light was murky. Crouched over an engine stinking of oil, hands rank with grease, he must have heard my thin voice and Tansy's babble and worked until we found him. When I stood in the doorway and waited, my hand enfolding Tansy's, he reached for a stained rag and wiped his fingertips down to his knuckles.

"Hal, didn't you hear me?"

He twisted the rag around his first knuckle joints, then threw the rag on the engine. "That's done at least. The syrup sold and gone." He walked out of the barn, the two of us trailing behind him, Tansy trying to keep up. Outside the barn, the chickens scattered, squawking.

"Hal?" I called.

He turned and looked over his shoulder. "I've got to go down and clean up the rest of sugaring." He hurried down the path.

At our small-legged pace, we followed, and he had long since disappeared into the sugarhouse before Tansy and I arrived. She had tired on the way down, and I lifted her to my hip, wishing I had thought to bring the backpack. Her weight tugged me down on that side.

When I entered, blinking in the dimness after the spring afternoon, he was on the other side of the arch, his hand in the pan soaking with sap, scrubbing. He wouldn't look at me. The light from the window cut in a shaft across his face, and I noticed his brow was furrowed, all the way down to lines between his eyes. The dusty sunlight caught in his brushy hair and voluminous beard.

I asked, "What's this about your brother and this guy Jorgensen?"

"There's nothing much to say."

"Who is Jorgensen?"

"You could scrub a pan if you're going to be down here."

"Why's this secret?"

"It's not secret. There are no secrets here! Jorgensen is a lawyer. When dad died, Jorgensen was the lawyer who handled his estate. What there was of it for an *estate.* This farm is hardly an English manor." His shoulder rose and fell with scrubbing. "I've told you Hidden View is encumbered with debt."

"Why's he looking for your brother?"

"The farm was left to my brother and me. Technically, Lucien owns half this farm."

I studied my husband, his face turned down to his work. "What does that mean for us?"

Without lifting his head, his eyes flicked at me, then back to the pan. From where I stood, I couldn't see his hands, hidden in that high-sided tarnished silver pan. He said, "My brother disappeared years ago. He never wanted jackshit to do with Hidden View. I'm not thinking about him, and I don't intend to think about him."

Tansy, heavy, slipped down, her knees trying vainly to tighten. I shifted her higher on my hip. "Hal, you think he's going to show up and want part of the farm?"

"I told you, I'm not thinking about my brother at all."

"Did the two of you get along?"

"Why in the hell would you ask that? Of course we got along. We're brothers, aren't we?"

"I just wondered—I mean, if there was an argument or something—since he's not here anymore."

The wet scrubbie whooshed by my head, flicking drops of soured sap over my face, and smacked against the wall. "I told you! I'm not thinking about my brother! This is what we're doing. We're farming Hidden View!"

I backed up, the sap drops trickling down my face, my arms clamped around the child whose face pressed against my shoulder. Across the cluttered dirty room, my husband's shoulders and chest rose and fell, his breath cutting through the quiet space like a stuttering engine.

I said very quietly, "All right, then, all right."

## CHAPTER 10

I OFTEN SAW Mary Atkins on my walks along the road. I walked every day, sometimes through the woods and fields, or otherwise far down the road. Mary's left arm trembled, and the summer Tansy was carried on my back, the palsy had spread to her face, now always tipped down slightly to the left. I saw her sometimes cutting gladiolas in the flower garden gone mostly to weed by the side of the barn. She always spoke kindly to me, while her good hand stretched out to baby's foot and brushed her toes. "I'll love to see," she said, "who this little person turns into."

That summer, Bill painted their house. When he worked on the side near the road, I paused on our walk, standing in the dooryard between their house and barn, shading my eyes with one hand and Tansy's with the other, as we craned back our necks to look. Even in the hot sun, he wore his green work pants and a long-sleeve shirt. The white topcoat of paint shone on the clapboards.

Mary opened the porch door and dragged out a bucket in her good hand. I hurried toward her, but she jerked her twitching head no, no, propped the bucket's bottom against one foot, and emptied it over the porch edge onto the tiger lilies. She straightened up and wiped her hands deliberately, slowly, on her pale pink apron, threading the ruffle through her joints. "Come sit. The sun's so bright."

I hadn't considered the sun sharp, but Mary tapped a chair back near her. I slid the backpack down my leg and unsnapped and pulled out Tansy. She gnawed my bent knuckle.

Lacy soapsuds rimmed Mary's wedding ring. Her hand lifted, trembling, and she puckered her lips to blow it away. The soap was tough and her breath was weak. I lifted the tail of her apron string and rubbed away the bubbles. She laughed a little, a quiet polite murmur. "I used to wash my floors all the time. Now . . . here and there. Sometimes."

Tansy's drool slid down my fingers onto my thigh, bare beneath my cut-offs. The day was so hot and still the humid air lay against my sweaty face and neck. Crickets thrummed around the house, an unseen chorus.

In the wicker rocking chair, Mary leaned her head back and swayed gently with one foot on the porch. Her eyes fluttered closed, and I wondered if she was nodding toward sleep. Just out of my sight, I heard Bill's boot steps creak down the aluminum ladder, the rope's pulley between the two aluminum sections jangling as he moved the ladder around the house.

Holding my plump little girl in both hands, I glanced sideways at Mary, where her throat was creped, her wrinkled cheeks spotted with pale red and brown splotches. Her lips were up a bit, as if thinking of something she liked, and I smiled, too. I stretched out my long legs and admired the solid curve of my calf muscles. From either her hands or apron strings, the scent of Pine-Sol wafted toward me, a cleanser my mother used. Without opening her eyes, Mary remarked, "This house was built in 1856. Bill's family has lived here for three generations, and I knew a lot of them. But who before that? I wish I knew. From the cemetery back there, I know there was a Hilda Mayberry. What a name. Who was that Hilda? Maybe a dullard. But I'd like to imagine she was a spitfire, and would rather have gone fishing than scrub the floor on her knees."

I laughed. I held Tansy up, the drooling chubby mite of her. Mary's shaking hand made its wavering arc to the baby and knocked the back of her palm against the baby's heel. "A good one," she said. "Her."

Shortly after, Bill appeared with glasses of cold well water. I tipped the glass's lip into Tansy's mouth and let the liquid wash over her flickering tongue. Then I stood to leave, child snuggled in my arm.

Mary laid her good hand on her knee as if to stand, too.

I said, "Don't get up," and slid Tansy on my back again.

Her eyes blinking rapidly, Mary said, "Bill, give Fern and her baby a ride up the hill. It's hot."

I assured them I was fine, that the sun wasn't a bit too much. I waved goodbye and walked up the road, in no particular rush that day. Hal and Nat had left early that morning for southern Vermont and planned to spend as much of the day as possible at a large and new sugaring operation. The garden was as planted as it needed to be that season, weeded well enough, and July sang around me, in full leaf and flower, the crickets just commencing their summer serenading. Somewhere in the ancient, half-dying maples, unseen, a wood thrush trilled her melody, the eerily beautiful song from a plain brown bird.

The day had grown sunnier and hotter. Tansy's cheek sank sleepily on my shoulder. Where old maples leaned over the dirt road at the town cemetery, I wandered off the road. The cemetery had only a few rows of markers, mostly rounded white limestone. At the metal gate, I slipped off my sandals and walked barefoot. In the back, down in a little dip of hill, where the earth cut in an odd sharp angle, was Hilda Mayberry's marker, the single black slate tombstone in the cemetery. Her stone was alone in a shaft of light near the crowded hemlock pressed up against the rusting metal squares of fence at the rear. In block letters, carved with some pencil-sharp tool was HILDA, and below that, in smaller letters was MAYBERRY. *APRIL 23, 1857*, and *Died at 30 yrs old*. At its flat-edged top, in the center, was etched a human fist, the index finger pointing skyward. In accusation? In solemn direction?

With my baby sleeping on my back, a little bit of breeze flittered across my bare calves, the grass around me not at all recently mowed, studded with pussytoes and buttercups seeded deep in the long green, studded with tiny purple speedwell flowers. Long ago, her bones must have been laid in the ground and watered with tears and spring rain. Hilda had been a young woman. Her lifeless flesh would have been washed and dressed, wrapped in a hand-sewn quilt, the lid of a wooden box hewn from these woods hammered down over her face. In April, spring season, I imagined the hammerhead ringing on nails and wood, echoing over the bare fields. Down, down, she had gone. I knew nothing of this woman, not a single thing except her name, her thirty years, and the date of her death. I didn't know if she had died bleeding or fevered in childbirth, withered away through consumption, or fell from a hayloft—maybe the Atkins' loft—to her death. It was entirely possible a babe had been buried with her, its grave unmarked, or the infant's tiny stone had ebbed away in the decades, washed to nubs in the wild Vermont elements and years of forgetting. Perhaps her eyes were sparrow-feather brown, or blue as the midwinter sky. Yet, somehow, I knew the hand that had born down through this slate likely mirrored the clenched and mighty fist at the stone's crest, fiercely pointing heavenward.

I had no way of ever knowing if that extended finger was a solemn *yes*, there this woman went, heavenward, in starchy Puritan acceptance. Or whether, in the raving madness of grief, the man or woman who marked this stone did so in a fury of castigation, of *fuck you!* to the cosmos' Almighty greatness. How dare you steal my beloved? How dare you wreak this suffering upon me?

Her dark stone lay to the side, unique in color and name and position. Alone.

In a tree's upper branches, the wood thrush scaled her haunting song.

Tansy's drool trickled over the curve of my shoulder, bare skin around my tank top. I walked back to the gate and pulled on my sandals, and then, without intentionality, I returned to that grave and laid my hand along its top. The slate had warmed in the sunny day, its coal blackness not of the cold hidden earth but of a fistful of soil, warmed gradually in the hand.

## CHAPTER 11

MIDSUMMER, in the longest of days, Hal returned from the evening milking. I had just settled Tansy in her crib for the night, the day's grub and food smears and sweat washed off her with a sweet lavender soap. I was running water in the sink over the dinner dishes when Hal came up behind me and kissed the tip of my ear. One arm circled around me. "Brought you something."

I tipped my head back into the curve beneath his chin.

When I turned around again, the water shut off, the dishes abandoned, I saw he held a flower, three violet buds slightly longer than an inch, closed up tight, on an oval-leafed whorl. In our kitchen of dirty supper things and linoleum counters worn through to wood, the three buds might have been a fairy apparition of a holy woodland offering. We bent over it, the two of us. An odor of soil emanated from Hal's stained hands. "Gentian. This flower doesn't open."

"It's not just a bud?"

He shook his head. "This one spends its entire flower life closed up. A freak of nature."

I lifted the nearly weightless flower. "It's lovely, though, isn't it?"

"A marvel."

We held that tender thing between us, in our conjoined hands.

## CHAPTER 12

THEN THERE WAS a dearth of flowers.

Hal and I trod different hard-working paths on Hidden View's acres. All day I hurried, rarely turning my face up to the sun. I planted, weeded, hoed, directed tottering Tansy from the tiny trees of broccoli plants, the bursts of leafy lettuce and spinach. The following summer she was two-and-a-half, chattering about the family of rabbits she said lived beneath the hilled potatoes. Their names were Ribbon and Cider and Mopsy and Sleepy and Strawberry and her favorite, Crabby. "Crabby not eat lunch. Crabby is craaaaaabby," she said gleefully.

In the busyness of our lives, with the farm and sugaring and Tansy, the seasons melded one into another. Our patterns were clear, even to near-frantic me: I did not go down to the barn, and Hal did not enter the garden. That knowledge lay in me quietly, simply there, not fermenting or frothing anywhere near the surface of our lives. As the frost crept assiduously into fall and the trees relinquished their leaves, I noted the accumulating pile of smashed bottles behind the barn, chucked against a molding round bale of hay, at first hidden in aging strands of loosening hay, then poking upward, revealed, sliver by sharp sliver, as the volume accumulated. The strangeness of it all was the unpredictability. Days at a time would pass when Hal didn't drink. We went about our lives, sometimes tired and quiet, sometimes talking all through dinner about his travels with Nat Gilchrist or the meat deliveries I had made to Chesterfield restaurants. We walked all through the woods around the farm.

One afternoon, he took me up the mountain to forested slopes where barbed wire was strung through trees that had grown lips of bark around the rusting metal. We stepped over stone walls built over a hundred years ago, stone upon stone, and now, stone by falling stone, tumbled back into the glacial till, buried again. "When sheep was king in Vermont, sheep were all the way up here." Looking around, we couldn't see any view, any fold of valley below; nothing but a forest on that mountainside now. How the world around us had once been was completely altered, entirely rewritten.

In her backpack, Tansy pulled my hair. "Ow!" I laughed.

I followed behind my husband, reaching for the empty loops of his work jeans. His legs were longer than mine, and he outpaced me. "Hal! Wait!"

He was so far ahead of us I saw only the red of his t-shirt as he moved through the thick forest.

"Wait!"

But he was already waiting, looking back through the leafy woods for me. "Look at this," he said as I came near, gasping a little with the bushwhacking over fallen branches in the slender woods trail. At his feet was a stone cairn, a rusty jab of rebar poking from its top.

I looked down, not sure what it was.

"This," he said, "is the northwest corner marker."

High above us, in the leafy canopy of maple and ash and cherry, the birds picked up their song again.

Hal nodded pensively. "It's a lot of land we've got here. It's way into the forest. I bet Dad hadn't been up here in twenty years to look. It's amazing I found this corner so easily."

I nodded and then looked back over my shoulder at the trail. Later, I didn't remember anything more than that. Perhaps I sighed. Perhaps I complained about the mosquitoes plaguing me, or Tansy's insistence that afternoon on jerking my braid. Perhaps I yawned. I didn't know; what I did know was that suddenly anger washed over Hal's face, and I immediately plunged down that cold well of his anger, abruptly deaf to the birds' songs and even my murmuring child. He walked ahead of me, striding angrily, out of the woods and back to the farm. At dinner, he didn't say anything. I could smell the bourbon on him, and after I had put Tansy to sleep, I came downstairs and he was at the table, drinking. His back was to me in the doorway, and I stood there, watching his hand around the blue jelly jar, lifting it and drinking, and setting it down again. The glass made a click on the wood. Gradually, not moving even the littlest bit, I realized I held my breath as tight as I could, as if my ribcage was a glass jar and a huge fist clenched me. In my bare feet, I slipped away, upstairs.

That night, he came to our bed late. I was sleeping,

and I woke with his hand on my shoulder. I was immediately awake, thinking something awry. "What is it?" Impulsively, I tried to sit up, but his hand clenched me, and I could not. The sleep was gone from my eyes, and I tried futilely to see in the darkness where the moonlight flickered on the wet bits of his eyes and teeth. His heavy-boned knee wedged between mine.

"Fern." That one word, my name, a scrap of flotsam on the river of his boozy breath.

I tried to squirm away.

"Fern."

"You've been drinking. Stop."

He lay on top of me, the great bulk of him, hard as anything.

"No," I hissed. "No."

"No? What's this no crap? You're my wife."

"Hal, stop."

His mouth chewed my lower jaw, gnawed away on me; any lightness or dexterity, any sweetness that might have come—his loving hand that had offered me the closed gentian—was swallowed up and destroyed by the booze. His knee came up between my legs, hard, and I cried out. I must have startled him, because he flinched a little, and then I squirreled out and away. I jumped to the floor, gasping, moving away in the darkness, but he didn't follow me. He lay in the bed and groaned. "Fern, give me what I want."

I grabbed my clothes from the chair and fled downstairs. In the kitchen, I dressed, shaking a little. I spent the rest of the night on the kitchen stool, knitting under the light over the kitchen sink. In my mind, I wandered over poetry lines from books in that little room.

*I scrub the long floorboards*
*in the kitchen, repeating*
*the motions of other women*
*who have lived in this house.*

At last, my fingers tired of knitting, my mind worn from too little sleep, chattery at the edges as if I had been drinking coffee for hours, I set my yarn and needles on the counter and stepped out to the porch. Shortly before dawn, the eastern rim of the sky was lined with just the merest scrim of rose, the palest possible tease of promise against the night still firmly entrenched. Clouds had dominated the night sky while Tansy and Hal were sleeping, and the gibbous moon appeared to duck in and out of a ghostly film that came and broke, and joined again. The moon that night didn't appear at all as the graceful Lady Moon. Instead, the light was blistering white, the lopsided moon darting crazily in and out of the shifting clouds. How had I gone from those sweet phrases of cows and pastures to the gray monotony of scrubbing floors? The dark possessed the upper hand over the moon who came forth only in sporadic jabs of light, while around me the nocturnal summer world hooted and called and chirped its auditory presence. Closing my eyes while the animal world thrummed, my face tilted up to the chaotic sky.

I thought again of the law of averages, and what would that mean? How would life come down for us? Would the law of averages mean I would have one point four more children? Two? Three? Or none. I wasn't sure that approximated even the least bit of sense. Hal's vision of the world was a march of numbers, a page in his handwritten composition notebook titled *maple*, with a plan of columns and figures he trusted would march this farm solidly into his vision of success. Could we live that way, he and I? Husband and wife? With his faithful adherence to what I believed was an arbitrary law? In the conifers, a raccoon howled its strange trilling hoot, a hungry curl of sound. I opened my eyes for Lady Moon, but she was gone, sailed off into the immense sea of clouds. And my own laws? Child, milk, my jumbled desires. I waited there as the dark wound down, waiting for the moon, who did not appear.

I leaned back against that old farmhouse, my eyes filled with the night's dark. I let my shoulders and back take my body's weight. My hands spread over my chest, my fingers pressing hard between the raised bends of my ribs. Within, my lungs spread those ribs, my body steadily working on at its living; within, my heart, mightiest pulse of my body and yet most tender, folded and bent, curved over in pain. My jaw clenched as spasms of misery washed over me.

When the dawn was just pushing up over the horizon, the time we usually rose, I went upstairs. Hal was awake in the bed, staring up at the ceiling. I stood in the doorway, and his eyes slid toward me. We looked at each other for a good long while, and then he finally sat up with a moan. He bent his face down away from me, rubbed the back of his neck, and then said, "Christ. Let's get on with it."

"It?"

"The farm." He stood up and dressed with his back to me. I went downstairs and started the coffee and eggs.

## CHAPTER 13

IN JUNE, the woodcutting season, Hal dumped a bucket load of split wood in the woodshed. I had run upstairs for Tansy's sweater where it had been left on a laundry basket in the bedroom we did not use. When I didn't hear the tractor drive away, I stood at the one window and looked down. Kneeling in the driveway, Hal bent over his chainsaw, sharpening the chain. In his gloves with the split thumbs, he rammed the file down each tooth, lips drawn back from his teeth, his jaw clenched, eyes narrowed. I stepped nearer the window and studied him, his shoulders hunched over his work, oblivious to the world about him. *Rasp, rasp, rasp.* He shoved the file against each slender tooth.

With increasing frequency, each morning as Hal went out to the farm work, or disappeared with Nat Gilchrist, he didn't bother to look at the child and me. Without speaking of it, he ceased to touch me. I wondered if I had been merely a need, something as physical as oatmeal, pork, whiskey. That need he was slaking somewhere else, in whatever way. I held Tansy's small red sweater in one hand. In my own tender place, I was red as the slender muscular tongues of birds, my internal flesh filled with folds and crevices as a peony bloom. What bit of joy I might have gathered there had quelled. Its absence was a loneliness, an emptiness in me.

From the window, I saw our small daughter crouching beneath the lilacs, in that curious little kid way, all elasticity, her hands gathering something on the earth I couldn't see from my angle. Against the green foliage, the long lavender flowers above her head withered to a rotting brown, she was a bright pink patch, her hair two spindly sprigs of braid. Hal kept on with his chain sharpening, the side of his face toward her as he knelt over that chainsaw, no more than a stone's throw from where she bent in the lilacs. He did not look at her. Nor did she turn to him. Instead, she glanced over her shoulder at the house—for me, I knew—and then returned to her child's work.

The window I looked through was significantly over a hundred years old, six panes over six, the once-upon-a-time white paint dirty, stained with mold where wood met glass. The panes were smeared with dirt in waves where condensation had slid down the glass, accumulating in ripples of stuck-on dust. My thumbnail chipped absently at a line of the debris.

*Rasp, rasp.* My husband's shoulders bent powerfully to the task. In her little blue mud boots with yellow polka dots, Tansy crabwalked further into the lilac thicket.

At the window's top, dusky clouds tore across the sky, immense and bunching, jostling as a great wind bore them along the mountainside. Stepping nearer the glass,

I tipped up my face. Would it rain? Would the clouds smash and empty, or would the inclement threat simply sail by? The clouds rushed by, so many of them, apparently without end. For just a moment, I imagined myself channeled saint-like up into that massive cloud bank, the freezing wet slapping my face and body, twirling around in that ethereal realm. Would I be able to tread cloud like treading water, dip my head beneath the hazy scrim, and observe the workings of Hidden View?

In June, this should begin the loveliest of Vermont's seasons.

As if I had been transported to the heavens, I saw the farm: the beaten down farmhouse with its rusting metal roof and the barn, bowed at the front, threatening to burst, its boards popping loose in places. As I followed the curve of path, the sugarhouse appeared with its sprawled trash of used plastic tubing, hodge-podge of things no one would ever want again, and then the fields with their stony poor soil, my garden where the slugs had set into the lettuce already, to the clothesline that had snapped that morning and dropped wet jeans on the muddy ground where I had abandoned them.

*Rasp, rasp*. He threw the file away from him. His hand knocked through the oily pouch of tools.

I had once believed the world so small, so microscopically possible. An *if you can imagine it, you can become it* kind of universe, a phrase you could write on an index card, thumbtack over a kitchen sink, and live by. I had come to Hidden View with my eyes open to the fields overrun with thistle, the garden buried beneath burdock, the asparagus eaten up by wild raspberry runners. Indeed, I had imagined my hands and my husband's hands, put to the land, would tip the inclination of this farm from disorder to order.

Below me, Tansy moved deeper into the thicket, so I saw merely a patch of candypink moving back and forth, back and forth, as she eased her way into the branches.

The farm was a ring I suddenly realized, a circle from house to barn, sugarhouse to garden, bending back to house. We had chopped that ring in two, the barn and sugarhouse his territory, the garden mine, and the house a nether in-between zone, center of strife. Without realizing it, our lovemaking and affection had quelled, evaporated. I couldn't recall the last time either of us had touched the other with mutual desire.

His searching hand hadn't located what it needed. Frustrated, he scattered the pouch, spilling the tools, and then leapt up and kicked at the dispersed things, his lips drawn back in that angry sneer.

From my vantage, how wide our world seemed then, the infinite challenges not in the permutation of weed or wood, sap or seed, but in our own inner worlds roiling with our chaotic rubbish.

His hands clenched into fists by his sides, Hal tipped his head back, his thick throat exposed from his raised beard, veins pulsing in his temples and along the hard cords of his throat. He howled, a wordless rage at the sky, eyes wide open, and then he swung his fists out into the air, whacking at a great nothing.

The patch of candypink disappeared in a flash. Hal stalked away, out of my sight, as if through the strength of his rage he could change the being of Hidden View.

## CHAPTER 14

IN THE FREE BOX outside the library, I picked up a hard-worn wool sweater. A score. The sweater, a hand-knit, was baggy, loose, a big mama triple X size, torn at the hem in half a dozen places, split under the arms, ragged and filth-stained at the cuffs and neck. Four or five times I washed the sweater in soapy cool water, gently squeezed the liquid from the wool, and laid the sweater to sun-bleach on a towel in the sun. As the wool cleaned, I found its green was gold-speckled, a summer's leaf color with bits of buttercup. In the evenings, while Tansy slept, I took my tiny scissors to the sweater, *snip snip snip*, and bit by bit, painstakingly, unwound that knitting, careful not to jerk or tear, determined to salvage as much of that yarn as I might. The yarn was curiously thin, and as I took the sweater apart, fresh as I was to knitting, I gradually realized the yarn was handspun, too, with variations of width. If it was handspun, it must be hand-dyed, too, but I couldn't figure out how the dye had set so well, and how the flecks of gold were genuine flecks and not clumsy smears. Where the yarn was knotted, I broke it and wound each section into a separate ball. These balls accumulated, ball after ball in a basket on the couch, in sizes that matched cherry tomatoes through Baby Pam pumpkins. In my hand, they had not even the weight of a fledgling bird.

When I had completely unwound the sweater, I put the yarn to my needles and began ribbing a sweater for myself, but after a few inches, I had to rip that out, too. The yarn was so thread-like thin I had to begin on different-sized needles, again and again, working my way from size sevens down to size two needles so fragile themselves that when Tansy knelt on the bag with my knitting, a needle snapped. Frustrated, angry, I stood in the living room with the ball of yarn at my feet, the short piece of knitting in my hands with its jagged broken needle. For spite, I broke the other whole needle, then wept.

Later that week, delivering pork with Tansy, I drove further than I usually did and went to St. Johnsbury. At the yarn store there, I bought one long circular needle, a twenty-two dollar purchase, worth five pounds of pork, and that night I cast on the yarn again. The needle tips brushing against each other were like ice skating, smooth and strong. This time around, I had it. The sweater worked up from the ribbing—knit knit, purl purl—for two inches. Then I worked the number of stitches into a wave pattern, the green being the sea with the yellow glimmers of sunlight. I knitted up, up, up, and then began a series of bumps that in my mind was the beach. Upwards from the beach was the wide yoke over the chest with a matching one over the back. I patterned in a fiddlehead fern, with a series of smaller ones all around it, a whole cadre of a background of ferns in different sizes and shapes, their fronds in variations of closed and opening and open. On either side, I patterned up bars of marriage lines, bracketed by small but elaborate cables. I put those cables in for no particular pattern but merely because I could, and because the pattern was lovely. Over the top of the ferns, on both front and back, I scalloped in clouds. That yarn was so thin and the needles so minute, I had to labor, tiny stitch by tiny stitch. As I neared the collar, I studied the sweater with my even stitches. On the back, over my right shoulder, I added in a crescent moon, a small one the size of a quarter, although I suspected Lady Moon would be concealed behind my hair tumbling over my back. When I joined the sides in a bar over my shoulders, I altered the pattern in the long inch-wide swathe that went from my neck down to the wrist bones: instead of marriage lines, I split the zigzag and made a broken marriage line, surrounded as it went down the arms by that pattern of scudding clouds.

When I had finished the sweater and sewn in the last of the small threads, I stood up and immediately pulled it over my head. *Ta-da!* I triumphed to Tansy.

She looked up from her bowl of applesauce and clapped. "Good, mama. Pretty-ful."

I rubbed my hands all over that sweater, over my abdomen, breasts, shoulders, and down the length of my arms, so deeply satisfied with those tight, even stitches, with the knitted landscape I had created, beauty and order emerged from a dirty cast-off.

## CHAPTER 15

THE SPRING Tansy was three, Hal planted with an intensity I had not seen in him before. After dinner, he stood at the kitchen windows, studying the barn and fields, and even then often went out, rather than to his chair and bookkeeping. Ten more auctioned cows appeared on a cattle truck one afternoon. I had had no glimmer of a warning, although he had mentioned he was determined to plow pieces of field this spring that had lain fallow for years.

That summer, things went awry. The tractor broke, required parts, broke again. Hal eked out the parts bill. A replacement tractor was impossible; the farm could not be encumbered with more debt. A violent storm blew the house shingles from the north side, and Hal spent the following day hammering and patching and swearing. Rain pummeled the fields, day after day, swamping hay, corn, alfalfa, every inch of my garden. The barn sagged at one end. He cut a tree and shoved it at an angle against that corner, shoring it up. The price of milk fell, as if into a long, eternally bottomless well. Squirrels nested in the eaves along our bedrooms. Mold blossomed on the wood furniture. Sedge invaded the north side of my garden and tore the skin of my hand when I tried in vain to pull it out. The truck transmission finally quit, and Hal and Nat Gilchrist spent two rainy days driving around until Hal bought another truck, a white heap pock-marked with scabs of rust. Days, that July, were stormy and sunless.

☾

The farm, chunk by chunk, was falling down around us. The wilderness, so near to us, held so tenaciously at the lines drawn—tilled earth, raised barn, inhabited house—slipped wily under those marks.

The evening he returned from buying the truck, as I was washing the supper dishes, he stood at the kitchen door, looking out, almost facing me but not quite. Rain poured down in a sheet so solid the fields seemed to rise in a green wave to meet the weather. I rinsed the bowls and set them, one, two, three, on the drainboard. In the window's pellucid light, I saw the wrinkles across his forehead and the bridge of his nose had deepened like carved grooves in wood. The distance in our ages seemed suddenly mathematically clear, a proportion that might favor neither one of us.

In her high chair, Tansy plucked raisins from an oatmeal cookie, piling the dried fruit like animal droppings in a corner of the wooden tray. She wore an orange cotton hat with a green pumpkin stem we had picked up in the library free box.

He cleared his throat. "Fern." He did not generally use my name. "Your mother give you any money?" He jerked his chin up and down. "When you left?"

"Why would she have? You know she didn't approve of you. You know she was angry I left school."

He nodded. I could see his jaws working, tightening. He nodded again, and turned to leave.

I asked, "Are we in trouble?"

"Trouble? You know what the price of milk is now? Shit. Shit, girl. There's no other way to say it but shit. This farm has been mortgaged too much and too hard." He jerked his chin. "We're sinking. Sinking, girl. Why produce this fucking milk if it brings in no cash? What a joke. The bank owns this whole farm, owns us, girl, several times over."

"What do you mean? Might we have trouble with the payments? Might we lose the farm?"

"Huh," he snorted through his nose.

I put my wet hands on my hips. "I don't understand what you mean."

"Why should you understand? You're just here to play house with that baby, to muck around. I'm the one who's footing this bill. I'm the one who's shouldering all this."

"It doesn't need to be that way. I can help you figure it out."

"How? It's pretty damn simple. It costs us more to produce that milk than we get out of it. With the sugaring equipment I ordered, we're going to have a yearly payment –"

"What equipment is that?"

"The arch. I bought a new arch and pans."

"What are you talking about, Hal?"

"How are we going to boil three times as much as Dad did? Five times? Seven times? Shit, girl, with that baby you have, you're not a full player here. We barely got through last season."

"What? What?"

"You know my plans down there. You know I've put in as many taps as I can."

"Yeah, I mean—"

"You think we can boil on that same shitty arch? Of course not. Bigger demands bigger."

"What's the price tag on that?"

"About thirty grand."

"Hal!"

"There wasn't another option. This is the best deal Nat can give me."

"You? Or us?"

"The farm."

Piece by piece, Tansy dismantled her de-raisined cookie, broke it apart, and arranged the dismantled pieces in lumpy piles.

"Hal, why didn't you tell me?"

"I did. In ways. But you don't want to know. Not really. Just like you don't want to go near the cows. You don't want anything to do with them except spend the check that comes in."

"Spend the check? Like I'm out shopping for high heels and makeup?"

Tansy clicked her tongue against the roof of her mouth.

Hal leaned his back against the door. His face, turned toward me, was masked in shadow. "Fern, the future of Hidden View is maple, not milk. What's going to happen when the world falls apart? When the oil's gone and the electricity's out?"

"What on earth are you talking about, Hal?"

"That's going to happen. We all know that. Fossil fuel is finite. This world we're living in is going to change, one way or another. What are we going to do then?" He jerked his chin at Tansy, sorting cookie pieces. "What's she going to do? Milk won't keep without electricity. Milk isn't worth shit now, with those industrial farms in the Midwest. But syrup—syrup is gold, Fern, gold. It keeps. It's food. It's here to stay for the long haul. Syrup's going to be our salvation."

"But, in the meantime, since the world hasn't fallen apart yet, and the banks haven't crumbled, it's our source of debt."

Tansy echoed a tiny, "Debt, debt, debt."

"Yeah," Hal said, with that *rasp* in his voice again.

I squeezed my wet hands together. "Hal, how is this going to work?"

He stood still. With the grainy light behind him, I couldn't read his face. "How does anything work around here?"

"What does that mean?"

"It doesn't mean anything," he said flatly. "It means nothing, Fern, nothing. This is just the way things are."

Abruptly, I was near to crying. I could feel tears bite in my throat, and I blinked to keep a mess from rolling down my cheeks. That vision I had of sweet pastures and warm milk and laughing little children had given way to what I perceived as unrelenting gray. I looked at my husband's hand laid on top of a chairback, the wide back of his palm, his knuckles. "Hal, remember how happy we were? Remember what it was like when we were first together?"

He shook his head.

"Hal, please. Please."

"I don't know what you want. I look at you and I think, I don't know what this woman wants at all."

"You can't mean that! Hal, I want our family. I want this farm to thrive."

"Do you? Do you, really, Fern? I don't know about that. I see you arguing and arguing about this maple. Your life is just tied up in this one little bit of this farm, just this house and that garden and the child. We can't thrive, as you say, just that way."

Tansy was quite still.

"I don't know, Fern. I don't know what ever we were thinking."

"We were in love."

"I don't know what that means. I don't know if you know what that means."

I was crying.

He said, "Don't be a sentimental fool. We're running a farm. We have to be practical. Now is the time to be practical."

"How can you?" I demanded. "I can't believe you can say that. Am I not the epitome of practical? I'm no Hallmark card woman. What makes you think I don't understand the farm? Don't I know I need to eat a peck of dirt, too? That this farm isn't all sunflowers and joy? I never expected an easy life, Hal. I never thought this would be easy. Give me a little credit, here."

"Credit? We're speaking different languages here, Fern."

"Don't we want the same thing, Hal, really? Family and farm?"

His hand squeezed the chairback.

With a fist, I wiped my eyes. "You didn't answer my question, Hal. I don't want to lose the farm. What are we going to do?"

He tipped his head to one side, said, "Yeah," and walked out without a jacket into the rain. He walked down the path, seemingly not in any hurry through the dumping weather, and disappeared into the barn door, wide open and dark.

At the table, coloring over tomatoes in the Shur-Fine flyer, the little one parroted, "Lose the farm, lose the farm."

I rinsed the last pan, pulled the sink plug, and dirty water spun down the drain.

"Mama, lose the farm? Where would it go?" She giggled. "Down the river. To Kingdom Come."

"Enough. Tansy, please."

The sink drain gurgled. "It's time for bed."

"Not bed! No. No! Flopsy and Crabby hate that."

"They very well might. But nonetheless."

## CHAPTER 16

A KNOCKING had begun in my head, an incessant maddening chatter of blue jays mobbing an evil cat. I could not shake myself free. There was a solution out there. I knew this. I believed I could find what was needed, like a cloth spread over tomatoes to guard against frost.

I thought of my mother and her presumed nest egg and that I was an only child. When I had packed the last of my things from her house, emptying out my bureau and packing a box of books, she had stood in the doorway with her arms crossed, frowning at me. She had wanted me to finish my degree and make something of myself. By that afternoon, we had argued too much about all this, and she said nothing more. She didn't walk out when I carried my things to Hal's truck. Later that fall, when I realized I had forgotten my winter coat—a good, expensive wool peacoat she had bought me a few years past as a Christmas present—I phoned and asked if I could stop by for it. She told me she had thrown it out. I asked, You threw out my coat? She countered at me, What are you doing pregnant? You should be in college.

We rarely spoke on the phone and saw each other even less.

Saturday morning, after I washed the breakfast dishes and swept the floor, I paced around the kitchen, wrapping and unwrapping a towel around one hand. I ceased my pacing and stared at my daughter. She was playing with a little orange kitten I had knit, jumping the creature over a purple-hued fungus we had found, the size and shape of a broken half of a dinner plate. She had laid the fungus on the floor under the kitchen table, and she was small enough to kneel without her head touching the table's underside. Even so, her head was crooked down to her play, murmuring. With her hair in two wispy ponytails, the bones of her spine pressed against her white skin. I wanted to crouch under the table and lay my hand over her vertebrae, over her coursing blood and electrical nerves, crazy mother that I was.

Tansy tucked her kitten in the bend of her elbow, rattling a purr in her throat.

Without planning, I picked up the phone and dialed my mother. She was home on a Saturday morning. "Hello?" she said, and, "Oh, it's you," as if I had caught her midstream, busily engaged in something else. Like reorganizing her kitchen cabinets.

I started right in and asked about the Water & Light, and the three women she had been friends with nearly forever, and I even asked about the neighbors, whom she always complained about, the people whose dog howled on full moon nights. I didn't really listen while she answered my questions. I leaned the small of my back against the kitchen counter and closed my eyes and listened to my little child's lilting voice as she rocked her kitten in her arms. Then the rocking ceased, and I realized she pressed the yarn animal to her ribs and was nursing her creature, her face bent down and smiling. The girl had no sense at all that I was watching her, that I was drinking in her childish joy, and that even as I did so, I felt the fleetingness of her childhood, how very brief this little bit would be, until her youth curled up like a fallen leaf and was whisked away in the wind.

Then my mother's strident voice came to me, wound over those wires and my own distraction and ruefulness, my mother's indignation and anger. "That deer walked right across my yard and up to the porch. I mean, can you believe that? I was standing right there in the kitchen. I mean, I was spooning coffee into the percolator and I looked over and saw its ugly lips. I never—and I mean never—leave my purse outside. But I had left it on the porch step because I had paid the paper boy and the phone rang. It was the middle of the afternoon on Saturday! That thing ate the handle right off my purse. But it didn't stop there. Oh, no. That animal bit right through the leather and into the purse. It ate a whole side of my purse, and a lot of what was inside. He left the lipstick."

I laughed, imagining the largely artificial contents of that purse churning through the deer's digestive tract and scattered randomly in pellets.

"Fern, I'd had that purse since before you were born. My mother gave it to me for my twenty-first birthday. And now that it's ruined you're laughing?"

"Mom, it was just a purse."

"But it was mine!"

I felt something trembling in me, and I licked my lower lip. I rubbed my lips together, and then I said, "So, you're really upset because your mother gave it to you. Not because of what was in it."

"I had that purse a long time."

"Did your father ever give you anything like that?"

"My father didn't believe in gifts."

Rain coursed down steadily, gray laced with white clouds of fog. I knew she would have ten thousand she could spare in a bank account; she was miserly. But if I asked for ten now, how hard it would be to ask again in a year, or even six months. I stared at the cascade of rainfall, the fury of it even through diaphanous fog, and pondered how much it would wound me to ask for thirty thousand, and if that would be enough to sail us into solvency.

When my mother spoke again, I realized she broke a silence between us I hadn't noticed. "I know what you think. You don't have to smear my face in it, Fern. You think I did wrong by you. You're out there pursuing your farm life, like it's some sacred mission, to prove me wrong."

"Mom, that's not–"

"Don't interrupt me, Fern." But then she stopped, as if she had forgotten what was coming next.

With her non-nursing hand, Tansy swept her pumpkin hat from the floor and tugged it askew over her black curls. Laying her knitted kitten by her knee, Tansy knelt on the floor and bent over scraps of paper she had torn into postage-stamp-sized pieces, coloring with her crayons. I wanted to cradle a piece in my hand.

"You don't know what my life was like, Fern. All you've done, ever, is judge me. Judge me. My father had an iron fence around us. We were the minister's children, and we were going to be examples to the community, whether we liked it or not. Here I gave you a nice house, in a decent town, with enough money. I tried to get you an education, so you could do with your life what you want. But no: you squandered all that. You're just going to end up working in a grocery store someday. Or waitressing. You watch. You mark my words. You're going to want something wholly different for Tansy."

"Mom, I never judged you."

A spitting sound came over the phone. "Your whole life is a judgment against me."

"Mom, I didn't mean . . . Hey, I wish we saw each other more."

"I don't think so. You wanted your life. Now you have your life. Go get on with it. Go on."

"That doesn't mean–"

"What? That doesn't mean *what*? Maybe because I never talked about my life, maybe because I didn't cry and weep and moan about how difficult things had been for me, that you never knew. But you never cared to know. That's all gone, Fern, long passed over. Let it lie."

"But Mom–"

"How dare you judge me! All I wanted to do was keep you safe."

"Safe? Safe from what in that little town? You wanted to put me in a box and seal up the lid. That was no kind of life."

"The world, Fern, is filled with terrible people, vandals and thieves. Look what happened here. Hal stole you away from me."

"That's not true. I'm not stolen. There was nothing you needed to keep me from."

"You're so young, Fern, so young and so naïve. You still think you can remake the world in whatever way you want. You'll see, Fern. You'll come to see."

"Do you want me to be miserable?" I asked incredulously.

"You'll be like the rest of us. You might come to want that box again."

I thought of that deer, a doe I imagined, its brown neck stretched out, long jaws opened toward my mother's polished black paten leather.

I couldn't do it. I couldn't ask her for money.

"I need to go," she said, and the line went dead.

"Furry Leaf," Tansy said solemnly, "needs something."

I squatted down on my heels and looked at her. "What is that something?"

She shook her head. "I don't know."

I stood up and stretched my arms over my head. "I'm going to clean the bathroom."

Tansy wrapped her arms around my waist. "Bleh," she said.

I nodded. "Bleh. But needs to be done."

By late morning, it had been raining steadily for hours, a solid sopping mess of continual rainfall. The barn had swallowed up Hal. I couldn't set my hands to anything. Tansy bumped herself along the walls and windows. "Crabby wants a small cake. Crabby is going to be so crabby, I mean really, really awfully terribly crabby, if she can't have a small cake. A little golden one that fits in my tweensy hand and smells like sunshine."

I ceased shoving library books into a sack and looked at her as if she had gone mad.

She smeared her stub nose against a window and sighed. "And Sweet Pea wants to have a tea party in the Queen's garden."

He would appear soon for lunch. I left potatoes and sausage in a covered pan, a plate of sliced tomatoes on the table.

"Come, little one." I slung the sack over my shoulder, clasped her hand, and we hurried through the sodden rain to the truck. Keys were in the ignition.

In the truck, strapped in her carseat, my little girl sat beside me on the wide bench. With all the rain, the road was greasy. I drove carefully as the road wound down Still Mountain, the creek beside it swollen, rising and gnashing on itself as if in a self-quarrel. We took our time in the library, and then sat together in a chair in the back corner. I read a stack of books to Tansy, then stood and stretched. My breath caught deep in my chest, lodged behind a bone or under an organ. I clapped my hands together. "Little one, let's go."

"Let's not go home. Flopsy and Maple and Mopsy want to run around the Common."

The Common was almost entirely under water. In the middle of that lake emerged an island, a puzzle piece of sodden emerald erupting like some tangible destiny in a fairy tale. My little wild child ducked under the white slat fence and splashed through the Common's lake. I followed her into the icy water, gasping. My jeans immediately clung to my shins. She ran ahead, laughing, rain slicking her curls down her back, and ascended that green mound in the gray cold lake. I joined her on the little patch, a pitcher's mound in a game field gone stormy. Laughing, her eyes sparkled like upside-down crescent moons. How much I loved her, this little girl. Wet as could be, all the way through, even under my arms and behind my knees, I crouched down beside her and spread my hand over her wool-soaked back. "Oh mama," she breathed, her arm pointing across the Common.

At the far fenced end, I saw a heron standing on one leg, the other bent in a triangle. Slate-gray blue, the tall incredibly thin creature simply stood there in the pouring rain, wings folded around its body, an awkward oval above its stick leg. Motionless, the ugly, ungainly creature exuded patience and raw grace.

Tansy whispered, her breath puffs of warmth in my ear, "Let's never go home, mama. Let's turn into birds and fly away."

We crouched there in the rain. The sheeting storm showed no sign of ever diminishing.

An old woman in a white raincoat and see-through plastic bonnet eventually opened the front door of a Federalist house along the Common, snapped open an umbrella and walked to the fence. "What are you doing there? That child is going to catch her death cold." With one elderly hand she made a shooing gesture at us. Tansy's hand slipped into mine. "Get out of the rain!" the old woman shouted angrily.

"Mama?"

I shrugged.

"Mama, mama?"

There was nowhere else left for us to go.

Hand in hand, we walked back to the truck through the driving rain. I dried Tansy's face and hands the best I could with my t-shirt, both of us beginning to shiver. The truck's heater was slow to warm, and I had to billow the defrost to keep the windshield even passably clear. Fog gathered at the edges and crept in. With the back of my hand, I swiped the glass, smearing it. How hard it rained. I crept through town and along Route 14, mindful of the deep bogs on the left, then on the right. I didn't have much faith in the worthiness of those tires and feared skidding us off the road into deep water.

Off the main road, up, up, up Still Mountain Road. We passed few other vehicles along the way. Tansy slept, her head lolled back on her seat, dreaming, I guessed, of Crabby Rabbit's tweensy golden cake, redolent of sunshine.

When I turned into the driveway, my heart frothed up. I clamped my teeth, determined not to begin weeping. If I began, I would not cease. My tears would rival this fierce storm, flood my garden, the fields, drown the cows and pigs and furrow away our thin soil. I turned the bend and, entering the driveway, the house appeared before us. Quick as could be, I set a cast-iron lid over the poisonous cauldron of my heart.

If we lost the farm, where would we go? I wrapped the damp tails of my long shirt around my hands, twisting, wringing. I envisioned Hal disappearing—how could he survive without this farm, this piece of working earth he had lived on his entire life? He would lie down in the manure pit and die. The little one and I—we would creep away, our few treasured possessions wrapped in my checked apron and hung on a stick over my shoulder. Down the road, bent over, clasping hands, we would escape, our feet to the road, fleeing. In the early morning, we would pass my mother's house in the quiet town, shuttered up for sleeping, and head into the cool unfamiliar morning. We needed good shoes and a nest egg, neither of which I possessed. Where would we go?

The drumming on the roof abruptly ceased. I pulled the single key from the ignition and slid it in my pocket. My fingers brushed paper and pulled out scraps Tansy had secreted there earlier, while my mind had been occupied with cleaning the bathroom. I pulled out the frayed-edge pieces and unfolded them. They were so small they lay in my hand, the paper softened from multiple folds and wearing against my pocket. The child had marked the pieces with bright crayon: hard-rubbed cobalt, a swirl of pink, four parallel lines of gold. In the cab that stunk of rags soaked in two-cycle oil and pervasive mold, I sat staring at those little pieces of paper, those offerings from my daughter. Then, the papers cupped in my hand, I unbent myself from the truck. A breeze was lifting as the storm shifted, and I walked just a few steps away where the grass clung stubbornly in ill-health at the driveway's edge. Spreading my fingers, I held my hand before me, and the breeze came little by little, gathering strength, and lifted one, two, then three, four, five pieces of Tansy's artwork and carried them away bouncingly. One disappeared in an upward curl of air. Two swept away in a flowing breeze. Of the remaining two, one dove down into a mud puddle beneath my feet, white paper soaking up the rich dark water, quickly consumed by the wet earth. The other flickered around like a darting hummingbird, then lodged on a high twig in the lilac bush, waving gaily in the rowdy wind. At its very tiptop corner, I saw a smear of peppermint pink rippling.

Abruptly, the clouds rent apart, sprinkling the house with fresh-washed sunlight, and I stood there, marveling at the sudden unveiling of beauty. In a shaft of sunlight, the house with all its crumbling paint and spreading rot appeared burnished bright, flawless, amazingly just built. The cornfield so glossy green held twinkling jewels of water in the myriad golden manes of tassels. Overhead, the ample sky spread its colors of roseate and sapphire and pearl. I had thought building the house and farm on this knoll a foolhardy vision, but I wondered keenly now what hands and eyes, what laughing voices and rampart lovemaking, had begun this farm.

Through the truck's rain-smeared window, I saw my little daughter sleeping, the tip of her tongue kitty-cattish between her garnet lips. The cold and wet had rubbed a rosy sheen over her round cheeks. If I left, got back in that truck and high-tailed my way down the road, I feared I would never cease fleeing. Tumbled behind me, irredeemably attached to my heels, perpetually dogging me, would gnaw my own festering failures, a shackle I would never be able to cleave apart. Somehow, I had fomented a conviction this iridescent beauty demanded a stony soil, rank offal, the misery of illness: that to pretend otherwise was a foolhardy and misguided notion. I could not flee toward a world of rainbows and sparkly unicorns. I believed, crude-formed as I knew my thinking was, that we had sown the seeds of Tansy and Hidden View, and now, in the midst of cultivation's hard haul, I had to grit my teeth and suffer through the trials of evolving growth. Howling in my young body, over the rolling flux of seasons, of dying autumn and bleak winter and joyous summer, rang the experience that this farm was earned with far more than a requisite pound of flesh. I believed Hal and I would come back to each other, this rift between us a rainy season that would, eventually, disperse and clear. I believed we would grow old together, that we would come to know the sharp lines around our eyes, the aged quiver of our hands, the thinness of spotted skin over knuckles as our hands gradually slowed. I believed to get to there, I had to endure through here. All things in due course. Hands to the shovel. Lean into your work. Persevere.

## CHAPTER 17

THE ARCH Hal had insisted on ordering was delivered in October. He and Nat spent the better part of an afternoon walking the path, measuring the sugarhouse, and figuring how to move the equipment down the hill and into the sugarhouse. Chilled, in a drizzling rain, they knocked off their boots and came into the kitchen. I was grating cabbage into an oversized pan for sauerkraut. Hal made coffee and heated a leftover half of an apple pie in the oven.

Nat sat at the table and complimented the size of my cabbages. "They're really terrific. You must have a green thumb."

I shrugged. Tansy stood in the doorway to the living room, twisting on her sock feet, two upper teeth gnawing at her lower lip.

In both hands, he hefted a cabbage, speckled over its top with cabbage worm droppings, its outer leaves laced like a clumsily constructed doily from slug chewing.

"Hey, Hal, your wife is pretty darn good at this cabbage growing thing."

With the back of my wrist, I pushed hair off my forehead.

Hal asked, "Fern? Coffee?"

"Yeah."

Nat laid the cabbage on the table beside his gloves, supple gray pigskin I wanted to clandestinely stroke. "You're both doing such a terrific job at this farm. This arch, too, you're going to love, Fern. I mean, this is the Cadillac for sugaring. It's not the most expensive, but it's the best, I'm telling you now. It's efficient with wood—and fast. You'll be amazed."

I held the cabbage still against the large grater. "What's the sticker price?"

"Well, now. You know how these things go. There's different things all wrapped up in the whole she-bang. But it's all tax-deductible. I mean, this is a straight write-off. And you'll get depreciation on this thing just about forever. That's a whole other tax advantage." He stretched his arm across the table. "Thank you there, Hal. That coffee looks just great. Pass that cream right over here." I laid the cabbage on the table, shredded center up. The table was strewn with cabbage and loose green leaves, a jar of salt I had carelessly spilled. "What makes you think we need a tax advantage instead of less expenditures?"

He raised one eyebrow at me. "You're not thinking right. This arch is going to enable you to make more syrup—and a lot more syrup—which will bring in a lot more money."

Hal dragged out a chair and sat down. He drank down his coffee as he usually did, quicker and hotter than most people. "We're not talking about the invoice. That's already been done. Finished. We're talking about borrowing Bill Atkins' tractor, and how to get that arch down the hill between his tractor and mine."

"That's how you're going to get it down there? Between two tractors?" I pushed hair off my forehead with a salty wet-puckered hand.

"I'm not carrying it, girl." He went into the pantry, returned with a bourbon bottle, and filled his half-empty coffee cup. He held the open mouth over Nat's cup. "Brown stuff?"

"Aw, why not? Always good to be near the end of getting equipment where it needs to go."

Tansy appeared by my side, her fingers furrowing into my jeans' side pocket. Roughly, I pulled out her hand and held it tight beside my thigh.

I asked, "When is it coming?"

"Tomorrow," the men said together.

The next day, tomorrow, a white delivery truck appeared. Hal and Nat had been waiting in the driveway for an hour by the time it arrived, drinking coffee again and joking about Vermont roads and how turned around someone could get with a GPS. The driver had come from Quebec, and he didn't speak much English. After the equipment was unloaded in the driveway, he sped away. With all the rain, the path down to the barn and beyond to the sugarhouse was soggy. Hal and Nat and Bill Atkins deliberated, drinking more coffee. Hal pulled a bourbon bottle from behind the seat in the pickup and filled his mug and Nat's. "Bill?" he asked. "Sweeten that for you?"

Bill glanced at me, a look with such intention it might

have been a tool he tossed to me, a ball of twine or a folded pocketknife. "I don't think so." He walked around the large crate, saying, "Now did you say there was a good place to tighten the chains on this thing?"

"Right under the bitch's belly," Hal laughed. Finally, with chains, they strung the crated arch between the two tractor buckets and crept down the hill. Tansy and I followed at a distance behind. The crate, weighty, swung between the tractors.

Hal and Bill, each driving their own tractor, kept their eyes on the wood-slatted crate oscillating between them. Nat walked behind, calling out, "Watch her now!" He clasped his gloves in one bare hand, swinging by his thigh. I couldn't help this: my eyes kept gravitating from that wobbling crate, those thousands of unpaid farm dollars precariously hung between the two tractor buckets, to Nat's leather gloves. The newness and suppleness of the leather irritated me. They sharpened for me how clean were his Chippewa boots, with keen treads, against Hal and Bill's ripped rubber barn boots, their work-crumpled gloves, seams of their right hands blown out.

At the sugarhouse, from behind, I heard them swearing at the front doors, heaving and grunting. Tansy and I crouched on the path. Somehow, the arch was twisted in, and they went back again for the pans, and then a series of miscellany, the float boxes maybe, and other odds and ends Hal had ordered. By this third trip, Hal and Nat had abandoned all pretense of the coffee and were merely drinking bourbon from mugs. They laughed. Bill Atkins said his goodbye and rolled away on his tractor.

Tansy and I walked around the sugarhouse, dank and cold in the dreary October weather. Hal and Nat stood in front of the uncrated arch, swinging open the insulated door and pretending to chuck wood in the firebox. They cackled. The door was enormous, a great swinging thing that squealed metal on metal on its hinges, and then smashed shut with a fierce *clang*. Hal slammed the door shut over and over. He practiced kicking it with his foot, then jammed it with a flat metal shovel. Wincing, Tansy covered her ears with her mittened hands. How dearly, too, we would have to pay for these things. I did not trust Nat had bequeathed us any fine deal.

"Mama," Tansy whined. We stood in a dark corner, my hands turning over and over a short length of stainless steel pipe, weighty as treasure, even gleaming a bit through the dusty window over my head. "I'm coldy, Mama."

The men, in the back of the sugarhouse where I couldn't see them, hooted with hilarity.

"Mama," she begged again. "Coldy, hungry. Carry me up to the house."

"You'll have to walk."

Their joke, whatever it was, went on. Jealousy stabbed through me. I could feel it like an infection in my chest, razor hot, breath-crushing, invasive.

My child wheedled again, "Mama, mama."

"Stop it, stop it, stop it!" Tossing the pipe back in the box, I grabbed her hand and hurried out of the sugarhouse. Painstakingly, we trudged up the hill, a cold wind cutting at our cheeks.

In the house, irritated, I chopped onions and carrots and potatoes, threw them into a pot with water and beef and garlic and the salt I had swept up from the table the other day, and turned the gas high, while Tansy sat in her highchair with library books. Hal came in, and his steps were off-kilter. I said angrily, "I can't believe you did all that without asking me."

"You could have helped. You could have lifted one end. No one kept you from it." He was looking down, where the toe of one foot was trying to jerk off the boot on his other foot.

"I don't mean that. I mean, I can't believe you bought all that stuff."

"I had to. I'm keeping this farm together, one way or another."

"Through debt?"

"Through maple."

"Let me see the books, Hal. Let me know, too, what's going on."

"It's enough that I know. And I know, Fern. I know what I'm doing."

I shook my head.

He said angrily, "Go ahead. Spit at me. We could have done this together, if you agreed. If you didn't keep fighting against me."

"I'm not fighting against you. You're the one who's making all the decisions here. This could be a bad one, Hal. That's what I'm saying. Why aren't we doing this together?"

"Because, girl, I know what I'm doing." He shouted, "I goddamn well know what I'm doing, and you don't know one thing about it!"

Tansy dropped her book, *smack*, to the floor. He and I stood apart, looking at each other. With an urgency, I willed him to leave. Inside, all through my torso, I could feel the imminence of crumbling, the tearing away of river banks by a tumultuous spring flood. Wrong season: late autumn is the season of stillness, of rest from the growing garden.

I said, "All I said was, I hate we didn't decide this together."

He nodded. "That's the way it was. Looks like that's the way it's going to be." He went out.

I stood on the porch, watching him walk through the frozen field, hoary from that morning's three-inch spikes of frost. The word *truncated* came to me. What a truncated kind of life we had evolved toward. Just how much more would we splinter? I thought of those almost impossibly small bluets, how the flowers sprang up in great clumps all over the fields, sunshiny golden at their centers, far too lovely for any sentimentality. Hal had told me, "Hope's free," and it was; it seemed to me that hope could indeed be free. Or I wanted to believe that, as desperately as I had wanted anything. I wanted to believe a man who had offered me wildflowers would weather with me through storms of discontent, and join back to our family—daughter, mother, father—stronger. The cold was just beginning to nail in for the winter. I longed to squeeze my fear in one fist, contain it under the arms like a mouse writhing to escape. But this fear of mine was no tiny plum on Little Jack Horner's thumb. "Mama," Tansy said, holding her arms wide out to me. I settled her on my hip. Together, we stood at the window, watching to see where he might have gone, but he had disappeared, and so we looked out at the long sprawl of brown field studded with daggers of ice. Crows dove into the shorn corn stalks, pecking at some tiny treasure they gleaned.

## CHAPTER 18

I WAS EMPTYING the garden one afternoon when my husband's brother appeared. Tansy and I saw him drive along the road and then his car disappeared behind the house. I didn't know Lucien then and assumed he was someone here for Hal, for milk or meat or wood or syrup. I thought nothing more than that whatever few dollars he might leave here could go toward the tax bill due the next week. I finished planting my long rows of garlic, those final seeds of this year I secreted in the earth. The slant of light was already narrowing, hovering nearer the horizon, a promise of that long cold season nearing.

The light thinned and petered. I gleaned the last scraps of frost-killed squash vines for the compost pile and eventually went in to begin dinner. When the scent of frying pork began to sizzle in the house, he came downstairs. He was at least six inches taller than his brother, although so thin through his chest he seemed almost pressed. His hands especially seemed wide and flat and empty. His face was grizzled with an unplanned beard, and his hair was matted in lumps. Looking at him, I saw that if his hair had been cared for, it would have matched Tansy's silky curls, as dark as hers, too.

"I'm Lucien Hartshorn," he said. "The younger brother." He opened the fridge and poured himself a glass of milk from the ceramic pitcher. He limped on his left side, a jerk so noticeable his shoulder dipped. He had been broken in some way that was impossible to conceal. Seeing me study him, he glared.

"Fern. This is Tansy. My daughter."

Tansy held onto the belt loop of my jeans and tucked her face against my leg.

Lucien dropped into a chair. He looked gray about the eyes, as if he desperately needed sleep.

I turned the chops over in their spitting grease.

Hal kicked mud from his boots and came in. He and Lucien nodded at each other, and then without a word, Hal washed up. We sat down to eat, the four of us, full darkness pressing tight against the windows.

# Part Two

## CHAPTER 19

LUCIEN LEFT after dinner. He said nothing, merely dipped his shoulder into his coat and walked out. Upstairs, his dirt-worn canvas bag weighted the twin bed where I often slept. Beside it, folded, was a hand-sewn patchwork quilt, comprised from dozens of different scraps of red. My fingertips drifted over one square, a deep glossy red, velvet worn smooth as a rose petal.

Tansy's eyes saucered. After she fell asleep in her small bed, I lay down in the double bed in the front bedroom. When Hal came in and undressed, the leather of his belt creaking, his buckle clanking, I pretended sleep. Lucien's car rattled in before I slept, and he dragged limping up the stairs. The house was so tight I could hear him shifting in bed, turning over and over, sighing, comfort eluding him.

In the morning, our world sparkled with a twinkling frost. Tansy pressed her nose against the window, her eyes glittering, too. "Jacky Frost nipped my nose, Jacky

Frost nipped my toes. So I went inside and slammed the door!"

After Hal did the barn chores, he sat at the kitchen table with his black notebook, drinking coffee and figuring with his pencil. On the couch, I knitted a sock for Tansy. Even though I had tossed out all the poor pieces of green yarn from my sweater's yarn—the too-knotted, or frayed, or dirt-stained cuffs—I had a fat ball remaining. Mid-morning, Lucien still hadn't come down, and Hal stood at the bottom of the staircase and shouted, "Lucien! Get up! Get your ass down here. I mean it. I need to talk to you. Christ, now. Get down here."

I was clothes-pinning Tansy a house of blankets near the woodstove when Lucien appeared. He hadn't bothered to dress beyond his gray long underwear and socks. He sprawled on the wingchair, his legs stretched out on the ottoman, his black curls tangled.

"What's the matter with you?" Hal stood in the kitchen doorway, drinking coffee.

"Nothing."

"You look like shit. Been out tomcatting last night?"

"Saw Tom Rayford."

"I thought he was in Boston or some such shit."

"Didn't seem to be."

"You went to Dewey's. What was going on there?"

Lucien shook his head. His fingers knifed into his navel.

Hal cocked his head to one side and squinted at his brother, studying him. "What's the matter with you?"

"Nothing." Lucien straightened up.

Hal whistled. "It's one frosty day out there. You can practically skate down to the barn. Supposed to get some snow and then freeze. Freeze up good and hard." He seemed almost light-hearted, buoyant, after his intense fury of the months before. He disappeared into the kitchen.

I said, "All right, Tansy, that ought to hold for a bit."

From inside, she murmured, "BerryBerry goes here, and Maple over here, and everyone needs milk."

I clattered at the stove and heaved in cord wood.

Tansy lifted the bottom edge of her blanket door. Her dark eyes darted at Lucien, whose face was twisted in a scowl, and then she dropped her curtain. I left the stove door open a slit for the fire to catch and roar. Through the front windows, I noticed the sparkling day had already been lost. While I wasn't watching, clouds had hurried in, and sleet began spitting.

Hal strode into the living room. I tightened, I could feel it all through my body, when I saw him. I said nothing, merely bent and latched the stove door. With his coffee, he sat beside Lucien's legs on the ottoman.

"In your own messed up way, buddy, your arrival here might be providence. Fancy that, huh? I've been talking to Jim Swenson. You remember him? He's buying for K&K Lumber over in Prattsburg now. He was never able to put two and two together. Still can't. Here's what I'm thinking. I'm going to lay this out for you, simple, buddy. Those pines down at the east end of the pasture. There's that stand in there, a good eighteen, twenty acres at least. Swenson says the price of pine might go down. Bullshit it will. Not appreciatively, anyway. He's just trying to dicker with me before I've even done the work. I could run the tractor down there. In this frozen shit, I'm not going to have any trouble skidding logs out." He spoke evenly, his eyes steady on Lucien. Even in Hal's still body, I could sense the strength in him, coiled, ready for the work to put his body to.

Lucien leaned his head back. "I'm riveted here, man."

"There's that turn-out, down there. I'll skid them there, for a landing, and I bet we could even get a truck down there, if this kind of weather holds. Here's where you come in. You can buck them up. That's not hard." He leaned forward just a little, toward his brother. "That's something you can do, easy. Measure and cut."

I pressed my elbows to my ribs. I was afraid of what, what, I wasn't sure. Hal was going on and on, steady as could be, as if we were a nice little family enjoying this foul weather, this time together as a family. As a farm family, to catch up on what we were doing and where we were going. My eyes sought the joint of ceiling and wall, seeking escape from these clustered little rooms, wanting to flee down ripe hayfields, piggybacking my child.

Hal went on. "What's possible? Five, six hitches a day? It's frozen up good already, I can testify to that. You're going to have to help with this, buddy. This is our answer. Maple in the spring. Logging in the winter."

"Our answer? What makes you think I need an answer? What makes you think I had a question?" Grimacing, he dug his fingers into his belly. "Don't think I'm here for the long haul, man. I got Jorgensen's letter. Obviously. Obviously. I own half this farm. I'll sell it to you, or sell it to someone else, but I want that money, and then I'm gone."

"Let me get this fucking straight." Hal leaned forward and set his hands on his knees. His face pressed tight to his brother's. "Before I beat the shit out of you. You'll sell me half this farm? Sell *me*? Buddy. You can't just appear from wherever you been in Buttfuck, and think you own half this farm. If for no other reason than the bank owns every bit of this farm. We're so close to breaking fucking scotch tape won't keep us together."

"That's not true."

"What's not true, buddy?"

"This farm has been in the family for how many decades? How can there even be a mortgage on it? Hasn't it been paid off, like five generations ago?"

Hal got up and went into the kitchen.

Lucien looked to me, as if I might have the answer. "Well?"

I picked up my needles and the ball of yarn and turned them over and over in my hands.

Lucien asked, "Fern?"

I didn't answer.

Hal returned with a glass of whiskey and dropped his accounting notebook on Lucien's thigh. I had never opened the book, a drugstore cardboard-covered school composition book, duct taped along the spine, the covers worn malleable with age and use, grime smeared so severely the notebook could have tumbled from a mechanic's toolbox. "It's all there, buddy. You can look at every last bit of it. This farm has run at a loss for years now. You can have half of less than nothing. Congratu–fucking–lations."

Lucien laid his long-fingered hand over the notebook. "I'm going back to bed."

"No, you're not." Hal gulped a long whiskey swallow, his right eye squinting at Lucien. "You got a lot to think about, you can do it on your feet. This is no fresh news to me. What's good is the plan I figured out. There's light ahead here, buddy." He finished the glass.

Lucien's thumbnail dug at the notebook's peeling duct tape. "Dad didn't cut down there. What was it about those pines? Maybe he said they must be rotten inside, from the water down there."

"Aw, bullshit. He just never got around to it. But we will. They're worth a lot now, you'll see. It's a backwards kind of gift he left us. You'll see what I'm going to do down there. You come with me. We'll do it together." He disappeared into the kitchen and returned with his glass nearly full.

I clenched my needles.

Hal clapped the side of his thigh. "Get dressed, buddy. We'll go check it out." He glared at me. "What are you doing? Anything you got to keep you busy?"

I hurried into the kitchen. Tansy was hidden in her house, quiet, quiet, as a little lost girl. I hid in the little windowless pantry, standing still. That bottle on the kitchen table was half-empty. How full it had been when he began, I didn't know.

I heard Hal say, "This is our chance. You got to remember, this farm goes back to the town and the bank, we'll get nothing, neither one of us. They're waiting for us to fail. They're out there like wolves, ready to shred us. What's wrong with you now?"

"Nothing. Nothing at all."

"You look like shit. Buddy, I'm telling you, I figured this out. You know what the price of pine is these days? We can clear some of this debt and more."

"Mama," Tansy called. "Mama."

I scooped her over the wall of blankets and carried

her to the pantry. I held the child in my arms, her forehead pressed against my shoulder. Hal had hardly ever been in the house for a whole long morning as he had this morning. I heard his feet tramp, tramp, around the living room. When he spoke again, his voice was vaguely furry at the edges.

"You're going to thank me for this, buddy. There's going to be no more talk of selling any bit of this farm. I don't know why I didn't think of this before. I'll show you just how damn well the farm can run. What the hell's the matter with you, anyway? Always whining about some crap. This is all coming together, buddy. I didn't know what to do before. It's not like I can use her down there. What with the kid and all. But now. Well, you're here. Right in the nick of time."

The sleet had let up. I bundled Tansy and myself into our outdoor things and we went out. We walked all the way down the driveway for the mail, avoiding puddles in the road frozen over with a scree of ice. Tansy bent down to see her reflection in those muddied waters. We stayed out well into the afternoon, the sky so thickly gray I had difficulty deciding how much time had passed.

Hal's boots and coat were gone. There was no sign of Lucien.

Tansy hid in her blanket house, curled on a pillow, whispering to her doll. In the kitchen, I ripped cooked chicken from the bone, listening to VPR. In a bit, I realized she was weeping, a quiet choke. I bent over the blanket wall and tried to lift her in my arms, but she pushed me away, crying openly now. "What is it? What is it?"

Sobbing choked her words. "Margy's dress is broken. It's *always* broken. This button is always off."

"I'll sew it back on."

"You never do it right. It always comes off. This is the one button on this one dress she has, and it *always* comes off."

"Tansy, calm down. Come on, calm down."

The girl was inconsolable. I went in the pantry and leaned my forehead against a cupboard door, willing myself not to cry. Her weeping wore down, and then I realized she was talking.

She was sitting on the couch beside Lucien, her face splotched with unhappiness. He was saying, "It's green thread, Tansy, that's strongest." Deftly, his fingers worked on the dolly's dress. He still wore only his long underwear, and his hair hadn't improved around his milk-white face. Standing there, watching them, I wondered when I had last brushed my own hair. "What's her name?" His voice was finely polite, like a porcelain cup of sweet tea. "Margy?"

"Margy Cream Cheese."

"And you have some rabbits?" His eyes flicked at her.

"Well, there's Ribbon and Raspberry and Bluet and Vetch. They moved under the woodstove for the winter."

"Vetch?"

"Vetch is the thin purple flower with the tags of leaves. There's Grade B, too. From maple syrup."

"I've heard of that." He tightened the thread, snipped it with his back teeth, and handed it to her.

She turned the dress over in her hands, testing the strength of his sewing. "Good," she said.

He stood, catching his weight on his better leg. When he saw me watching, his face hardened. "I think your mother wants you back, Tansy."

"I'll be in the kitchen," I said. My hands smoothed my hair.

Tansy looked from him to me.

I said, "Do you want some tea? There's mint in the garden yet."

"No," he said, his voice a door closing.

Tansy said, "Margy's coat needs sewing, too."

I went into the kitchen. The winter season was rushing right in at us, the kitchen floor cold, so worn free of any coating or polish it was dully gray. Dark pressed up against the windows like wolves in a famine. I embodied winter, too, hungry-eyed and rangy, wild and careless. I took my cleaver to carrots on the board and brutalized the vegetables into pieces.

At dinner, Hal droned on about the price of hogs while Lucien stirred his spoon in his soup. Soup dripped into Hal's beard, such a tangled brush he didn't realize he spewed dinner as he pontificated numbers: hogs, poundage, market value. "Gold. You mark my words, all of you. When the rest of the goddamn world is going down the drain, falling apart every which way, we'll have maple. We'll have Vermont gold."

Lucien dipped his head slightly toward Tansy and asked quietly about a tiger named Spool.

"He's okay, but Raspberry has better stripes."

"When I was driving up, I saw Spinach crouched at the edge of the drive, under the lilacs. Who else do you know?"

"Are you listening to me, buddy? This is serious shit. Those two hogs are going tomorrow and then she–" he pointed his fork tines at me "–is going to pay the tax bill. I'm not walking in that clerk's office. That old bitch has been trying to snag me into some trouble or other for years."

"Trouble? What kind of trouble might she be trying to snag you into, man? Looks like you found enough already."

I clattered a steaming tray of biscuits on the table.

Nearly inaudible, Tansy murmured, "Larkspur."

Lucien said, "Birch Bark."

"I'm looking one hell of a lot better than you, buddy. That's no competition you're ever going to win."

"Butter?" I offered generally.

Lucien's spoon rattled against his bowl's edge.

"Or maybe," Tansy breathed, "the Sun-is-Green-Cheese." The sliver of a smile bent up one corner of her mouth.

## CHAPTER 20

I WOKE in the night to Hal's drunken breathing sawing through the night beside me. He reeked of cowshit, sweat, and booze. Even sleeping, his breath rattled and beat and fought. He slept as he always did, on his side, his shoulder rising up in the night like a mountain ridge. I eased from the bed and stepped into the hall. Tansy's steady breath filled her room. Under the cover of that clotted snoring, I slid downstairs, my hand on the wall to guide me in the darkness.

When I came out of the closed staircase, I saw Lucien lying on the couch. He had taken the small table lamp and set it on the floor beside him, half-covered with a dark shirt so there was but a spill of light near his hands and the open book they held. He had covered himself, toes to chest with that red quilt, his knee crooked over a couch cushion. The room swelled wide with darkness, around that defined patch of light. Hearing my steps, his eyes slid from the book to me. His hand reached down and snapped the light off.

I stood over him, my body a skinny shadow in the night, my head bent like a giant sunflower, closed up, but leafed all over, not yet in bloom. I thought of Tansy asleep in her little bed, dreaming maybe of snowflakes or icy puddles, or perhaps something else altogether. She was the seed I needed to cover, stitch myself as the prickly hull around her. The stove had died down, but I didn't want to open the clanging door, risk rousing Hal from whatever slumber he was choking through.

A scent hung over Lucien, an odd mixture of candy store sweet and intensely medicinal.

"You must be freezing, Fern. Go on back to bed."

"How long have you been up?"

"Night," he said, in a low voice, "is never my best time. I hate the dark."

I sat on the edge of the wing chair. The stove embers suddenly settled, tumbling in the iron box of the woodstove. The room was lit by vague starlight and wandering trails of moonbeams. Around us, the night felt infinite, borderless. The shadows of his hand reached out and rubbed his knee. "What happened to your leg?"

"This cold wet. Rotten Vermont weather."

"I meant, how did it happen?"

"You don't know? How could you not know?"

"I don't. I never knew anything about you, really."

"I could put that right back at you. I don't know anything about you, either, except you married my brother, you poor fool, and you have a daughter."

I asked again, "What happened to your leg? You break it or something?"

We spoke in undertones, as if complicit.

"We can talk about my leg, fine, if you don't want to

tell me why you married Hal. I was fifteen, Fern, and my dad picked me up at school. We had argued that morning during chores. The school bus wouldn't come up here in the winter, and it's a two-mile walk from the highway up Still Hill. It was a big pain to me. Hal usually drove the pickup and so it didn't matter—I usually got a ride with him—but dad wanted the truck that day, and so he said he'd pick me up. Hal wasn't there. He was working on a math teacher's house, some little shingling job or something, and he had a ride back to the farm. Dad did errands that day, and then he picked me up, drunk. He was late and drunk when he showed up at the high school, and I asked to drive. We argued about that, too, but he insisted on driving, and—Jesus, Fern—he was my dad. There was nothing I could do." He exhaled. "He smashed the truck up against a maple. We were arguing—I'm really sure we were arguing—when it happened. He took the curve too fast, simple as that, swerved all over the road, and the pickup went right over a stone wall and hit the tree. Everyone said he walked away, and it was a miracle because he wasn't wearing a seatbelt. It was me that went into the tree. A sugar maple. The maple's still fine, too, by the way. On Jessamyn's Corner, south side. I drove past it, coming in. I hate maples. The great big ugly things."

"My God."

"I thought I would die, but I didn't." He laughed. "Sure felt like I was, though, for a long, long time. You ever run up against a tree and get a dashboard pushed right into you? It's not a good feeling. It's not something you ever want to do again."

I shook my head.

"You know, you hear all that stuff about the white

light, and your life flashing before you, and all that. Some kind of inner peace, etcetera, and all that. Nothing at all happened like that for me. I know we were arguing, and I was mad. I was so *mad.* I was fifteen, and he showed up at school, late again, in that awful truck of his. He'd painted that truck maroon, some cheap oil paint he'd gotten somewhere and decided one stupid afternoon needed to go on the truck. To keep it from falling into absolute pieces of rust or something? I don't know. But he painted it with a paintbrush, and so not only was he late, he showed up when the football team was out in front doing their cool jock warm-up thing, and in this ramshackle truck that looked like a retarded kid's project. When I got in the truck I knew he was drunk. I could smell it and I could see it. Believe me, I knew drunk."

"But you drove with him?"

"Fern, I was fifteen. What was I going to do? Have a come-to-Jesus reckoning with my dad in the high school parking lot?"

"Right."

"I was under his thumb. I was under his thumb for years, Fern. Come on, I was fifteen. You can't shoot any blame my way for this."

"I wasn't, Lucien. I was just thinking: how painful."

"Pain! I didn't black out. I sat pinned in the truck screaming. And then in the hospital it was just a black misery of pain. They did a couple of operations on me, and probably screwed those up. I don't know. I was a kid."

"You've gone back in since then?"

"Why? What's done is done. That's over. What am I going to say? Cut me open and do it right this time?

Don't mess up my bones? Who's going to pay for all that? Me: with suffering. And there's no money for that. You think I have Blue Cross covering my sad body? But why are we still talking about me? Why not get to know you a little more?"

"Lucien, this was what, ten years or more ago?"

"I guess so. I don't care. We don't really need to talk about this. I just gave you the facts. Truck. Drunk dad. Equals busted leg. I got a lot of reading time in. Improved my skills there, quite a bit. Would have had a whole other different life if not for that. So, when that silver lining phrase appears in a fortune cookie someday, think of me, Fern."

"You're the silver lining?"

"No, no. I got a silver lining. There's a big difference." His legs moved restlessly. "What's your silver lining here, Fern? How'd you end up with my brute of a brother? What are you running from? Or are you going to tell me he's not so bad? That I misjudge him?"

The darkness lapped around me.

Into the silence, I said, "I wish he wouldn't drink like he does."

Lucien's chuckle rolled toward me. "Wish on. That's rich. Wish on."

"You think I'm crazy?"

"Not at all. I'm not new to the scene here at Hidden View, Fern. Tell me, though, why'd you marry him? You love him?"

"I don't know. I did, I do, I thought I did. No, I *do*, Lucien. I was in school, and I was working on a farm for the summer, interning and living in a shacky camp on that farm. He showed up, and he was working in the sugaring part of the farm. He seemed, I don't know, so full of . . . possibility. Like we could have a life together."

"You thought he was the silver lining?"

"I guess. I guess, yes, I did." Saying that, I squeezed my hands between my knees, my body full of nothing but grief, the rawness of it like the late fall weather outside.

"Marriage isn't exactly a rainbow, is it?"

I shook my head. "You've been married?"

"Me? Married? Are you kidding me? Who'd want me?"

I leaned forward toward Lucien, my forearms pressed over my knees. Quietly, quietly, under the cover of darkness and my husband's drunken, oblivious breathing, I whispered, "We could leave, Lucien. This isn't crazy. You, me, and the little one. Come with me! We could take your car and leave today. This morning. While he's doing chores. We could go."

"You're crazy, woman."

"Why not? You must have some money. I have a little saved. Maybe a few hundred dollars. Maybe a little more."

"A few hundred dollars? We won't get out of Vermont."

"You want to stay here? With him? Come with me, Lucien."

"Fern, why am I here? I don't have anywhere else to go. It's not as though I haven't tried."

"Why not? Why not?" I screwed my voice down. "Why couldn't we leave?"

"Where would we go? And what would we live on? You have a very young child, I'm a messed up cripple. I can hardly make it through the nights. Jesus, Fern. I can't take you on. I won't."

"This is no kind of life for the child. Lucien–"

"Quiet, quiet. We can't talk about this now. We're not going anywhere."

"I can't stay here."

"Fern, I own half this farm. I'm going to get that. When Jorgensen's letter came, I thought, Jesus, yes, hallelujah, my prayers are answered. I had hit every dead-end possible." His voice hissed through the dark. "You know what I can get out of this farm? You know what I can walk away with? Enough to start. Enough to really begin. I've paid my dues here, woman. Paid them in spades. I'm not going to slink away in the night like some criminal again. Some sad-ass broken up loser. I'm walking out of here with my half of the farm, God willing."

"I own half this farm, too," I said much more loudly than I expected. I froze, my heart clit-clat-clattering in my chest. Overhead, Hal's breath caught and resumed snoring.

Lucien pushed himself sitting. "There's a lot of halves going around here."

"You haven't done the math correctly. At all." I went upstairs.

Sometime later in the night, Lucien limped up to his room. Again, I could hear him turning over and over, sighing in the night.

## CHAPTER 21

BEFORE DAWN, Hal was up and banging at the woodstove. I rose while he was washing and fixed coffee and oatmeal, poached eggs and toast. He shouted up the stairs for his brother. "Get dressed! Get your ass on down here. Fuck! The day's waiting." His eyes were red-rimmed rheumy but he forked down a plate as light began easing into the house. Clouds pressed low, promising snow.

Lucien came in the kitchen and sat down without looking at any of us. He wore jeans and a brown flannel shirt that didn't reach the joints of his wrists. His shoulders hunched forward as if he were cold.

Hal studied his brother even as he kept shoving runny eggs into his mouth. "We're going to load the tractor with tools and head down." Bread crumbs spewed from his lips.

"I'm not wholly up to par."

"You never were, Mr. Half a Farm, my ass. And you," Hal turned to me, "you need to put that hog check in the bank. It's Monday. And then get over to the town clerk and pay the rest of that tax bill. I got a list here I need from Leo's. You stop there, too. Put it on the account. You're not eating?" he said to Lucien. "Then let's go." He hurried out of the house.

Tansy lifted the hem of her blanket door while Lucien rummaged in the closet for outdoor clothes. She scurried over to him, her hands twisting the back hem of her shirt. She wore the funny shirt with green and white stripes on one side, black and red polka dots on the other. What she whispered I couldn't hear in the kitchen. Lucien bent over and said kindly, "This afternoon, Tansy."

When he had left, Tansy and I watched him walk down to the barn, his good leg pulling ahead. He wore a gray coat ripped at the back left shoulder and black rubber boots, mended with duct tape flapping at one heel, that must have been his, waiting in the closet for his return.

Tansy and I spent the morning driving in moderate snow. The truck's heater didn't work well, and our jeans soaked from traipsing through the sidewalks' drifts of snow, then froze unpleasantly around our ankles. At Leo's, I bought files and a chain, squinting to decipher Hal's crabbed handwriting. The man behind the register gave Tansy a chocolate doughnut with pink and gold sprinkles. Sitting on the counter, she ate it with great delight.

I spent the remainder of the morning tidying the house from our long day yesterday, ordering some chaos.

The men were back before noon, snow drenched. Hal bolted lunch and went through the mail I had brought up from the box. In the living room, Lucien sprawled over the couch. Tansy begged to eat near him so persistently I let her carry in her little bowl.

"Spoil her, you do," Hal said.

I was buttering a plate of toast.

He held up the box. "This is the wrong fucking chain."

"Leo said it was the one you wanted."

"I own three chainsaws. He thinks he knows everything about me, huh? Fucking genius?" He lifted his bowl and slurped broth. "I don't have time for this shit." He grabbed the box and tore off in the truck.

I washed up the dishes and poured myself tea. In the living room, Tansy busily picked carrot pieces from her soup and lined them on the lip of her bowl. "These are terrible carrots," I heard her say.

"What's so terrible about them? They have a good orange color. I bet your mother grew them."

"They're *cooked*."

"Is that some sin against carrots?"

"What's a sin?"

"Something you shouldn't do, I guess. Are carrots not supposed to be cooked?"

"They get mushy and terrible."

"Well, I didn't realize."

"Yes," she said primly.

When I came in, Lucien asked, "Hal take off?"

"I got the wrong chain."

"He wanted more hooch, anyway. It was a mess down there. Not the funnest time."

"Do you want any soup before I put lunch away?"

"No."

I looked at him, a book spread pages down over his

chest, his knee on a cushion, and then went back in the kitchen.

I put the soup away, and stepped out on the porch for more firewood. In the driveway was Lucien's silver Toyota, the hatchback covered with an unblemished layer of fresh snow. The sight of a car in the driveway was unusual for me, and, seeing it, I did a double-take. Beside it, two curved tire paths from Hal's truck led down the snowy road, the marks blurring under falling snow. I guessed a good five inches had piled up since morning. The air was wet and clean after the closed-in house, with its layered scents of chicken broth, coffee, laundry detergent from the clothes drying on the rack, and the underlying trails of mold and booze and bodies.

The wood piles on the porch had diminished. I pulled on my jacket and gloves and, with my face tipped up to the whirling flakes of snow, took my time restocking the porch piles from the woodshed. The wood smelled damp, redolent of forest. Finished, I leaned against a porch post and listened for the chickadees or the blue jays who often swarmed the compost. But the birds had either flown off or were silent, and the snow came down without a sound, weighting the twiggy lilacs, the immense two maples with their bark stained black.

Down at the barn, the tractor was parked, its winch mud-covered. The back wheels' chains with their fat spikes had clawed up the hillside, torn through the snow and into the earth that was just beginning to freeze for the winter, the sharp knobs gnawed through to the underbelly of wet soil. At the field's far end, down that slope, the line of gray trees had already toppled in a crisscross mesh, a black gash against the winter landscape, not yet obscured beneath the steadily falling snow. By the day's end, I guessed, all that disturbance would lie hidden beneath a pristine surface of new-fallen snow, wet enough it was near to rain.

I clapped wet bark from my gloves and went inside.

Lucien had moved to the wing chair, his legs spread over the ottoman. Tansy stood beside him, matching up pairs of her rainbow-colored Go Fish cards, shaped like the classic fish oval with a triangle tail "Yellow fish," she pronounced solemnly, "never win."

"What happened down there?" I asked. "With you and Hal?"

"Dumb shit. It's not frozen up, not deep down. And that tractor's not made for logging. He pulled out a couple of hitches and then got stuck. Took us forever to winch the thing out. What he's thinking, I don't know."

"You know what the price of milk is these days."

"I don't know. But I don't see this as any solution. All that pine is just going to pulp. What kind of money is in pulp these days? In toilet paper?"

"I don't follow those things. I didn't even know he intended to log there until yesterday. You hurt your knee down there?"

"It was a mess. You know what he kept saying? We need a skidder, we need a skidder. What do you bet he's looking for a bigger piece of machinery now? We don't need a skidder. What we need is a better plan."

"A skidder?"

"How much more can he draw against this farm, anyway? Do you have any idea how badly he's managing this farm? Any idea at all? What a complete waste of time and effort it is to slop around down there, for so little?"

I looked steadily at him.

"My guess, Fern, is you never venture down there. You're just here, in the house or the garden, pretending if you ignore all the other crap, it will just go away. It won't, woman. This farm is a disaster. I've been here a few days, and already I can see it's complete chaos down there. The equipment is filthy and cobbled together, the animals are ill-cared for, that barn is a hovel. It doesn't need to be that way. And all that crap about how he had a bad sugaring year, so complain, complain, about the taxes? He doesn't even have wood for next year. How's he going to make syrup without dry wood? How long has this been going on this way? It was never bad like this."

"But he's gone all the time. He's always out there. Down there." I gestured. "What's he doing?"

Lucien narrowed his eyes at me. "I would have thought you might have figured that out by now."

He shifted in the chair. "Anyway, things aren't the way they used to be. You can't farm without an outside income, without some other cash coming in. Unless there's a trust fund, which I don't see kicking around here. If you haven't brought it with you, it's not here."

Tansy leaned her cheek on the chair arm. "Mama, can I have some hot chocolate?"

"It's getting cold in here."

"Getting cold?" Lucien asked. "This house has always been a sieve."

I clenched my elbows in my hands, arms over my chest.

"Lucien, what's he doing down there?"

"You know what's going on."

"I don't. Lucien, I don't."

"Uncle, there's grumbles in your belly. Maybe you want some hot chocolate. I think hot chocolate is a good idea."

His fingers nuzzled her head. "How did we get on this, anyway? Hal's Hal."

I cast around the room. For what, I didn't know.

Tansy, bored with our talking, squirmed, her cheek on the armrest.

I looked down at Lucien, his legs in jeans worn tissue-thin at the knees, draped over that cracked leather ottoman, his dark eyes intent on my face. I asked, "What am I going to do?"

"Don't you have some family, your parents maybe, you could go back to?"

"No," I said. "I don't."

"You must. Or some friend from high school. Come on, Fern."

"He's back," I said. "I hear the truck."

Hal was in the house, stomping snow and rain. His eyes were wild at the edges with drinking. I lifted Tansy from the chair and took her into the pantry. The floor beneath my feet was cold as the yard's ice. I offered her shards of broken graham crackers, all I could find for a treat.

I heard Hal say, "Let's go. I got the chain."

"It's raining now."

"It's fucking snowing and raining."

"I'm not going. I'm not going to slop around in that crap."

"Get up."

"My knee's knocked out. I'm not going."

"The fuck you're not. I've had it with you lying

around the house moaning about this and that. Get the fuck up."

"Who are you? Dad?"

"Get the fuck up," Hal said, malice rimming his voice.

With my heel, I closed the pantry door. "Here, little mousie. More cracker crumbs?"

Hal was shouting, shouting. I heard a knocking over of something, more shouting, and the door slammed.

"Lick sugar off my fingers, little mousie." We sat on the pastry counter in the pantry and recited the alphabet, A to Z.

"My favorite letter, mama, is M. After that, T. What's M for, mama?"

"Mousie?"

"No . . . mama."

"I thought so. And T? Is it for tree or toad or tasty or Tansy?"

"Chocolate," she said.

"That's C."

"What does Uncle begin with?"

"U. That might be a hard one."

"I actually like T because of Tansy."

"I thought so, little one. Actually, I did."

When we came out, Lucien lay motionless in the wing chair, one hand over his closed eyes as if he were sleeping. The house was quite cold, and I knelt before the stove and raked the coals forward, jiggling them to get the ash down. Tansy stood beside me, sucking the tip of one finger and staring at Lucien. I stepped out on the porch, searching through my pile for the driest pieces. The sky was open, flicking snow against my cheeks as I looked up, searching for a lightness in the clouds that might mean clearing. Newly turned back to snow, the flakes were melting as soon as they touched my black sleeves. When I came in, I saw Tansy had taken the red quilt from his bed and was lumpily spreading the heavy blanket over his legs. The quilt warmed the room like a wide hearth.

He said evenly, "Thank you, Tansy. That's fine." His voice was very calm, like the Common's grassy lawn on a July day. "If you get that Madeline book I see over there I'll read to you."

She placed it on the armrest. He laid his long hand on the book and looked at her. "If you'd be more comfortable, Tansy, you can sit beside me. Just look out for that knee there. The rest doesn't matter much, but steer clear of knocking that knee."

She climbed over the armrest and into his chair. He read those lines I knew by heart, with twelve little girls and two straight lines. I divided my bread dough, set it into pans, and slid them in the oven. Then I stared out the window at the half-snow, half-rain dripping against the glass, smearing any clear vision of the outside world. Cold wound through the house like a pack of feral cats. When he finished *Madeline*, I said, "If the two of you are okay, I'll go out for a short walk."

Tansy said, "Go."

Lucien nodded.

"Sure?"

"Yes."

"You're up to her?"

"Go."

"There's bread in the oven. I'll be back before it's ready."

I shrugged on my coat and wound a scarf around my neck and over my hat. It was windy as well as sleeting now, and I sank my mittened fists deep in my pockets. With my face down, away from the wind, I knew right where I was going. I heard the tractor far down below the field and the grind of the chainsaw, too. I headed into the barn, where, it was true, I rarely ventured. The great space stunk of fresh manure and rotted hay. In the dim light, cows lowed. Just inside, where he often parked the tractor, was strewn with a jumble of oily tools and balled up rags. I pressed on, into the milk room, which reeked of rotten milk. The sides of the bulk tank were crusted with yellowish dried milk. I did not go in further. The cows lowed in their stanchions as I passed them, on my way outside. I stood in the blowing wind, lifting these things in my mind, turning them over, over. I trudged through shin-deep snow. Around the back I abruptly stopped. My shovel was there, the garden shovel I had used now for five years, its straight hickory handle snapped jaggedly off, halfway down. Both pieces leaned against the barn, strips of dirty red paint curling in some crude mockery from the siding.

I covered my mouth with my hand, clenching in any sound I might make. I studied it, my broken shovel. Then I turned away into the wind.

At the edge of the barn, the wind caught me full-face in a torrent of icy snow where it tore up the long fields, unbroken by trees or hedgerow or building. The snow pelted my face with its needles, and clawed down my chest where scarf and coat collar parted. I leaned against the barn's cornerboard, wide as my back, stretching from my heels to far above my head. Make myself so, I thought, *for my child*, as solid as this barn that has stood here, uncomplaining, for so many decades. The weakness of my careening heart I could stamp into the earth and set my foot firm upon it. Who would need a heart when I had my strong hands? I pushed off from the barn and headed up the drive, snow whirling. Wind blew icy and wet on my face. It filled my bones and muscles, swooped me up in its great embrace, slitted my eyes.

When I stepped in the house, warmth and the heady scent of bread baking greeted me. Tansy knelt beside Lucien, smiling, her face alight at the story he read her. She held her tiny hands over the red quilt as if it were a magic carpet that carried her up and away from dungeons and ash-stained knees and wicked trolls. When Lucien finished the story, he closed the book and she curled against his side. "It's warmy under here."

Lucien asked, "How was the walk?"

I nodded on my way upstairs. In the bedroom, I tugged my hair from the elastic and brushed until my hair crackled. Then I looked through the closet and found a clean blouse at the back, a light rose-hued one I had not worn for several years. It was too big and hung like a smock beneath my waist. Whatever had I wanted? A wood-handled tool in my hand to spade the soil, turn it over, and tend some seeds. I was out of that house I had grown up in, where I had been swathed in sterile nothingness.

Whatever was it I had wanted? To live, to live: I had thought it was that simple.

No garden dirt or crumbles of dried leaves from the yard tracked into the house of my childhood. Dull white carpet and walls, with none of the sparkle of new-fallen snow, none of the shifting hues of a cloud-filled spring sky. A box I had longed to burst beyond, into the wild world, and make my own way.

"Mama! Is the bread done? Don't burn it!"

I smoothed the smock over my hips and went downstairs. "I've never burned your bread, little one."

Curled against Lucien, she giggled. "Uncle didn't know."

"He does now."

Giggles. Giggles.

I took the golden loaves from the oven and set the kettle to boil. In my boots and sweater, I walked out to the garden, reached down into the snow, and pulled out a handful of mint. Icy rain stippled my cheeks like frozen tears.

Lucien was reading *Mouse Tales*. Dropping the mint in the teapot, my hands trembled. I spread my palms and fingers flat on the kitchen table, setting all my weight to the task, pressing as hard as I could. He read with great animation about a bird and a rock and those clever mice.

I sliced hot bread, buttered it, and cut the pieces into triangles. Listening to his voice in the other room reading that familiar story about the old man who called children horrid things, I stared down at the bread triangles. My mother had always cut sandwiches in this way for me. I had always eaten the inner points first.

Lucien said, "What a mean old man."

I put tea, cups, bread, on a tray and carried it into the living room.

"Tea time!" Tansy sang.

Lucien said, "Tea time?"

I handed him a mug of tea. "We'd go mad as hatters in the cold seasons, without some civility."

He leaned over the steaming tea and breathed in deeply, his eyes closed, smiling. "Mint," he said with contentment. He sipped the tea. "That's good."

His smile drew at the awfulness in me, how near to tears I was.

Tansy asked Lucien to read the book's table of contents to her. At each story title, she said, "Ooh, I love that one. That one's so funny."

Lucien rubbed a hand over his skinny belly, as if he could feel the warm tea settling in.

I handed him a triangle of bread.

He took it from me.

## CHAPTER 22

THEY SETTLED into a pattern, those brothers, logging after morning chores and past noon. Lucien was sometimes in the house in the afternoons, and sometimes gone, where I knew not. Tansy sulked on those afternoons. He was often absent at dinner, and late into the night. I reminded myself he had grown up on Still Mountain and a town of friends might yet be around him.

The afternoons he was in the house I sometimes went walking alone, down the fields or up into the woods. Ranged high above me were the snow-frosted shimmering mountains. I let the stillness of winter creeping in fill me.

Lucien did things I had not considered.

He oiled away the creak in Tansy's bedroom door. He mended the broken board on the front step, so we no longer had to double-step, Tansy hanging from my elbow. In the staircase where I could not reach, he replaced the lightbulb that had been burnt out for two years. He filled the woodbox. Before dinner, he had Tansy set the plates and silverware on the table. Yet he also spent considerable time in the wingchair, reading. "Not now," he'd tell Tansy. She'd curl under his chair with the little animals I had knitted her, whispering to them about the rabbits, who apparently were having some difficulties with the mice.

One afternoon Tansy and I drove the truck to town for errands. When we pulled into the library, Tansy shouted, "Uncle's car! Uncle's car!"

He was alone in the back, reading in a chair with his heels stretched up on a radiator. When he saw us, he closed his book and smiled, his face full of pleasure seeing us. "Where are you headed?"

"Chainsaw store," Tansy said. "Fill the diesel cans. A huge chocolate bar for me. This big." She spread her little hands wide.

"Is that so?"

I rolled my eyes, and he laughed.

She scrambled over the chair arm and curled herself in his lap, facing him. "Uncle, did you see the moon last night?"

"I did."

"That's Lady Moon."

"Oh? Whatever happened to the Man in the Moon?"

"There's not a man in the moon. That's Lady Moon. Did you see how she made the clouds all pretty?"

"I did." His fingers wove through her curls.

"I thought she did that very nicely."

"I thought so, too."

I gazed out the window at the wide lawn spread behind the library, a smooth plane of hardened snow. A brisk wind blew crumpled leaves by.

Tansy chanted, "Higher than a house, higher than a tree. Oh, whatever can that be? A star," then giggled.

"No stars last night," Lucien said. "Your Lady Moon outshone everything in the sky."

I had heard him in the night, downstairs. The moonlight had lain on the pillow beside me like a cheerless friend. "Come, Tansy." I hooked one finger on the back of her collar. "Let's get a stack of books for you."

"Uncle, read to me later?"

"Of course."

"Come, little one," I said, although I wanted to linger in this warm place, filled with books and cleanliness, where a trapezoid of late autumn sunlight edged across the parquet floor toward my boots.

On his lap, Tansy studied me. "My mama knitted her sweater," she told Lucien. "It's a fiddlehead pattern. See? It's opening, like the ferns in spring. See the way the yarn moves, all twisty? Just like a fiddlehead."

"I've been admiring it for a while now."

"Tansy," I said.

She wrapped her arms around Lucien's neck. "Come with? Come with?"

"I'll be along soon."

"Don't miss dinner."

"I won't," he said. "Go with your sweet mama now."

As we left the room, I glanced back over my shoulder and saw he hadn't opened his book but was turned crookedly around, watching us go.

# CHAPTER 23

ONE EVENING at dinner, Hal told Lucien he had bought a skidder.

"The hell you did," Lucien said. "With what?"

"That mill check put a start on it."

With the heel of his hand, Lucien shoved his plate of potatoes and chicken and squash across the table. "That wasn't yours to spend."

"The hell it wasn't. I got a good price on it, too."

"A good price? This isn't a bushel of corn. A skidder. Jesus. What were you thinking?"

"I think it's pretty damn clear what I was thinking. We're going to log. We need a skidder. I found one at auction that fit our price of cheap as hell. You think I'd let that pass by? That tractor we've got down there isn't doing the job at all. I know you don't give one rat's ass about machinery, but it should be clear to even you that that tractor isn't the equipment we need. This isn't rocket science, man. This is thinking. Thinking! This is putting the pieces together and figuring out a plan, getting the farm back to where it should be. So, shut up and thank me. That's right. Thank you, big brother Hal, for keeping Hidden View together."

"Put out your boot then, and I'll kiss it. Is that your intention? Come on and stick it out. I'll kneel right down there and kiss your dirty foot."

"Look here, crazy brother. When the chips go down—and, believe me, they're going to go down—this farm will have maple. I'm the one with the vision here. Not you. Not Fern. And if we need a skidder to log, to get that cash to keep maple going, then I'm goddamn well going to buy it. With no apologies."

"Who's the crazy brother here? You're planning for the apocalypse?"

"I'm planning for what needs to be done."

Abandoning the table with its dirty dishes, I scooped Tansy in my arms. The brothers argued, back and forth, around and around. Upstairs, I put the child to bed. They were yet in the kitchen, under the harsh double-ring of fluorescent light, when I came down to brush my teeth. Hal's words had razors at the edges, divots of whiskey, clawing at Lucien. As I went into the bathroom off the living room, I glanced into the kitchen. Supper dishes with uneaten piles of food were piled unevenly at one end of the table. Lucien had the accounts book open and was reading aloud, biting over every expense, every milk check, every scrap of our torn life.

I snapped off the lamp in the living room and sat on the bottom step of the staircase. In the tight house, I was concealed from the kitchen and their sparring voices, in my narrow plaster and wood perch. Nimbly in the dark, my fingers worked four knitting needles, around and around, on Tansy's sock.

"How could you do it?" Lucien demanded. "You know damn well the farm is going bust."

"What was I supposed to do? *Give in*? Lie down and die? That might be you, buddy, but it's not me."

"What's that mean?"

"It means this." Hal's fist banged the table, rattling the hodge-podge dishes. "You can just show up, after years and years, and I mean *years*, and think you have any say at all about this farm? Any fucking say in the least? You don't know one thing about what I've been doing here *all my life*. Don't you tell me what to spend and what not to. Go back to fucking Tulsa or wherever you've been, you want to pull that shit."

"You haven't been here your whole life. I can do math, too. Add it up. You joined the army. Then you took that money and went to college. You think I wouldn't have practically given a testicle to go to college? Then what'd you do with that? You came back here to this broke down farm."

"This farm is going to succeed, one way or another, and I'm damn sure it's going to be my way. The world is changing, brother, and the farm needs to change with it. I'm the one with the vision here. I'm the one who sees where the farm needs to head. And I paid my dues in that army. I put in my days scrubbing potatoes and kissing asses. I'm not going to apologize for anything. You could have signed up for the army yourself, if you weren't such a lazy prick."

Lucian laughed, scoffing. "Me? With this leg? What did I get? A busted leg. What did you get? A college education."

"It's hardly a Harvard degree. I got an associate's from

a community college. It's a gumball machine degree, brother."

"Still, it's more than I got. I didn't even make it to a high school degree. You got Fern and Tansy, too."

My hands folded over my needles. I was so still I hardly breathed.

Hal said, "I don't want to hear any whining. I don't want to hear any snot-nosed complaining. Why are you here, anyway?"

"I came because I got a letter. Half this farm is mine, brother."

"I'm so goddamn sick of hearing about that half. You want half, you take half of nothing, and pack up and go like you did before."

"Pack up and go? You think that's what I did?"

"I didn't see you sticking around. Turned seventeen, bought that damn truck, and left. Just about the time you might actually have been useful, you leave."

"What? I should have stayed here with you and the old man?"

"You just fucking skipped out. Left the old man on my back. I ran this farm for years, by myself, before I joined the army. I held up that falling down drunk bastard at the same time. I bet you never gave two thoughts to that."

"You can be sure I did. Why the hell do you think I left? You could have gone. What kept you here?"

Hal laughed, that nasty snicker: rat-like.

Lucien said, "I didn't do anything you couldn't have done. What tied you here so tight? Don't go blaming me for anything. You were stupid enough to stay. Let it all fall down. Good riddance I'd say."

Hal's heavy boots *tramped tramped tramped*, walking around the kitchen, the whiskey bottle glugging. Lucien had been in the house long enough now that I knew the step and drag of his injured leg, strength and weakness, strength and weakness. Hal's steps were solid as rocks. Knitting held in one hand, I pressed my cheek against the wall, cool plaster under my cheek.

"You don't know shit about anything. You were always a spoiled brat, buddy. The baby, the baby."

"Spoiled by whom? When did I have a chance to be babied? What nonsense are you talking? She was dead before I was two. I don't have a single memory of her. Not one. Nothing!"

"You had plenty of her. She favored you, just favored you. Always carrying you around and brushing your hair. As if no one else existed. And then your ridiculous knee. Mary Atkins coming all the time and waiting on you. Poor Lucien, poor fucking Lucien. Gets to lie around and eat pudding and not do a damn thing. Read his books. You think I don't want to read? Just you and that wife get to read!"

"What's wrong with you? Why are we even talking about this?"

"He never asked a thing of you again."

"He broke my leg. Let me say this again: he ruined my leg. He smashed me up so bad I'm never going to walk right again. My body hurts every day. Every day I'm going to remember him smashing me into that goddamn maple. What was I supposed to do? Stay here for the rest of my life as *thanks* for that?"

"Get over it, will you."

They were quiet then. A light wind brushed the house.

The sticks of a lilac bush scraped at a window, raked over the glass like a witchy fingernail.

Lucien cleared his throat. "What did you mean, she favored me? No one ever told me that."

"She cared about nothing else after you were born. Didn't look twice at me or the old man again. Like Fern. Wrapped up in that one kid and nothing else. What Ma saw in you I never figured out."

"What was she like? Come on, Hal. Since you started this."

"She's been dead a long time. Twenty-five years is a long time. There's nothing of her left here. As you said." A glass rattled against something metal, a knife or spoon perhaps.

Lucien asked, "What was he like at the end?"

Hal's marching again, *tramp tramp*. Was he going to the windows to look out? "He didn't ask about you. If you're wondering. He never said one word about you after you left. I don't think we said your name for years in this house. You were mud."

"I wasn't asking."

"He wasn't sorry in the least. For anything. Especially not for anything you think he should have been sorry for."

"I wasn't asking. Did you hear me ask?"

"You want some of this? A shot to help you sleep?"

"No."

"I'm just pointing out, there's a lot to do tomorrow. Those four hitches. Another truckload the next few days." His words tumbled against each other, like poorly stacked firewood, near to the falling point. "We can rattle on about this . . . this crap. That's what it is. Crap. But there's still tomorrow coming on up, and we've got to be working. No one else to do it. The work."

I slipped my knitting in my smock pocket and eased up the stairs at their edges, to keep from creaking the treads.

In the dark, I lay awake. Downstairs, Hal lumbered around, his voice flaming occasionally. When he crashed up, he seemed not to know I was in the bed. Almost immediately, he drunked out, his breathing clattering through the dark.

I must have slept and woke abruptly, my own breath caught against my breastbone. Under his jagged breathing, I heard water running in the plumbing. I slipped from the bed and stood on the landing, listening a long while to Tansy's sleeping breath, downy soft, like feathers rustling in a thick-walled nest.

My sight eased into the dark. Downstairs, Lucien lay crookedly on his side on the couch. He stirred at my footstep, turned, and lay on his face, arms locked over his head. Out of sheer inertia, I sat in the wing chair, listening to the loose rattle of Hal's snoring, Lucien's haphazard breath, and the lilac bush's branches scritching now and then against the window. After a bit, Lucien sat up, pushed his hair from his face, and said, "It must be very late, Fern."

"Three, I think."

"I hate how everything's worse at night."

"I don't mind the night, so much. There's no housework, at least."

"That's so."

In the dark, I couldn't see his face. A bit of white light

from the kitchen bulb over the sink lay on the floor like a stray moonbeam.

"I don't know how he does it. How he gets so badly into me."

"He's a mean man," I said, before I thought about it.

"Could be the answer." He stretched forward and touched his knee. "How'd you end up with him, Fern?"

In the cold, I crossed my arms over my chest, hands locking on my shoulders.

"Fern?"

A dry scratch caught in my throat and I coughed without covering my mouth.

"Fern?"

"Lucien." I shook my head. "I didn't know. I told you, I thought—I thought–"

"Was it lust? Is it that simple? I know my brother's strong as can be, all muscle. He must have desired you like crazy, I'm sure."

I didn't answer.

His hand rubbed over his knee, one side of his mouth curled up enough that even in the night I saw his grimace. "It's none of my business, I know. It's all prurience on my part, isn't it, about your life with my brother? Maybe it's nothing more than my own raw jealousy, just the sulky self-pity Hal keeps pointing out in me. What could I ever offer a woman? Nothing. Nothing but my broken up, bad body." The woodstove clicked-clicked one, two, as the metal cooled around the failing embers.

I coughed again, and again didn't bother to cover my mouth, hacking into the room, my hands clenching my shoulder knobs, and then the room stilled.

He said suddenly, "Tell me, Fern, was it just lust?"

"Of course not. Or not just sexual lust. Lust for the farm maybe? For a family together? For a life I thought we might create?" My voice cracked a bit. "I don't want to talk about this, Lucien. You weren't drinking with him, were you?"

"No."

"Are you going to stay?"

"Stay here? On Hidden View? For what?"

My fingernails burrowed through my nightgown, into my shoulders.

"Fern, I went through every bit of that book tonight. He's ruined this farm. You know that. What could I get out of this?"

He didn't seem to be asking me, so I didn't answer. "I don't think I'm a great materialist." His head was down, as if talking to the floor or himself. "But I've got to have something. I couldn't make it out there. It was one dead-end after another."

"In love or in work?"

He looked at me. I knew he was looking for me through the dark. "Work. I never got very far along the other path."

"You might clear some money on the wood yet. That might happen."

"I had thought so. But I was wrong. Dead wrong."

As if in pain, he hunched over his folded arms. Without thinking, I stood up and touched his shoulder. "Lucien?"

He rolled back on the couch and drew me fully over him, chest to chest, hip to hip, knee to knee. His arms folded around my shoulders, my face caught in the hollow under his chin. I heard Hal's vicious breathing from upstairs and, under that, a gurgle teasing through Lucien's belly, some wayward bit of that ruined dinner, the steady churn of his heart.

Then he shoved me from him so brusquely I half-cried out. He stood shaking in a dark corner of the room and shouted, "Leave me be! Leave me be, Fern."

I fled upstairs.

## CHAPTER 24

THE BROTHERS were in ragged shape the next morning. I set a full breakfast on the table. Hal drank coffee and twisted into his barn coat. Watching him walk to the barn, I wondered if he was yet drunk. Lucien didn't appear.

Tansy chattered through her oatmeal about a whale named Lindy who had risen out of the cornfield last night and visited her in her room. "She's a blue-gray whale, with a little bit of orange behind her ears. Mama?"

"Yes?"

"Do whales have ears?"

"I don't see why not."

"They might get a lot of ocean water in them."

I nodded. "True."

I set to cleaning the pantry shelves. In the gray November, the house echoed the season's dearth of color.

Tansy appeared beside me, sprong-haired sprite, her hands clasped before her. "Mama."

"Yes, Tansy?"

"We need to make tea."

"You're switching from hot chocolate to tea?"

"Mama, it's for uncle."

I looked behind her but saw no one. "Did you go into his room?"

"I knocked on his door first. He wasn't coming down for breakfast. He says he's not hungry. At all. I think we should bring him tea."

I was on my knees, cleaning out the lower cabinet of pans.

"Mama, we need to make tea. Tea would be good for him."

"All right, all right. You go find a cup you want. I'll heat some water."

When the tea had steeped, Tansy poured it into a hefty ceramic mug. She added milk and maple syrup and then looked at me.

I wrapped a towel around the mug to soften the heat against her skin. "Go ahead," I said. "I'll finish this and then come up."

She lifted the mug in both hands. Her black eyes shone through the rising steam. "It's hot," I said. "Careful now. Careful."

"I am careful."

One after another, her small footsteps ascended the stairs. I stood at the bottom where she could not see me and leaned against the wall.

Lucien spoke quietly. "Tansy, how nice."

"This is tea."

She must have set the tea down as I heard her fussing about him, offering a pillow behind his back, saying, "Here, here. Here."

She said, "This is really good tea. Smell how nice it is? Mama made it, from things in our garden. Say your tummy feels bad? This is really good for a hurting tummy. Or you're really really cold? This is good for that. Once we were walking in the woods in the spring, or the winter, I forget. It wasn't summer. There was snow. And it started raining? I was *so cold*. I might have cried a little coming back. Mama was mad at me, but then she made me tea, and I warmed right up!"

"Is that so?"

"You need to drink that while it's hot. I'm sure it'll help your knee. Do you think whales have ears?"

"No."

"Why not? Mama thinks they might, but I think they might get too much water in their ears."

"What would whales need to hear?"

"Their *babies*, uncle."

"That's true."

I went up and leaned in the doorframe. Lucien was sitting up against the headboard, the red quilt spread up his chest. His eyes flicked sideways to me. Tansy knelt on the bed beside him, heels tucked under her bottom. The room was suffused with the camphor and lemon scent often trailing Lucien. A greasy jar of liniment sat uncapped on the little table. Beside Lucien's hand, a library book lay open, pages down, on the quilt. I lifted it and read silently,

*Now wind torments the field*
*turning the white surface back*
*on itself, back and back on itself,*

*like an animal licking a wound.*
*Nothing but white—the air, the light . . .*

I closed the book and laid it facedown on the small table beside his bed, near the label-stripped jar of liniment and the stack of books I had devoured when I slept in this bed with a nursing child, in that time before I knew Lucien. With nowhere else to go, I sat in the single chair.

"So, Mama, I was telling uncle about the whale with the orange behind her ears. Not at all like earrings," she informed us.

Lucien sipped the hot tea, his gaze on the window and what bit of sky he might see there, his head leaning back against the high headboard. "The whale jumped like this, like this." Her hand swooped. In the daylight from the single window I saw how drawn he looked around the eyes. From where I sat, the window was filled mainly with the mass of maple branches, a tangle of wilderness. Midday, this was all the light we were going to get that day.

I pulled my knitting from the pocket in my smock.

"The weird thing about whales, you never expect them in a cornfield, do you?"

"That's so," he said.

Tansy chattered about whales and Jack Frost. My needles worked through the yarn. We were all near each other in the little room, the sky at the window great shifting clumps of clouds.

In a lapse in Tansy's story, Lucien said, "I was wrong last night, Fern. I wasn't thinking very well."

Tansy and I looked at him.

"You weren't thinking well about what you said, or what you did? That last part at the end."

He paused, then: "What I said."

Tansy rubbed his hand. "You're cold, uncle."

"You heard Hal and me?" he asked me.

"I did, some."

"He couldn't have meant all that. He was pretty far gone."

"He certainly did mean all that. He meant every bit of all that. Why fool yourself?" I set my knitting on the chair and stood at the window. Snow was falling again, a steady pace of lightness accumulating into fields of tundra.

"Is he out there?"

"Yes." I pressed my forehead to the glass.

"How can he do that? You think he'd be falling over. Does he have no weakness in him at all?"

I studied that landscape of snow and the giant skeletons of leafless trees. A single crow flew over the garden, black wings flapping steadily, and disappeared in the snowing sky. When I spoke, my breath fogged the cold glass. "Where did you go, when you left?"

"I stayed a little bit in a lot of places. The UP, Whidbey Island, Salt Lake."

I raked my finger through that cloud of fog, cut it right in two. "Where are you headed next?"

"I don't know."

"I can't imagine what that would be like. To just up and leave, go."

My hands moved over the windowsill, wanting to grab onto something, tight.

"It's not all it's cracked up to be."

I turned around and sat down in the chair beside him. The room was so narrow I could have reached over and brushed loose the strand of hair caught in his eyelashes.

Tansy laid her head against his belly. “You need to get better,” she exhorted. “Uncle, we need you well.”

His hand stroked her curls. I took up my knitting and began where I had left off.

## CHAPTER 25

All afternoon, Lucien slept. Tansy and I were quiet in the house. The downstairs rooms felt as though jars of glass had been hurled and smashed the night before, and if we trod too carelessly rogue slivers might pierce our feet. I picked two handfuls of kale from the garden and made a soup of kale and beans and pork. Hal came in and went to bed without eating. Tansy and I played Crazy Eights and went to sleep early, too.

Again in the night, sleeplessness plagued me. Beside Hal, I lay awake, my toes pointed straight toward the footboard, as if in rigor mortis, my hands curled at my shoulders. Hal's breath churned steadily, like a chopping maul. At last, unable to endure my distraught thinking, I slipped from the bed. In the tiny hall between the three rooms, I listened to Hal's steady snores, Tansy's light wheeze, and Lucien, too. At first, I couldn't hear him and imagined he had gone downstairs, too, but then he muttered, sleep-choked, "Yeah, yeah," and the bedsprings creaked as he rolled over.

Downstairs, I fed the woodstove as quietly as I could. In the kitchen, I sat on the stool drawn near to the sink and jerked the pullchain for the small light. The sink's white ceramic was stained brown in a great ugly splatter. With my heels hooked over the stool's rung, I worked at Tansy's green and gold-flecked sock, my thoughts easing into the scalloped pattern of yarn. A mouse, startled by the light, scurried beneath the range. Around and around and around I knitted, decreased, and then finished, biting the yarn free with my teeth. I held up the sock to the light. The sock was ridiculously small in my hand, so small I knew it probably would not even stretch over Tansy's heel, let alone serve as a sock. The library-book pattern was so mesmerizing, with its lacy scallops, I hadn't studied it for practicality. I laid the sock and the ball of yarn with the needles stuck through on the counter. A single sock, its mate not yet begun.

Deep in the night, so deeply dissatisfied, I slid into my boots and coat and hat and went out the kitchen door, hurrying down the frozen, rutted up path, then veered off that and ran into the field. Under my boots grew the winter rye, still green and pliable despite the winter hammering in. I stopped, gasping. Overhead sprawled the cosmos, Orion a sentry in a universe I did not understand. A gibbous moon rose waxing in the east, sailing in its own course of destiny. The cold drilled into me, and I bent my head and trudged back toward the house with its small glow of the light I had left on, hands fisted in coat pockets.

As I neared the house, the overhead kitchen fixture blazed on. I stood on the path, cloaked in the night, and gazed through the windows. Lucien, in his long underwear and plaid shirt, limped back and forth in the kitchen, one hand rubbing his forehead, the other his belly. I was near enough to the windows to see a distressed pain zigzag his mouth. He stopped at the range and lifted the steaming kettle, and I realized he had come downstairs for hot tea. The mug steamed on the counter. With one shoulder bent down toward his crooked leg, he lifted the green sock I had finished and held it under the light, his lower lip nipped between his teeth. Then, surprising me so that my breath drew in sharply, he pressed the sock to his face and closed his eyes. He stood there for the longest time, with the pretty-patterned, newly made sock against his lips and nose, his other hand cupped around a belly pain, before he finally laid the sock where he had found it, lifted the hot mug, and killed the light. I waited in the dark; no other lights gleamed on. At last, I entered the house, but Lucien had taken the tea upstairs with him, and I did not see him that night.

In the morning, Hal wrote me a list before he went to the barn. Gasoline, bar oil, kerosene. The leaves were gone now, every bit of them except for the tan furled beech hanging on stubbornly. Frost hiked up the windows. I told Tansy to put more clothes on before we left.

"I'm wearing tights and two dresses and one vest and panties, mama."

"Put on some pants, too. It's cold out, little one."

"Over my flowered tights?"

"Yes, over your flowered tights."

"Hmph." She stomped to her room.

Lucien appeared in the kitchen as I was counting the money Hal had given me. I looked up and said, "How are you this morning?"

"Cold. Are you going to town?"

"For him." I folded the money deep into my pocket.

Lucien limped to the front window and leaned against the wall, looking out, all his weight on his good leg, his complexion sallow. "It looks nasty out there."

"Can I get you something in town? Something you want?"

Tansy ran in and wrapped her arms around Lucien's waist and kissed his hip. "My uncle."

By the collar, I tugged her back with one hand. "Don't be rough."

I was about to say something when Bill Atkins appeared at the door. Someone had called him about buying a hog from us, and he asked about the skidder and when it was going to be delivered. I gathered our things together while Lucien spoke with him. Tansy dressed in her coat and hat and hurried out the door, standing on her tiptoes to talk to Bill's dog Lyle in the truck.

Bill went to let Lyle out for a run. Lucien headed upstairs.

Just as I left, I hollered up the staircase, "We'll be home in a few hours, Lucien!"

"Take care of yourself and the little girl." I heard him shuffling around.

Bill and Tansy were at the door, and I had to go.

## CHAPTER 26

HE WAS GONE when we came back. I knew when I pulled in and saw his car missing that he had left. Beside me, Tansy chattered. I said nothing, merely clenched my hand around the steering wheel, and then I got out.

## CHAPTER 27

Making biscuits for dinner that night, my hand reached in the flour bin for the scoop and found an envelope. I was alone in the pantry and ripped it open. Inside, he had left me six twenty-dollar-bills and three tens, folded up in a page torn from a book of poetry. In one poem, two lines were circled. I read, *There is only one heart in my body, have mercy on me.* I read the poem over and over, then folded the money and poem back into the envelope and buried it in the flour.

# Part Three

## CHAPTER 28

THAT WAS a winter of much ice, of snow falling and turning to rain, and the rain icing the world around us. Many mornings I looked out the windows at a sea of ice surrounding the house, miring our house like Shackleton's ship. Tansy resented her uncle's absence. But why, why, did he need to go? And where did he go?

I had no answers for her plaintive questions and little sweetness to offer as consolation. I taught her the alphabet instead. By sugaring season, when the days gradually lengthened and the sun gave some vague promise of warmth, she could read little words, *cat* and *bed* and *rat*. I had this, at least, to offer her.

In the winter, the farm tightened around us. Tansy and I ceased going to town. There was scant gas money, and what money we had, Hal kept. He worked steadily at the lower field, and those pines were shorn by the end of February. Tansy and I went there only once. The forest was gone. What remained was stumps and brush debris. One pile he burned. From the house, Tansy and I saw the fire leap wildly all night. In the morning, it smoldered as a giant ash heap. When we walked down, we saw the deep pile of ash falling over the electric-hued coals.

In March, he left the skidder there and tapped the sugarbush. The work in the sugarhouse began then, the five thousand taps' worth of sap pouring in through the days and nights of thaw. The new arch was fast. When the fire was lit, we began and did not stop until all the sap had distilled into syrup. There were no longer those lulls where I stepped outside the closed up sugarhouse and leaned against the rough-board exterior, listening to the redwing blackbirds nesting in the pines. The boiling was so rapid on this arch we seemed to be perpetually drawing off syrup, or else on the verge of it. In the buckets of snow we melted against the stack, I washed filters as fast as I could, my hands stinging in the icy water, swollen and clumsy. Tansy was there all those long working hours, sometimes happily playing with a rusted dishpan of mud or standing under the edge of the roof in the rain, head tipped back, dripped water splashing into her laughing face. But she tired, too, of the closeness of the sugarhouse, how frantically Hal and I moved around, worried about burning syrup, keeping the fire at a maximum ferocity, and wearing ourselves down into crabby and unpleasant beings.

The worst of the new system Hal and Nat had designed was the noise. No longer could we hear the fire's crackle, the bubble of sap as it thickened toward syrup. Only the monotonous spin of the two fans ground through the sugarhouse, over the generator's stuttering background. The contemplative roll of steam toward the open cupola's sunbeam-shot light was chewed up by the machinery's unrelenting chaos, the thrusting drive of metal on metal. At the end of a boiling session, late afternoon or deep in the evening, my head throbbed. I was sore all through my shoulders and back and feet as I had always been after hours in the sugarhouse, but these times I was also hollowed out to a dull headache. The steady noise served to separate us three even further, as we could not even really talk to each other. Tansy and I mouthed brief things at each other. If we really needed to talk, we had to step outside behind the woodshed.

With my broken garden shovel, Hal opened and slammed shut the arch door, a bone-jarring clang, repeating over and over.

Six days into this, Tansy stomped her feet rather than follow me down the hill. "No! Won't go."

"Tansy, this isn't an option. We need to work."

She shook her head. "Won't go."

"Tansy."

"Hate it down there. Crabby hates it down there. Flopsy and Mopsy aren't going either."

I picked her up and tucked her under my arm and carried her down the hill, her legs thrashing and kicking me. I dumped her in a snowbank beneath the sugarhouse eaves and stomped inside. Hal had already started the fire and glared at me over the front pans. "This is going to come right up," he said. "Get the filters and bucket ready."

Outside, Tansy howled.

"What's wrong with her?"

"She doesn't want to be down here anymore."

"Get the filters ready." He disappeared behind the high back pan.

At last, Tansy finally dragged herself hangdog into the sugarhouse and rubbed her tear-messed face against my thigh. "Sorry, Mama, sorry, Mama, sorry from Crabby and Foxglove, Mama."

I bent to kiss her damp hat, when behind me Hal screamed. A high-throated peal of raw emotion. Somehow, he had gotten his glove stuck in the huge arch door's latch, the leather thumb pinned between the metal, and his feet stamped wildly. This time, I merely stood there and watched as he undid the latch, pulled his thumb free, then stood back, breath heaving in his chest. His eyes, wild, scattershot around the steamy interior, and I soundlessly wrapped my arm around Tansy, and we stepped out.

☾

A few weeks later, the sun higher and significantly warmer, I began to think of the possibility of spring. One afternoon, driving back from errands in town, Hal met us walking to the mailbox and said he had sold that logging site and thirty acres more below it.

"To who?"

"Karl Jaspers."

Jaspers and his son were loggers. "Not for much," I guessed.

"Enough."

Sitting in the big pickup, he didn't look down at us, but higher, over our heads, up the wooded mountain slope. I glanced at Tansy. She had run ahead on the dirt road and tapped her boot on ice sheathed over puddles, her toe breaking through the skinny film. With his head tipped back like that, I saw black grime rimming the lines of his neck.

Tansy squawked, and I guessed she had dunked her foot.

"Hal, you really want to do that? Sell off pieces of the farm?"

"I used that piece up, Fern. There's nothing there for me anymore. Turn it around. Get rid of it. That's how I'm thinking. What's encumbering this farm? Debt and beholding. There'll be less of that, now."

"Is that what you're going to do? Put that money toward the bank and mortgage?"

His head leaned over the seatback against the rear window. Not seeing the track of his eyes, I had no way of knowing if he was looking out the dirt-smeared window or, instead, was merely focused somewhere in his own mind. "Milk," he said, not turning to me, "was my dad's life here. That, and other little, piddly things, a little syrup, a little firewood. Those days are gone. I've got to make this farm in my own way, or it's going to be in someone else's hands. It's as simple as that, girl."

"I'm going, Mama!" Grinning at me, Tansy ran around the bend in the road, disappearing.

He leaned forward and held his hand around the keys in the ignition.

Waiting for his final words, my eyes flicked away from him to the hemlocks along the road, the branches low enough that Tansy liked to pick their tiny pinecones. Right at eye level, a small saw-whet owl stared at me, unblinking, its wide face white-feathered with tuffs of gray. "Hal," I said quietly.

He cleared his throat. "Enough's going to have to be enough." He put the truck in gear and drove away.

I stood there alone on the muddy road, staring at that owl, intensely alive, miraculously motionless.

"Mama!" Tansy shouted. I turned to look at her running back around the bend, jacket flying open around her. When I pointed at the hand-sized owl, the creature had disappeared without a sound. "Mama, I'm wet and very crabby."

The sale was none of my affair. I had rights, perhaps, by marriage, but not by deed. At dinner, he was ebullient, busy with his glass and liquor bottle. "Nothing like getting a check to put a shine on the day." He headed down to the sugarhouse after dinner to boil that day's sap, the last of the season he said. "I'll do this boil slow by myself. You don't need to come. It's a frog run, this year."

Tansy said, "Frog run? You're boiling frogs? Yucky."

"Frog run is the last sap run of the season, when the peepers are out." He lifted his glass as if saluting the sap gods. "The season doesn't often run this late. It's a lucky one. We've had a good year."

He sat at the table, drinking and smiling. With Tansy on my hip, I leaned against the sink, watching him. He didn't look to me for confirmation. A good year, he said again. A good year.

Tansy and I had been outside all day, spading the garden, planting optimistically early spinach and peas. She was nearly sleeping as I read to her. The sun hung with us in these lengthening days.

I cleaned the kitchen and swept the ashes from beneath the woodstove. For a few minutes, I stood on the porch, the sunset bleeding over the horizon, then sinking quickly into dark. I inhaled deeply, the earth soaking with thaw. In a while, I went upstairs and dressed for bed. Tansy slept in pink pajamas. Through her window, moonlight lit her face with a luminescent glow, her lips crimson red as they had been at her birth.

In the warm evening, I stepped outside in my nightgown and mud boots and leaned against a maple. Around the house, snow had mostly melted. I leaned my head back and smelled wood smoke, the richness of thawing earth, opening up after such a long hard season. In the swamp, peepers sang and chirped, an amphibian cacophony.

Then a different sound cut in, a car engine winding up the driveway. I leaned against the tree, motionless. Whoever was driving drove without lights, and the engine stopped before the car turned the final bend. I waited, and in a few moments a figure in a white shirt that caught strands of moonlight appeared, walking with a jerky dip on one side, a broken body badly put back together. He came up the driveway and hovered at the lilacs' twiggy edge. Far down below, at the bottom of the field, the sugarhouse's two small windows gleamed, the stack shooting sparks into the unbounded night.

Either I moved or he found my white nightgown in the moonlight. Quickly, he was beside me, his hands on my shoulders. In the moonlight, his hair was wild around his head, shading his face.

"Lucien?" I whispered, although there was no need to whisper.

"I came back for that closing, for the cash, and he said not to come here. We met at Jorgensen's office. He couldn't sign that land over to Jaspers without my signature, and I came to be sure to get that check." He pondered the sugarhouse. "I heard him tell Jorgensen he'd be finishing up tonight."

"You're not a moonlit dream?" In the dimness, I reached for his hand but got his waist instead, my hand tugging cotton and flesh. We were all body, hands over skin.

He pressed me against the tree, bark prickly through my nightgown. His hands moved over my thighs, up my belly and around my breasts. I heard his zipper breaking, and he was pushing at me, questioning. I opened my legs and let him in. I was wide and rich as the earth, the great mawing opening singing around us. He slid right in and filled me up. Over and over he came out and in, and my belly swelled round and tight with his seed. I drenched him, my water flowing down my legs, sticking the two of us together. "Fern," he said. "Oh, my lovely Fern."

He knelt before me and held my nightgown up, his mouth sucking at me as if I were a welcome rain, and I believed I must be pouring into him. I trembled all over as if a hail pounded me. He slid into me again and leaned his arms over my head on the tree. My lips reached up for his. He had undressed no more than unzipping, but my gown was around my neck, my nipples hard in the spring night. "Oh, Fern," he said and ran his hands over me, over all of me, my chin and my breasts, my belly so full, my lips there and legs and down my calves into the tops of my rubber boots. "Fern. You must be the most lovely woman. I can't believe just how lovely you are, Fern, the dearest thing in the world." Then he covered me with my nightgown and led me by the hand to the house. Overhead was the sky spread with winking stars, all the way down to the edges of the earth and the glowing sugarhouse.

"You come, too. He won't be up soon."

"I'll be in later. Let me walk around a little, get my bearings." In the light from the house his face was serious, no longer greedy with my name.

I went in, washed, and lay down. Chips of bark from the maple itched my scalp.

He didn't come in. I went to the window and looked down. In the moonlight, he stood before the house, looking around, down to the sugarhouse still glowing in the darkness, then up at the sky spread with those tiny bits of stars like jewelweed. He looked over his shoulder, as if searching for me. I wanted to open the window and call down, but the storm windows were still latched. I lifted the lower sash and held the cold latch's metal without opening the lock. "Coward!" I wanted to shout. "Coward!" Or, equally, "Come in, come in!"

He tugged his untucked shirt tighter around his body. Then Lucien was walking away, toward the lilacs. I ran into his room and stood at his window. With that jerk in his walk, looking back over his shoulder at the house and then up at the sky, he disappeared down the driveway.

## CHAPTER 29

YARN. How I craved skeins and balls of the colored stuff, something I might work my wooden needles through. One Saturday, on my meat delivery route, Tansy and I pulled over at a rummage sale. Threateningly overcast that morning, the sale had been moved inside a garage on Chesterfield's Main Street, double doors rolled up. I had no intention of buying anything, yet I pulled over at the sidewalk. Tansy and I walked through the long tables spread with bric-a-brac, and then in a corner, on an armchair with the stuffing sticking out of it, I spied a clear plastic bag of balled yarn. My little girl and I bee-lined. Relinquishing five dollars, I bought the bag.

I envisioned knitting a rainbow sweater for Tansy, a fair isle hat for myself, mittens of warmth and many colors.

None of that came to fruition.

Where I had wanted wool, the balls of yarn were mainly acrylic, cheaply made and overly bright, knitting up in a false and cheap way. Where I had craved durable wool redolent with lanolin and not too distant from the earth, the acrylic slipped between my fingers with no warmth or living presence. But in the bag's center, I discovered three skeins of the thinnest gray wool that had not been wound into balls, had not, in fact, even had their labels split. From the faded labels I guessed the yarn had been bought a number of years ago, probably in a department store. What could I do with that gray yarn?

I rubbed it between my fingers. I tried knitting Tansy a hat. She curled her upper lip in disgust and announced she would never wear such an ugly color. To myself, I wondered where she had discovered the liberty of choosing beauty over practicality. Evenings, while Tansy slept, I ransacked that bag of yarn and experimented knitting small pieces with the needle sizes I had. Dissatisfied, I unraveled it all.

Waking in the middle of one night, I had a sudden vision of a gray vest, with a regular seeded pattern. In my mind, I saw that vest spinning out from my knitting needles, growing in width and length to a woman's-sized sweater, for me. I could not sleep. When Hal dressed and went out to the milking, I put on the coffee, oatmeal, and poached eggs, and then I looped yarn over my needles, pulling firm as I cast on. Over the next few days, stealing minutes from the garden and house, I worked furiously at my knitting project. When the initial ribbing at the vest's hem was finished, I began the seeded pattern, winding in bits of that frou-frou acrylic yarn as I knitted, intending to create a field of blooming flowers. After dinner, while I read *Charlotte's Web* to Tansy on the couch, my fingers kept busy with that project. Beside me, Tansy sorted through the yarn, picking colors for the next row of yarn blossoms.

In a plastic grocery bag, I carried the emerging vest and a handful of yarn to the library story hour on a rainy Wednesday morning. I had nearly reached the armpits.

The day before, Hal had shattered the pickup's rear window. Nat Gilchrist, having switched his house's heating from wood to gas, had offered us what remained of his woodpile, in exchange for pork. Chucking the cord wood in the truck's bed, Hal had lobbed a piece through the rear window, and the safety glass had crazed into tiny pieces. He mended this not by going to Gates' Salvage and purchasing a used window, but by duct taping plastic over that hole. As I drove to the Common, the duct tape ripped free and the plastic snapped with the drive's wind. Rain sputtered on my neck. "Mama!" Tansy complained. I pulled over and vainly tried to mend the cobbled repair.

I had hoped by the time story hour was over the rain would have ceased, but instead I drove back to Hidden View with the rain lashing my neck and shoulders, and Tansy kvetching in her soaked carseat. Not until that evening when Tansy and I were settling on the couch with E. B. White did I think of my knitting in that plastic bag and ran out to the pickup. The truck, jammed with tools and Hal's chaps, did not contain the plastic bag. Disbelieving, I searched all through the cab, even under the seats, and then climbed through the torn plastic over the broken window and kicked through the piles of bark. I remembered placing the bag behind Tansy's headrest, tucked in a corner behind the seatbelt where I believed it had been secure, away from the mud on the floor. While I was driving with rain and wind blowing in, and Tansy complaining, the bag must have lifted in the breeze, its thin plastic hardly rustling, and tumbled out. The next morning, I retraced the roads we had driven, Tansy's face pressed against the side window, scanning the ditches for that white bag. We never found it.

## CHAPTER 30

SPRING MARCHED into early summer. Tansy and I worked in the garden every day. As if in an attempt to salvage our farm life, Hal and I implicitly spread ourselves thin. Or perhaps we didn't know what else to do. I pushed the garden boundary further. He was out the door before light. We met up at supper, bleary-eyed with exhaustion. In the hottest days, Tansy generally didn't dress beyond underwear, which saved me laundry.

Nat's syrup check was delayed and didn't arrive until June. Lifted in my arms, Tansy picked it out of the mailbox one late afternoon. I opened it on the walk back to the house. The check was smaller than I had hoped. But still—it was a sizable check. In the driveway, I stood turning the check over and over, pale blue with dot matrix printing on one side, made payable to Hal Hartshorn. Tansy squatted in the weeds, naked backed, her teeny fingers picking apart a vetch leaf, slender lobe by lobe. I held the long check up to the sunlight. The dot matrix printing blurred, strands of dusty spiderweb.

I set the check on the table beneath the salt shaker.

Coming from the barn, Hal glanced at it before he washed his hands, then folded it into his wallet.

I'd steamed the spring's first peas, robbed a bed of new potatoes just large enough to boil and mash. Over this, I poured cream Hal had brought up in the silver pail from the barn, these round gems of peas and potatoes sweet in delicacy, slathering the vegetables in yellow-hued buttery cream. Tansy happily spooned into her dinner, murmuring, "And then Flopsy said to Mopsy, we can eat peas all summer." She smiled at her spoon. "This is the bestest dinner."

Hal and I served ourselves. We ate with great appetite, all three of us, this fresh farm-grown meal our variation of manna after a long winter and endless meals from the freezer and root cellar. I said, "Let's buy blueberry bushes with some of that check."

With the back of his hand, my husband brushed drops of cream from his mustache. "Why?"

"There's that level area beyond the garden. Tansy and I have been scoping it out. I think we could put twenty bushes there, easy, and in a few years, we'd have plenty of berries."

"What's a few years?"

I shrugged and filled Tansy's bowl again from the skillet. "Six." I blinked. I had been thinking eight. "It's long-term planning, Hal."

We ate heartily, the three of us, sunbrowned and sweaty, dirt and chaff flecking from us over the table, our chairs, onto the floor.

I said, "I wonder why no one ever planted berries here."

"There's wild apples."

I nodded.

Hal said, "And wild raspberries."

"Never more than a few handfuls of those."

"How much are these blueberry bushes?"

I took my mail-order catalog from the cabinet and spread it out over the table. "See, if we get twenty, there's a discount." I showed him the two varieties I had circled in blue pen, and talked about peat. Hal flipped through the magazine.

I said, "Let's use some of the maple check for this. To put back into the farm."

"Hm," he said.

As the angle of light gradually diminished in the kitchen, we ate every bit of that mash in the skillet, Tansy finally pulling the cast iron pan toward her and gathering leftover drops of cream onto her fingertip and sucking them clean. As we talked and leafed through those glossy pictures, I could see our berry bushes ten years from then, their branches drooping down toward the earth, laden with fat purple berries ripening blue. The vision was so real to me, so nearly perfectly tangible, I could almost close my eyes and imagine I might walk out the door and along the garden, and there, instead of the scrubby burdock-ridden field, I could kneel down and cradle white berry blossoms in my hand.

The three of us sat there long after the meal was eaten, my husband and I talking about the garden and berries, and just how delicious was blueberry pie with whipped cream and maple syrup. Her lips smeared around the edges with potatoes and peas, Tansy looked from one parent to the other. I boiled water for tea. The meal seemed a perfect ripe berry in itself, a bit of savory sweetness we held in our mouths.

Later, I bathed Tansy. After I had read to her and tucked her, soap-smelling, into her bed, I came downstairs to look at the berry catalog again. As I walked through the living room, graying into twilight, I heard Hal's muttering voice in the kitchen and paused. I stood in the dim room, peering into the kitchen lit unforgivingly by the overhead double-ringed fluorescent light. His hand flipped Nat's check back and forth, like a flash card with the problem on one side, answer on the other. That blue jelly jar sat on my opened berry catalog. "Goddammit," he muttered. "God fucking dammit." He lifted the jar and drank. The back of his hand holding the check smeared across his lips. I could imagine the ring stains that jar would leave on my catalog, how that wetness would pucker and distort those pages, edging them toward ruin.

I turned quietly around in the living room and eased as soundlessly as I could up the staircase and sat on the floor in Tansy's room in the dark, my hands clenched over my knees. In just that little space of time, I realized I would never set the blade of my shovel to that burdock-ridden piece of earth. That night, I dreamed of opulent berries in my mouth, sun-warmed, sweet, succulent, dripping juice down my chin. Then I woke, and the dream was gone.

☾

In our perpetual cash hunger, Hal arranged for restaurants and stores in Chesterfield to buy our syrup and frozen pork. Although he preferred to be the one out and driving around, he was often too busy to make the drive into Chesterfield, and Tansy and I went every few weeks. We kept to ourselves. This I was able to do: with every grocery bill I paid, every bank deposit I made, I was able to pilfer just a few dollars, sometimes five, sometimes no more than two. But those I slipped into my pocket and then hid in a back corner of the bottom pantry cabinet in a chipped butter dish. If my little one and I were ever to leave Hidden View, I would need that nest egg, that clump of prudence.

There is but one heart in my body, I whispered to myself as I repeated that drive back to Hidden View, the road along the river twisting and winding. Have mercy on me. Have mercy on my working flesh and my bones and my coursing blood. Who was there to have mercy on me? Surely not my little child. Myself: but myself having mercy on myself would get us nowhere. I kept my hands industrious as I could, staving off an increasing panic.

At the end of August, when the garden and fields were at their lushest, bent under fruit and blossom, Bill and Mary Atkins drove up one evening as I was clearing the supper table. He helped her out of the truck. Mary moved woodenly, placing her feet deliberately before her. He reached in the truck, quick as he was, and slid a pie dish into one hand. With the other, he cupped her elbow. I stepped out on the porch. She had never visited the house as long as I had been here, and it seemed ages since I had seen her. When had I abandoned my walking habit? "It's a pleasure to see you," I said.

Bit by shaking bit, she looked up from her feet. "With

all these blackberries," she said. "It seemed a shame not to bake a pie."

Into the back of my thighs, Tansy whispered, "A blackbird pie?"

I reached behind me and laid my hand on my daughter's head.

Mary and Bill came steadily toward us, not having heard. "Where's Hal?" he asked.

Quietly: "The king was in his counting house, counting all his cows."

I wondered if I was hearing voices. I stepped back against the house, knocking Tansy free from her hiding game.

"Milking," I said.

Mary labored up the three steps. Tansy, whirling on a porch post, singsang, "The queen was in the kitchen, eating bread and stew of rue."

We settled Mary into the wingchair, and Bill said, "Guess I'll go check on that milking."

I offered her tea but she wanted only a glass of water. Tansy stayed on the porch, looking through the screen door. We chitchatted about gardens, the warm weather, how quickly Tansy was growing. I offered her a slice of the pie, but she said, "No, no, dear, that's for your family." Then, "Have you heard from Lucien?"

I shook my head. "He can't call, and he doesn't write, I guess. I'm," I shrugged, "I'm not certain where he is. He never talked about those things."

Tansy pressed her small nose to the screen mesh, a divot on the fragile material.

Mary closed her eyes. I looked at her carefully, wondering if she were faint. Then she opened them and looked around. "I was just wondering, was all. I haven't been here, in this house, since after his accident. He was a nice boy," she said.

I nodded. "He is. He is."

"They never seemed to have gotten over his accident, the three of them, Harold and Hal and Lucien. The two of them just wanted to pretend it hadn't happened, and Lucien, of course, well, he couldn't."

Mary had a way of blinking her eyes rapidly, then winking her right, twitching her head down a little to that side, and then beginning the blinking all over again. She wore a long pale pink dress patterned with chickweed, tiny flowers, leaves and stems.

"He seems resigned to it," I said.

"Does he? That's good. It was such an awful time for him, when it happened. I would visit him sometimes, bring him something he liked, stewed chicken or mashed potatoes, vanilla ice cream. I sewed him a quilt, a red patchwork from scraps, that I began the night I heard."

"Did you? A red quilt you said?"

"He was in the hospital for so long that I gave it to him while he was still there. He was young then, but yet he wasn't a child anymore. He was fifteen and on his way to growing up. I used to wonder if that marked him, if he wasn't able to ever grow up and that's why he never came back." One trembling hand rose, as if with a will of its own, hovered about a foot over her lap, and then shook its way back down again. "But then he did." Her eyelids fluttered as if a light streamed in. "He would come see us, some evenings. Just for a bit. He and Bill would talk. He spoke of Tansy a lot. And you, too."

"Is that so? I didn't know."

Tansy opened the door and curled into my lap. I asked the child, "Did you see father and Bill?"

She shook her head.

Mary's shuddering eyes wandered around the room. "Didi would have been glad to see you here, I think. Keeping things together so nicely."

"Didi?"

"Deidre. Harold's wife?"

I had not known her name.

"He was not a good husband to her. I knew her well, quite well, and he was not at all kind to her."

I nodded.

She went on. "I'm sorry for you, all alone here. I wish I could help you some. Didi and I had our boys together, and then we did so much together, canning and cooking. We spring house-cleaned together. Here, it's just you and the child."

"I don't mind."

Her eyes went over me like sprinkles.

I wondered if she knew I was lying, and I said, "It's a beautiful piece of land, isn't it?"

Mary said, "It is. True, it is. The view this farm has, especially. The way you come out of the woods and the sky and earth are all spread out. Of course, Didi would have wished the boys didn't cut the pines at the far end. Cathedral pines, she called them, the way they pulled the sky to the earth."

"Cathedral pines," I echoed.

I stood and tugged a panel of curtain free from its hook, to shade her face from the late afternoon sun. "Thank you, dear," she said. She raised her hands and touched her hair on either side, as if to affirm her tidiness. I sat nearer her, on the ottoman. Her dress came all the way down to her sturdy black shoes. I wanted to rest my cheek on her pale pink knees with their lace of chickweed. This near to her, I sensed the faint tremor all through her upper body, shoulders and arms, a palsy she mostly checked by clasping her hands in her lap.

"Lucien was a different child from Hal from the get-go. Hal was always so *strong*, so busy. He was more interested in rolling over, and crawling and walking and running, than he was in Didi or nursing. But Lucien was a quieter baby. He wanted to be in Didi's arms, or on her back. Even at two, he would crawl into her lap whenever she sat down. She kept his hair longer than Harold approved, and she would stroke those long curls. She kept them silky clean and brushed his baby hair. It's impolite to say so, but she favored her younger. It wasn't a secret." Her eyes blinked at me, her right side dipping a little deeper. "If she'd known what was going to happen to him, her heart couldn't have borne it." Her lips trembled slightly. "Harold thought everyone blamed him for the accident. Maybe they did, and that was true. But he took it out on Lucien. When Lucien came back from the hospital, he was on crutches and slept on the couch. Harold and Hal couldn't escape him. They left him alone all day. I would come and make him meals, help him around. He just couldn't seem to get better. Harold finally told me not to come anymore. That it was Lucien's leg, and he had to figure out how to get around." Her voice dropped low. "I was afraid of that man, and I didn't come back. But I felt terrible about it. Whatever would Didi have thought? It seemed merciless of me, that cowardice."

"She couldn't have thought that."

"She might have. He was her boy, alone and hurt."

From behind, Tansy slid into my lap and nuzzled against my chest.

Mary smiled at her. "You're a pretty little girl. Your Uncle Lucien has a sweet spot for you that I'd never seen him have for anyone. He thinks the world of you."

Tansy squeezed my hand. "Do you know where he is?"

"I don't." Mary shook her head. "You must miss him."

My little one sucked on a strand of curl.

There was no longer any need for the curtain to be pulled. The sun had shifted far enough along the ridge that it ceased suffusing the room. The men's feet were on the porch, stamping. I leaned toward her and asked quickly, "What did she die of?"

"Heart."

The men stepped inside the door. "Well, now, Mary, have you had enough, and we can let this family get back to its evening?"

I stood and drew back the curtain panel again, to let more light into the room. As my fingers tied the sash, I scrutinized Mary. Her palsied body was clumsily tied together, coupled with her wooden legs and feet. I was so caught up in reading her that I hadn't realized she was studying me.

"I had been wondering," she said, "but now I see. You're expecting."

Without moving, I felt the three adults' attention focus on me. Its unwanted weight burdened me.

"It's time, Mary." Bill cupped her elbow.

I followed them out. When she was settled in the truck, I leaned against its door and thanked her for the pie and the visit. She raised one quivering hand but it could get no further than a few inches off her lap. She did not realize what she had said, and that, more than her head tic and worn body, caused me to wonder if she was dying.

Bill nodded to me and turned the key. I stepped back, and they drove away.

## CHAPTER 31

WHEN THE TRUCK turned the bend in the driveway, Hal ordered, "Go in the house, child."

Tansy looked to me.

"I said, go in the goddamn house right now!"

She ran up the porch and into the house.

He shoved my smock up and yanked my shorts down to my knees. My belly jutted out before me, a life of its own. His hard-worn hand spread over the round of my body as if deciding whether to wring that small life out of me. His face pressed closer to me than he had ever been, so near his breath poured into my nose and mouth: an enormous presence he was, mightier than a thunderstorm. He smelled of rot. My breath held still, my eyes frozen open. He hissed, "You fucking cunt. I can't believe you."

I didn't see his hand move, the other hand. His bone and nail clenched the lips between my legs. A cry smothered in my throat. I feared he would rip me into pieces.

He stepped back and stared at me, my half-nakedness. "It's his, isn't it?"

I nodded, once.

He twisted my left breast, my swollen tender flesh, as hard as he could, his teeth set together. "I ought to fucking kill you." Tears poured down my face. "I ought to beat it right out of you. I could fix it right now." He did it again, that awful thing between my legs.

I whispered, "Please. No!"

"When did you do it? When he came back this last time it must have been. You goddamn fool." He laughed. "This joke's on you, not me, girl. He's not coming back. He got his money. That's all he cared about. That and poking his pecker around."

His bloodied hand jabbed my taut belly. "That thing is mine, you hear me? No one but you would know any different, and you don't any longer. That child is mine."

With his hair and beard shorn so close, he seemed not flesh but wood, stone, a bludgeon.

"Answer me, now!"

I nodded.

"What did I say? Whose child is that?"

Quietly, my face turned down, I said, "Yours."

"Right. Mine." He grabbed two fistfuls of my belly flesh and squeezed. "You fucking cunt." He turned and strode down the mud-rutted drive.

I fumbled my clothes together and caressed what I could of that tiny being. Nausea twisted in me, and I stamped it down, willed myself steady.

## CHAPTER 32

I WAS RAVENOUS, snatching at scraps of bread while I cooked, filling myself with ripe tomatoes and beans and cucumbers in the garden. I drank from jars of maple syrup, swallowed leftovers on Tansy's plate, crunched cold pork chops as I hung out the laundry. My belly swelled rapidly, lumpy and hard as a giant's fist. I was spared early sickness, but the size of my body wore into me. By summer's end, I had a boulder of a belly that I bent over awkwardly in the garden. Weeds crowded in. I failed to pick the last of the beans. I longed to lie down in the dusty path and sleep.

Hal began making any deliveries we had. I didn't care that those few stolen dollars eluded me now; with this child, I knew my years at Hidden View had been inexorably extended.

By the end of October, Tansy and I had managed to put away everything we could from the garden. The very last bit, planting garlic, I could not bear to skip. All that long winter I might envision those gems of garlic, sleeping in the earth. In the spring, those green shoots would be the first to burrow up, tangy and succulent. I assured myself I would have a whole new life then.

On my hands and knees, I planted those cloves, my belly swaying and tearing at my back. The baby lay low in my sack of skin, dragging toward the earth. Finished, I hobbled to the house, my belly spread before me, sank down in the wingchair, and picked up my knitting.

# Part Four

## CHAPTER 33

WASHING DISHES I stood back from the sink and leaned over my belly. Tansy huddled in her bed, feverish for the third day. I had not turned on the electric lights against the dim morning. Steam from the dishpan masked the cold windows. Although I had stuffed cracks in the old wood windows with twisted bits of insulation, rogue drafts wandered chillily through the house. The tea kettle blew, and I whirled, pushing my hair from my forehead with the side of one wrist. Who was in the kitchen door? Lucien. I lifted the kettle from the flame and its whistle cut off.

"Oh," he said, "Fern."

"That's me," I said, and poured steaming water into the teapot for Tansy. My wide stomach swayed.

Upstairs, she bleated, "Mama, mama, when you coming up?"

"Where is he?" Lucien hadn't come any further into the kitchen.

"Why are you always asking where he is? I don't know." I flapped one hand at the wall. "Out there, out there. Not here." I banged the teapot on a wooden tray, two cups, a pitcher of milk and a jar of maple syrup. A spoon whose handle spread into an ear of ripening corn.

He stepped in and took the tray by its handles. "I'll take that up."

"She's fevery. She's been fevery for days. Don't see her if you're just going to leave tomorrow, or the next day. Or even next week. Better yet, get out."

The baby twisted in me. I spread one hand over my belly's jerking bulge.

"Mama, you said you'd come up!"

He raised the tray.

I grabbed one edge. "We hardly know you."

"Not true," he said. His chin jerked. "Go sit down. Find your knitting."

"Mama, you said!"

"Coming!" I shouted. But Lucien went.

I hobbled to the wingchair and eased down. I had long since given up on that pink smock and wore a gray-and-navy plaid shirt I had found in Lucien's room, buttoned over my great middle, jeans abandoned for long underwear safety-pinned down low. I sat in the poor end of November light without turning on any lamps, the baby kicking against my organs, restlessly squirming in that little cage. Exhaustion seeped through me. Tansy had been awake most of the night, and much of the two before. I was drifting toward sleep when Lucien appeared beside me, squatted down low to look at me. I struggled awake. "How's Tansy?"

"Feverish. I told her I was getting you tea." The back of his fingers stroked my cheek. "Fern, I didn't know. Didn't guess."

The baby rolled, flipping over. I pressed a hand to where little heels stretched my skin.

Tansy bleated for him.

He called up gently, "I'll be right along." The tea he brought me was milky, sweet with maple, and his lips grazed over my forehead, a warm brushstroke. Between my legs, a gush of warmth. Fool, I thought to myself. Fool.

The tea warmed some inner place in me the baby had not sought. I did not remember Tansy's pregnancy as such a vast ordeal. This baby had size and weight; I felt as though a planet swelled inside me, rotating on its own gravitational intention. My pelvis ached as though it would split apart, my digestive organs, clanging along, were smeared and twisted. I could no longer lie down to sleep or the child would clamber high and wrest my lungs empty. My heart, more than anything, plodded slowly, jerking along, stumbling to keep us alive.

Once I had lowered into the wingchair, that mound made it difficult to rise. Hunger clawed at me but not greatly enough for me to wrestle myself standing. Vaguely, I wondered where Hal might be. I recalled something mumbled about delivering hogs to Enosburg, in that pinched early morning, and wondered if he might be gone all day. Through the windows, I saw the morning fog thinning to patches of cloud shot through with crimson, the distant mountains rising from the scrim like immense, ancient blue stones.

I slept and woke ravenous to the scent of savory cooking. A dream lingered with me of an encompassing warmth, a fire with heat but lacking danger cosseting me. He had wrapped Mary Atkins' red quilt around me, tucked it over my belly and hands and sock feet. I lay in the daylight, rubbing my fingers over a quilt square of gilt curlicues embossed on maroon velvet. My bladder forced me up and when I returned to my nest, Lucien appeared from the kitchen.

He loaded the stove with wood and sat beside my feet, rubbing them through the quilt. "It's damn cold out," he said. "I don't think it'll get much above zero today, and it's only November."

In the daylight, I saw his hair had been trimmed recently but the shade of his beard had grown in over a week or more. His cheekbones, under his almond eyes, pressed wider than I remembered.

"What are you cooking?" I asked.

"Beef stew with potatoes."

"I'm famished."

"What happened to the right burners on the stove? I cleaned the jets, but I still can't get them to light."

"I don't know. Is Tansy sleeping?"

He nodded. His kneading hand moved from my feet up my legs, over my great mound. Both his hands caressed my belly, his eyes locked tightly on mine. I was too tired to move, to even lift a finger in acknowledgment, to offer an extra blink.

"Fern?" he asked, his hands at the quilt's hem.

"What?"

"May I . . . ?"

I sighed. "Oh, for goodness sake. Go ahead then."

"Fern." Hesitatingly, with no quickness, he tucked the quilt down and then his hands unbuttoned his own navy-and-plaid shirt over the great bulge of my middle. The shirt had gone through so much living and so many washings that the buttonholes themselves were frayed, spitting bits of white thread that might have rubbed apart between his fingers. He spread apart the sides of the shirt, and then gently pushed up the undershirt that came from his old bureau as well. The white cotton had long since lost its brilliance to a toneless gray. The white skin of my distended belly rose up in the daylight, streaked all over with a wild spatter of grooved scarlet and plum-hued stretch marks. I had not done that; I had not bared this pregnancy to the world's eye. With his long hands, he explored every bit of me, where the baby lay, and how the baby moved, fluidly rolling under his cautious touch. My milk-wide breasts with their dark aureole spilled over that belly and down my sides, under my arms. In both hands, he held them gently, one at a time. I closed my eyes and tried to keep my heart beating, my lungs opening and closing.

A few minutes in the spring evening, listening to the peepers and inhaling the thawing earth, had led to this profound weight in my middle, this deep exhaustion, the ebbing away of my own life.

He whispered, "God, you're lovely, Fern."

"Don't be ridiculous. I've gained about fifty pounds and my belly's just about hanging down to my knees."

He kissed the plug of my turned-out navel. Through his lips I felt no sucking need on his part, no draining of my scant vitality. I was vaguely aware of the foulness beneath my armpits, the days-old accrual of my unwashedness. Gently, he tucked the undershirt back over me, buttoned up that well-used shirt, and folded the quilt around me to stave off the cold.

In a yellow pottery bowl, not our everyday use, Lucien

brought me a bowl of stew, savory with root vegetables, beef, and thyme, buttery in my mouth.

Limping, he paced the room, looking into the kitchen, out the front and back windows. "Where is he? Where has he gone?"

"He's delivering hogs. Maybe." I set the bowl on the floor. "I need to sleep while Tansy is."

"It's horribly cold out." He tightened the quilt around me. "This house is a sieve of draft."

Sleep dragged me down. In that other world, I dreamed a circle of small children, with red faces and pointed heads, surrounded me like a palisade. Their little hands chucked stones at me, pegging my face and chest, the swollen target of my middle. I tried to shift under the weight, but they pummeled me with rocks, then vanished into the forest, howling with laughter. I dreamed my mother sat in the kitchen, eating key lime pie. "She has a baby in her," my mother said. "How did that get there?" The baby tried to burrow an escape hole through that weak spot below my ribs. I woke gasping, a sharp pain just under my ribs. I rubbed that place, in vain trying to nudge the small being to move.

Lucien and Tansy were camped on the couch, she in her paisley pajamas and mismatched socks, Lucien brushing sweat-soaked tangles from her curls. When she saw me awake, she jumped off the couch and snuggled under the blankets against me. "There's a baby in Mama's belly. Did you know?"

Lucien nodded. "I see that."

"I can feel the baby move. Even the baby's bottom, sometimes." She giggled, one hand over her mouth. "I'm going to be a sister."

"I need to get up, Tansy." As I struggled up, Lucien rose as if to help me. I let the blankets fall to the floor and went in the bathroom. On the cold toilet seat, I wanted to lay my head to my knees and weep, but I couldn't bend over at all. My back and my ribs ached. My feet stung with the cold. As I tried to get comfortable in the chair again, they covered me and brought me buttered toast and hot tea. From the light, I thought it was yet morning, but I wasn't sure. Tansy's fever had burned out. Her hands nestled cool in my hot ones. She curled beside me and laid her head against that mound. "Our baby's in here, kicking my ear."

The baby had jammed under my ribs again, and I worked at that stitch.

Tansy whined for more toast.

"Sure," Lucien said.

I heaved myself up and walked around the room, my palm on my sore ribs, trying to coax the baby down. Lucien picked at a snarl in Tansy's hair while she munched a crust, his eyes following me, appraising. I was cold and hot all over, and irritated. I snapped at him, "Where were you this last time?"

"Out there."

"Out there, where?"

"There." Tansy's hair crackled with static as he brushed.

"Why did you come back?" When he didn't answer, I pressed. "You didn't know about this."

"Uncle, will you read me *The Three Billy Goats Gruff*? It's really good. There's three billy goats, little, medium, and big, and a bridge, and a troll who's as *mean* as he is *ugly*. Ow! That's a snarl."

"I mean, are you just passing through in the night? At least you came in the house this time."

"Fern."

"Uncle, you'd actually really love this book. And it ends, always, Snip, snap, snout, this tale's told out. Always. Mama says it's–" she took a breath "–predictable."

"That's a big word." Lucien laid the brush on the couch.

Tansy said, "I don't know at all what it means. I can just say it."

I said, "We need more firewood. That's predictable."

He said, "I'll get it after this book."

In the kitchen, I saw he had left the gas on under the pot. The stew was drying out at the edges, and burned a bit at the bottom. I snapped the gas off. Then I put on Hal's old coat and went out without a word.

## CHAPTER 34

THE NOVEMBER light was sparse but clear as water. As no snow had fallen, I walked down the stalk-stubbled cornfield, skirting wide of the barn. I walked far down to the pines at the southern side where Hal had never cut. There, I leaned back against a white pine, its immense trunk stretching straight and true, its distant crown concealed in the many layers of wide-spread branches, soughing a wordless song. Far above, on the hill, the house perched tiny, its windows glittering chips of mica. Under the great pine, my body did not appear so immense, so terribly cumbersome. A coat button had slipped undone and I tucked it closed again.

That fear reared before me, of the great travail I would suffer to end this pregnancy. I had been handholding that fear tighter and tighter as my belly stretched and the baby's coming neared, and I had kicked it vehemently away to the corners of my mind, refusing to acknowledge how that fear was swelling in me alongside the growing child. I folded my hands over the stained coat, over the shifting in the jut of my belly, my throbbing blood and hollow bones, the massive trunk behind me. I had not been without Tansy for months now, and the cold and my trembling whooshed through me. I remembered the ending of Tansy's birth as pure, inviolate darkness. With each contraction, I descended into a stone-lined well, upside down, my hands stretched over my head, and only the completion of the contraction reeled me back up. I knew quite clearly, in the way I knew the sun rose dependably every morning and set every night, that the well's bottom was my death, and my outstretched fingertips would greet my demise. I knew that to bring my second child into this world would demand a journey again to that place so separate from the things at hand: from the dailiness of my hands at work, from dressing and eating, from the simpleness of walking and speaking. From my own little daughter. I was afraid I could not endure it again: that I would not be able to return. Hard as this cold-bitten life at Hidden View might be, the ice in the hoarfrost beneath my boots gleamed like Orion presiding over the night's cosmos. Alone, I saw that fear before me, a shaggy beast. I tightened my mittened hands over my great middle. I had no choice. I had to go there and return. I leaned against the pine for as long as I could bear the cold chewing at me, listening to the wind's wordless murmuring. Then I began that long trudge back up the hill.

## CHAPTER 35

HAL'S TRUCK was parked beside the Toyota. I heard them arguing as I neared the house. "You need to go!" Hal shouted. "You need to get in that heap and fucking go! I'm not fooling around this time. Fucking go! We had a deal, brother." Through the kitchen window, I could see rage pulsing in the veins on his forehead and neck. His fist and pointed finger jabbed through the air.

I opened the door and stepped in. I suffered an impulse to conceal my belly.

"This is my house, too." Lucien stood in the room's middle, Tansy on his hip, her legs curled around him, her face pressed against his shoulder.

"The fuck it is. If you don't leave, I'm going to kill you." Hal's fist waved before Lucien's face. "No one will give a shit. No one will ever know, and the world will be better off. That's fair warning, brother. I am going to fucking destroy you. Don't doubt me on this."

Without removing my outdoor clothes, I took Tansy from Lucien. She kept her face down, hidden. I carried her upstairs and sat on her bed. I closed her door to lessen their shouting. "He's going to leave," she sobbed, tears streaming down her reddened cheeks, into the snot streams beneath her nose. "I know he's going to leave. And he just got here!"

In my arms and narrowed lap, I rocked her.

Hal shouted crazily, "You're not staying here! You are nothing but a burden on this farm. You get that? A burden. You're just a broken down, no good fuck up. What'd you screw up now that you had to come back with your tail between your legs? Huh? Take your fucked up self somewhere else. I had straightened you out. You weren't coming back." His voice dampened off as he went into the pantry.

I struggled out of the heavy coat and made a clumsy nest around us, my little child sobbing into the crook of my elbow, the blankets half over our heads. Weak from her illness, she cried herself into sleep, her breath gradually shuddering, her face messy with tears and mucus. I slipped my arm from beneath her head and lay beside her, my hips and stomach muscles and back sore to the point of misery. Downstairs, the brothers' voices beat against each other. I willed myself not to think of Lucien, not to remember that spring evening teasing at the edges of my mind, not to hunger for the weight of his hands on my aching body. I willed myself not to think of Hal, either, that furious black wind. Intent to keep Tansy asleep, I lay as motionless as I could, dredging back through my memory to my own childhood for some bright spot. What surfaced was a memory of myself at Tansy's age, standing behind my mother's opened bedroom door, staring down at my toes lifting and curling in a shaft of dusty sunlight. I must have been wearing shorts or a skirt because the sunlight truncated my bare knees. From somewhere in the house I heard my mother calling Fern! Fern! and yet I didn't jostle the door, didn't reveal my hiding place, didn't step out of my own secret little spot, the sun caressingly warm on my feet.

Downstairs, Hal's voice banged, and something slammed against a wall, shaking the farmhouse, and then again, and again. The kitchen door slammed. I crept out from under the covers and stood at the window, looking down at the silvery roof of Lucien's car, pocked with a splatter of rust. I eased the bedroom door open and stood on the cramped landing, listening. I didn't hear the brothers' voices.

"Mama! Mama!" I hurried back into her room. Awkwardly, I lifted her to my hip and carried my child downstairs.

Cold swarmed through the living room like needy cats. The brothers had let the stove go out. Not just down, not just embers, but out. On my knees, I stirred the poker through the powdery ashes, finding but few sparks.

"It's coldy, mama, coldy."

"I know, I know. Crawl under those blankets."

I stepped out on the porch, looking for kindling. A sharp wind blew up and raked across my cheeks, through my thin shirt. I ripped birchbark from a log and piled the smallest pieces of wood I could find on the shelf of my belly. The afternoon was passing rapidly, evening gray creeping night in. I slammed the door and knelt before the stove.

"Coldy, coldy."

I could not get the fire alive. Once I lit the stove in September, I didn't allow the fire to die. I had no kindling nearby, and did not know where the hatchet was. I leaned my face into the smoky newspaper and blew. My eyes streamed sooty water.

"Mama, I'm so hungry. I'm so big hungry. And coldy."

The cold drove into my hands and feet and face. That stitch in my side was not a stitch but a knot under my ribs, a giant fist bruising me. On my knees, my legs and back throbbed with the strain of contortion and cumbersome weight. I could not get that fire to spark. I pressed the heels of my hands to my eyes.

"So big coldy. So big hungry."

I lumbered up and into my boots. I had left Hal's old coat upstairs and so I went out in my shirtsleeves and pinned up long underwear, found the hatchet in the woodshed, and split a pile of kindling. Bending over my huge stomach, shirttails flapping, I choked down tears. With my final *thwack*, right as I dropped the hatchet, a pain ricocheted through my lower abdomen, as if my muscles had split apart. I stood spread-legged, gasping, then crookedly bent over and gathered the splintery wood. I was shivering when I came back into the house. I was so large I could not bend over to take off the snowy boots and relied on my toes and heels to claw them off.

On my knees, I built the fire again, struck a match, and lit the paper. Fire whooshed up the chimney.

"Some little cheese sammies, mama? Please? I'm so hungry."

I added sticks the width of my wrist.

"Little cheese sammies?"

"I can't right now. I need to get the fire going." I

blew on the little flames, catching some warmth on my face. When I turned around, Tansy was gone. Perhaps she was in the kitchen, pleading her sad case, coldy and hungry, to the scrabbling mice. I hunched over the stove, my forearms stippled with goosebumps. The fire drew lustily. Outside, Hal's truck cranked over, and he rattled down the driveway. No one had turned on any lights, and the room was darkening. I added larger logs, one, two, three, four. The stove metal creaked as it heated.

Behind me, I heard the door open and Lucien's voice, his step and subsequent limp. Tansy was yet murmuring about those little cheese sammies. In the kitchen, I heard a match strike for the gas stove. "The cheese all the way to the edges, that's the way Mama makes them, and don't burn them."

"Tansy, have I ever burned you a sammy?"

"No. But don't. And never any cooked mushy horrible, *horrible* carrots."

Glancing at me, he settled Tansy on the couch under the quilt, her favorite forget-me-not flowered plate filled with triangles of bread and melted cheese.

"Fern?"

I shuffled to the wingchair, gasping, pains scurrying over the curve of my pregnancy.

He stood before the stove, warming his hands over its top.

I accused, "You let the fire go out."

"I shouldn't have."

"More cheesy sammies?" Tansy lifted her plate to Lucien. They disappeared in the kitchen.

The heating stove warmed me, bit by bit. My stomach clamored for food, but I was too tired to bother rising.

Hal would come back seething liquor and hatred. The mere thought of more drama, more screaming and arguing, exhausted me. I could not see the way to the end of this night and into tomorrow.

Lucien fed the stove and warmed his hands there. "What do you want, Fern?"

"What kind of question is that? What do I want? Do you mean, I want to go to sleep? I'd rather he didn't come back? I want this pregnancy to end? I don't understand you."

"Uncle. Please read to me. Please, uncle, please read, please read. My nice, nice uncle."

"You know what I'm asking. You asked me before to leave. Now I'm saying yes. Yes. We can do that."

"You're ridiculous."

"The three billy goats gruff book. You really like this book, Uncle. Remember the troll? And the bridge? And the clever billy goats? And always daisies at the end. Snip snap snout?"

She stood beside us, her arms pressing *The Three Billy Goats Gruff* to her chest. Her eyes flitted over us. I could see she was afraid of my weakness, of the tears I might gush, of her beloved uncle heading for the door.

"Go ahead," I told him. Was it merely the different planes of pain in my body? The room and the three of us appeared to be fragmenting, Tansy and her worried face in one triangle, myself and the cavern of pregnancy, and Lucien in a third, his eyes knotted at their corners, standing with his weight on his one good leg? "Go read to her. Keep the fire going, will you. That's what I want."

So he read to her, stacking the finished books in

a pile beside them, and then he brushed her teeth, washed her, and had her kiss me good night. When they went upstairs, I shelved her books and tidied the room, awkward in my heavy body. While sweeping, a contraction gripped my lower abdomen, harder than steel, and I gasped at the sudden force of it, toppling to my knees and hands. When it passed, I stayed in that animal position, my breath heaving. I feared what that kindling chopping had brought on. I tried to shift back and forth, to ease my muscles, quell any further contractions, settle that baby into slumber. But my too-heavy belly dragged down, cracking my back, and I gradually pushed myself upright and stood with my feet apart, leaning back and my stomach pushed out, ridiculously still holding the broom.

When Lucien came down, he said, "Fern?"

"Stop staring at me. I feel rotten, and I'm not in a beauty contest."

He took the broom from my hand and led me to the wingchair and helped me lower down, then he lifted my feet on the ottoman and spread Mary's red quilt over me. Then he swept the floor, closed the curtains against the night, and turned off the lamps except for the small one over the far end of the couch.

Hal's truck roared up the driveway. From the wingchair, I saw the kitchen door open, and he came in and unlaced his boots, hung up his coat, and cleared fresh snow from his beard with a quick jerk, one two, with his hand. He strode into the living room and stood with his back to the woodstove. Lucien followed from the kitchen with the teapot wrapped in a blue towel, steam curling from its spout. He bent and set it on the table then stood up, folding the towel into thirds and holding it in both hands. I saw by the way he stood and the steady way he looked at Lucien that Hal was sober. I curled my hands into fists, hidden behind my back.

"How much do you want?" he asked Lucien. "Five? Ten? Twenty thousand? How much do you want to sign over your half of the farm and go away? And I mean, *go away*. This is over. This is done. You are finished here, forever."

"I want what's fair."

They stared at each other. I sat below them in that wingchair, under the quilt, not moving.

"I'll go see Jorgensen, first thing in the morning." He nodded once, curtly, at Lucien, and went upstairs.

Lucien poured a mug of tea and set it beside my chair. The steam drifted toward me, smelling of mint and the sharpness of dew-wet earth spaded open. He moved around the downstairs, washing dishes, sweeping the kitchen. I drank the tea and dozed in the warmth, woke when he fed the woodstove and screwed the dampers tight. In the meager red-hued light I saw how crumpled the corners of his eyes were, how pressed tight his mouth. I remembered he had arrived only that morning, and he must have driven from wherever he had been, all night perhaps, the night before. He stood looking out the glass door, his forehead to the cold pane. What he could see in that darkness I might only hazard. He didn't turn to me, and, worn as I was, I slept.

I woke in the darkness to someone feeding the woodstove. I lay without moving, listening, as the wood was laid in, piece upon piece, then the door shut. "Lucien?" I whispered.

"I didn't mean to wake you. It's very late. Or early, I guess." His voice ebbed through the darkness to me.

I blinked. A thin stream of white light from the kitchen sink light flowed across the floor. In the pale light, I saw him standing with his back to the stove, undressed now to his gray long underwear. I lumbered up to pee and then returned to the deep chair. From the mug he held, I could smell the sweetness of wild mint. I rubbed my hands over the crest of my belly. "What time is it?"

"Two or so, I think. Go back to sleep."

"This baby won't let me sleep for much at one time." I worked at that sore place.

"How soon is it?" he asked. "A few weeks?"

"That's what I figure, too. Good math." I closed my eyes, trying to gather what rest I could.

Lucien squatted beside me. The thin light from the kitchen caught wetness on his lips and eyes. "It's freezing in here, Fern. You have any idea how fucking cold this house is? I'm sure you don't."

The baby began to stir.

"You going to let your brother buy you off?"

"Ah, Fern."

"That's what it comes down to, doesn't it? He's going to force you one way or another."

He pulled away from me and walked around the room. Even in the dim light, I saw how badly he moved, how jagged his lameness.

He limped back through the dark room and stood beside me. I reached for him, pulling him toward me by the cuff of his sleeve. I was so glad to have his familiar body beside mine, the sticky scent of liniment trailing him, the scruff of his face prickly against my hands. "Ah,

Fern," he said. He sat beside me on the ottoman, his hand pushing hair from my forehead, my cheeks. "I haven't any right, I haven't any right at all, but is the baby ours?"

"Of course."

He held me, awkwardly, one arm around my shoulders, the other over my middle, murmuring, "Fern, Fern," rubbing that soreness under my ribs. The baby moved in a way that I breathed easier.

I murmured, "I'm never going to make it to the end."

"You're lovely, Fern."

"I'm as big as a house and, good lord, do I feel miserable."

"Fern, Fern." His hands on me were satisfying, like chunks of fresh bread are to hunger, easing me into sleep.

I must have been hungry, as I dreamed of bread dough rising, yeasty sweet, over the lip of an enormous bread pan. In my dream I turned round and around, gravity free, weightless, no longer tugged down to the earth. My belly became that bread dough, rising and swelling beyond any womanly pregnancy, and then I simply reached in and pulled out an infant, easy as slipping my fingers into glutinous dough.

I woke alone, the comfort of that dream wicking immediately away. Insistently, that baby pummeled my ribs, squeezed my bladder. The weight of my body pressed my spine. I had so far yet to go. The heavy door between the living room and kitchen closing woke me, the door we rarely shut. Over the years it had swollen beyond its jambs and so it shut imperfectly, leaving a crack of white light. Hal's voice seeped through the crack. Without rising, I listened hard, as the voice was unfamiliar at first, an easier tone than Hal had ever used with me.

"You want some toast at least?" Frying butter hissed, a fork scraped over the skillet: Hal scrambling eggs.

"No."

"Toast is good. The woman can bake bread."

"I know," Lucien said quietly, his words laying down.

"Look, buddy, she wouldn't have been right for you. The sympathy in her heart runs damn shallow, I'm telling you. She'd never coddle you and your weaknesses."

"I never asked her to." Lucien's voice was thinner in timbre than his brother's. "You don't want her. You don't, Hal."

"I want this farm to go on." The skillet clinked against a plate as he dished up eggs. The hot butter stirred an involuntary hunger deep in my belly. "You don't give a shit about this farm. Turned seventeen, skipped on out. Left me with that drunk bastard. There wouldn't even be a Hidden View if it wasn't for me, all these years I've been breaking my back. You sure you don't want some of these? Last chance."

Maybe Lucien shook his head. I didn't hear his answer as I shifted, aching, in that chair. I thought of a plate of scrambled yellow eggs and cheese, buttered toast, milky tea.

"You may think you're due some part of this farm, but it's mine. Mine. And Fern is mine, too. God knows, we're nowhere near the perfect couple. We had six good months or so. What more could I expect? But she's holding up her end. Even big as she is, she's holding her own."

"Is that all you want from Fern? That she hold up her end? You don't want a wife."

"Sorry here, but did you get some notion of a wife out of one of your storybooks? She won't fit into that, I can spare you the pain now. That'd be like getting a picture book vision of a farm. Cows, fields, barn, silo. Smiling farmer man."

"Hal–"

"Hidden View wasn't made by one person. You never got that, did you, you dumb fuck? Not one person made this farm, and I'll be goddamned if one person loses this farm, the old man or you, I don't give a shit. It's not going to happen. This isn't about you, or me, or Fern, or any baby. Which brings me to that."

I had to pee but I didn't rise.

Hal said, "She's carrying my child."

They were quiet in the kitchen. What were they doing, those brothers? Staring at each other over an egg and butter smeared plate? The baby's head pushed against my bladder.

Hal said, "She and I agreed." That quiet again, only the wind murmuring wild around the house. Then a chair shoved across the floor, and dishes clinked in the sink. "Let's not be stupid. Go back to Jorgensen's sister, what's her name. You liked it there. I'll settle up with you. Then you're going to sign that deed over to me, and we're done. That's the answer."

"Hal?"

"What now?"

"Don't go talk to him."

"I'm going this morning."

"Hal, don't. She doesn't want me back. I wasn't, I wasn't doing so great there." Lucien's voice wavered.

There was a long strand of silence. I shifted again. The lid clanged on the coffee pot. Hal asked, "What'd you do?"

"Nothing. Nothing. It wasn't anything I did."

"It was what you didn't, huh?"

"Hal . . ."

"I went to some effort there."

"I know, I know. I know you did."

"What happened?"

I listened: wind scritched the lilac branches against the window.

"Don't fucking shrug at me."

The wind scratched again. Hal's boots tramped, tramped, tramped over the kitchen floorboards. Then his voice came, low and steady, persistent as a tunneling rat. I strained my neck forward to hear. "You're a mess. I can see you're falling apart. You didn't sleep last night, did you? I'll do the chores and go talk to Jorgensen, see what he says. Then we'll talk later this morning, the two of us, and see what we can settle. I'm not the old man. You know that. We can squeeze something out of here for you. We'll settle this deed thing, once and for all."

"But Hal . . ."

"I'll work it out. You know I'm not him."

"I thought maybe I could stay here for a bit. Until I got back on my feet a little steadier."

"No."

"Hal, I don't have anywhere else to go."

"Don't pull that shit on me. I got you a job and a place to live, and you had to go fuck it up. No. I'm going to straighten this out today. You're going to sign that deed, get your money, and leave. You go upstairs and stay there. Keep out of Fern's way. She don't need you nosing around."

A contraction clamped me abruptly, bending me forward as I gasped through its duration, and then I laid my head back, hands cradling the orb of my belly as the baby flipped and swam.

Hal's boots tramped, tramped, over the creaking floorboards. His voice cracked angrily, frightening me. "What is it with you? You blame everything on the old man and your goddamn knee. Why are you still on the fucking payroll here? You're a grown man, Lucien Hartshorn. You're going to sign that deed over, and you're out of here. Gone. We have enough problems here without you. This isn't your marriage, brother. This isn't your life. Stop looking that way at me."

"I'm not. Hal . . ."

"Too bad you had to screw up down there. That was a good deal for you."

"Hal . . . Maybe don't go to him today. I don't know. In a day or two? I need a little time to think."

"No you don't."

"But Hal. I can't just leave here."

"Of course you can. You did it before. You can damn well do it again."

Lucien made a sound, a half-choke.

"That's not going to get us anywhere. You're not thinking straight, I'm telling you. You listen to me. You go upstairs and stay there. I'm taking care of this. Of you. Today. All right? *Today*. You listening to me?"

"Yes."

I kept my eyes closed, my breath sucking in and out. Hal strode through the room, jammed on his boots and coat. He opened the door and left.

I waited a few minutes and then got up to pee. I was so pregnant my belly lay on my cold thighs, and I had to wait while the pee emerged in bits and dribbles.

There was no sign of Lucien when I came out. Like a sparrow, a contraction fluttered across my belly, and I stood with my legs apart, my hand on the wall to brace myself as the sparrow metamorphosed into an alligator tearing at my muscles. When the beast had passed, I breathed again, once, twice. My shirt was clammy with rank sweat, and I made my awkward way upstairs to change. I dropped Lucien's plaid shirt on the bedroom floor and tugged over a pink t-shirt I had found in the free box. My stomach was so protuberant I had to wear whatever I could find. This shirt had *Rio! Happiness!* silkscreened over my breasts. Exhaustion tearing at me, I lumbered downstairs and stood leaning against the window, sipping tea. In the garden, mammoth sunflowers I had not cut hung with their heads facedown, a sprinkling of snow on their tufted crest. A chickadee darted among the flowers' thick stalks. Beyond the garden was that flat stretch of weedy earth where I had once wanted to plant twenty blueberry bushes. Ruefully, I studied that barren place. That was the rub about growing: planting was a hopeful act, the belief in a rich and abundant future. The sky teased a promise of snow. Snow might be a small gift, some consolation in this dreary day, a fresh brightness over the earth frozen so hard and lifeless a mattock would merely chip at the frost-jagged ground.

Light ebbed into the kitchen, beginning over the sink and counter and spilling to the floor. I braided my hair, then mixed and kneaded bread dough, wrapping the bowl in a towel and placing it on a chair beside the woodstove. I was emptying a dustpan of ashes swept from beneath the woodstove into the compost pail when Lucien fumbled with the doorknob and came in, his cheeks and lips red raw with cold. He glanced at me and then away.

I listened for Tansy, hoping the child had woken at the sound of the door and would appear between the two of us. My eyes flitted toward the window and its square of pale blue sky. Myself, I felt sullied, dirtied irreparably down to the marrow of my bones.

Lucien brushed snow from his jeans and straightened up. "I split some kindling and filled your porch box, if you need it. But you shouldn't. I'll keep that stove going fine."

As I turned to go back into the living room, to burrow in the chair, my hand, clumsy with my size, knocked the ladder back chair. To steady myself, my fists clenched over its points. I stared at Lucien's socks, black, with fraying holes over his protruding big toenails. His feet shuffled near the door, as if waiting for an invite in.

Lucien cleared his throat, once, twice, raspy in the quiet house. "That's a good hot fire, Fern. It's cold out there, I'm telling you."

"You never told me this: where did you go when you left here the first time? When you were eighteen."

"Seventeen. I was seventeen."

"Where did you go?"

"I told you the truth, Fern. I did."

"What was that again? That truth again?"

He leaned back against the door, arms crossed tight over his chest, clumps of snow on the cold floor around his sock feet. "I had an old truck I'd bought, and one day I got in it and drove west. I just kept driving and driving. I'd saved up money from odd jobs I'd done, and I didn't think I needed much. I'd had an argument with my brother, about something dumb, I can't even remember what it was. I was cooking dinner for them. That was my chore, and it came to me that I could just leave. Fern?"

I didn't answer.

"I stuffed some clothes, a couple of books, in my backpack, took that jam jar of cash, and I got in the truck and left. I laughed out loud as I drove down Still Hill, thinking they'd have to cook their own stupid supper."

I raised my eyes to him. He watched me intently.

"I just kept driving and driving, I'd sleep in the truck a little, and then get up and drive more. I bought a map along the way, and then eventually I made it to the ocean."

I clenched the chair's wood. "What happened?"

"Happened? Heck, I don't know. I got a job, then another one when that one didn't work out. I went south when it got cold."

"You've been doing that, all these years?" I studied him, his eyes unfathomably dark like Tansy's, his hair a scrawl around his head. He was at once so familiar to me, as if I had known him forever, and also as strange to me as if he had just walked in the door.

"More or less."

"More or less?"

He shrugged, halfway, wincing, as if he met some pain. "More or less."

"What's more or less mean?"

"Well, there's a little more."

"What is that little more?"

He pressed a hand to his navel, then thrust his hands through the back of his belt. "Well, a few years into that, I got in a jam. I was running across a street in the rain. It was just the stupidest thing, Fern. I had a library book under my shirt and it was pouring rain, and I didn't want the book to get wet. I slipped on the pavement and screwed up my knee some more. It was such a stupid thing. And all I could think of when they hauled me off was that damn library book I'd dropped in a puddle."

The baby stirred up against my ribs.

"So, well, what little money I had was gone soon, and I was laid up. I called Bill Atkins, and he had to get my brother involved. So Hal sent me some money then."

"Where were you?"

"Bellingham. Winter. Do you really want to hear all this? It rained all the time there. How could a place be green and dark all at the same time?"

I scraped the chair back and sat down and tugged my shirt as far over my belly as I could. A false pink like bubblegum, the shirt was too tight and a great swath of my bare middle hung over my stretched-out, safety-pinned, long underwear bottoms, my skin mottled gray and goose-bumped with cold, hacked at with stretch marks. Ugly as dead plucked fowl. "Go on."

"Well, then, I just, I don't know. I had trouble pulling it together."

"It?"

"All right, my life I guess. My knee was still messed up, and I had trouble getting another job. So he sent me some more money. Then my dad died, and I came back here." He pushed aside the curtain and looked out the window. "He's going to be up soon. He won't want to see us talking like this."

"So Hal was taking care of you?"

"I thought maybe I could get enough cash not to feel so ragged all the time. Like maybe I could buy something real cheap somewhere. It seemed to me that if he had Hidden View, then I should be able to have a place, a shack or something. I mean, I guess I was thinking that." He looked at me as if I might have a better answer. I stared evenly back at him. He lifted the curtain again and looked out.

I said, "You're not being clear with me. Hal was taking care of you?"

"He gave me money I guess, yeah. Then I was going to stay here, after my dad died, and work on the farm. It was the old man I hated, I just *hated* him, and when I came back, it seemed like maybe I could work here for a while. The farm was falling apart."

"You had really thought of staying here?"

"At one time, yeah. I didn't, at first. I just wanted some money from the farm, and then I was going to split. But I couldn't figure out how to get any money from this farm until it sold, and so I thought I'd stay here and work for a while. It seemed okay. I didn't have anywhere else screaming for me."

His eyes flickered over the band of my bare skin.

I tried unsuccessfully to tug down the shirt's hem. Beneath my hands, the skin was cold as dead things. "Stop staring. I'm about to have a baby. This is what women look like then."

"Fern, I'm not—you're lovely–"

"Stop, will you. Go on now. I want to know why you left."

He glanced out the window, then back at me. "All right, so I was here. And then Hal and I had that huge argument. I didn't know what to do. As soon as you left that morning, he came and found me. He'd figured it out with Jorgensen. He said I wasn't able enough to work on the farm and he'd found a place I could stay."

"He told you to leave, and you left?"

"That money I left for you, Fern—you must have found it—he gave it to me. I figured it was yours, rightly."

The baby squirmed, kicking against the confines of my body. I pushed at that stitch under my ribs.

"Fern?"

"I don't get it. Your brother told you to leave, and so you did?"

"Fern, I didn't know what else to do. My knee was all messed up, and I went to lie down while you and Tansy were gone. He came into my room, right after you left, and he told me I was going to go live with Jorgensen's sister. She was a widow, and she had an inn in Maryland and needed someone for maintenance and crap. He packed up my things, and he made me get dressed. He said it would be warmer there, and I would get better. Don't keep shaking your head at me. He took me outside. He told me to get on the interstate and keep driving."

"And that's what you did?"

"He said it was the best thing."

"Hal, we're talking about?"

"Yeah."

I looked at him. "Hal Hartshorn? Your brother said it was the best thing?"

He nodded. He crossed his arms, tight, over his chest.

"So," I said. A twitching shiver jerked through me. "You liked it there?"

"Enough." He turned and searched out the window for his brother.

"Why did you come back then?"

He looked at me, his hand still holding the curtain from the glass. "Fern."

"Why?"

"Fern." He shrugged. "It wasn't money. I still have that money from the sale of those twenty acres. That's something, Fern."

"That's not an answer."

"He's coming up. I see him."

I asked deliberately, as if I had all the time in the world. "Why did you come back? If it wasn't the best thing and all?"

"I missed Tansy?"

"Are you asking *me*?"

He wrapped the curtain around his fist. "I had to come back, Fern. I had to." He let the curtain fall.

I struggled up. I was no longer so nimble. I stepped into the freezing pantry, leaving the door open a crack.

Hal came in. I heard him at the closet, unzipping his barn coat and switching it for the one he wore to town. "I told you to stay upstairs," he said.

I heard Lucien's voice, the words not clear.

"What the fuck is the matter with your head? When was the last time you ate? The last time you slept? You're falling apart, buddy. You're going around the bend. I'm leaving now." Hal slammed out of the house, got into the truck, and tore off.

I filled the kettle and set it to boil. Lucien stood at the door, watching the snow whirl behind Hal's departed truck.

"I put water on for tea. I thought we could both use some."

He reached for his coat. "I'm going to split wood." He went out.

The house clamored around me to be tidied, cleaned, scrubbed, but I was so far along in this hard pregnancy that I felt like a listing clipper ship in a novel, my hull taking on water, crazily trying to land on some unfamiliar shore. I sank into the wing chair, a scrap of woman beneath my weight.

Lucien returned with an armload of wood and fed the stove full. He stood near me, his hair disarrayed, his shirt untucked and crumpled, as if he had not changed his clothes in days. "Fern, I didn't explain myself right."

"What was the book?"

"What book?"

"The library book you dropped in the puddle."

"It was Tolstoy. Fern?"

"What?"

"I didn't lie to you."

"About what?"

"About where I'd been, where I was going. I just wasn't, wasn't, fully open."

"How much of a habit is that with you?"

"Fern, I can see the way you're looking at me."

A vehicle pulled up the driveway.

Under the weight, I could not lift easily and asked who it was.

"I don't know." His eyes flashed from the window to me. "You know what was in that book? That a man has a choice in this world: to either save his soul or destroy it. I know what my brother's doing. I see it. I know it. I'm trying to save mine, Fern. God knows, lame as I may be,

I'm trying. I don't know who that is in the drive. Fucking hell! What does he want?"

I forced myself standing with my arms. "Right there," I said, "we part company. I'm not a man. I can't walk out that door and leave." I gasped a little. "Even when this baby comes, you think I could do that? As if my soul were my own? As if I am just creating *myself* here?"

The stranger was on the porch, knocking at the door.

Lucien walked over to answer him. On the way, he said, "I didn't mean that at all."

The stranger wanted to buy pork and syrup. He stepped inside while Lucien dressed in his coat and hat and boots. "It'll be good to have it in the freezer this winter. My wife, she's been buying your pork at Green Bowl Market and suggested I just come up here myself, see if I could get a good lot. Maybe a better price? I've got cash."

Lucien said, "Cash works for me. Let's go see what he's got stashed down there, in the freezers." He searched through the basket for gloves.

"You folks have got one mighty fine view up here. Hidden View, huh? Keeping it all to yourselves."

"We didn't intend that," I said.

The stranger pondered me. I turned aside, busying myself with folding the quilt. "You're Fern Matthews," he said. "James Matthews' girl, aren't you?"

Lucien's hand paused halfway up on his zipper.

"I thought you looked familiar. I'm Doug MacAlary. I used to work with your dad, before I retired a few years back. I was sorry to hear of his passing."

"Aren't we all headed that way?"

The stranger squinted at me.

"Fern," Lucien said.

"The freezer in the old milk room," I told him. "That's the one Hal is selling from."

"When's the baby coming?"

"Few weeks, I think."

"Well, now, you fine folks. Congratulations. You're into the hardest stretch now, aren't you?"

I was still nodding when they walked out in the gathering storm.

## CHAPTER 36

TANSY DRESSED herself in jeans and her winter coat and soldiered by herself down the snowy drive, looking for Lucien. I straightened her bed and then watched her from my bedroom windows. In her red snowsuit with the pointed hood she flittered like a cardinal, flying across the glittery snow. She returned between the two men, her little face turned up to Lucien, one mittened hand touching his hip. The stranger laughed, his mouth a wide open cavern. He and Lucien shook hands and then he drove his truck away, and Lucien and Tansy loaded their arms with wood and came in.

He cooked her a bowl of oatmeal and cream and syrup.

"Ribbon, she's a nice rabbit but she's awfully naughty. She undid the shoelaces on the old woman who lived in a shoe and let out all her children. They ran away in the woods. Naked!" she giggled.

I unpacked the box of Tansy's old cloth diapers, then dressed in my coat I couldn't stretch to button and hung the diapers on the line to bleach out in the blowing snow.

Tansy came running, her hood tied in a tight bow under her chin.

"I'm going to make snow angels!"

Heavy as a rock, I dragged myself back inside, the swirling snow lightly filling my plodding steps. I unwound my scarf and draped my coat on the rack near the stove. As the coat didn't button, my clothes were soaked with snow. I dragged upstairs to change.

"Fern?" he asked from his room.

"Who else." I struggled into the only other clothes that fit, a thin old housedress I despised. The huge thing had arrived in a box from my mother's Water & Light companions when I was pregnant with Tansy. Smaller in that pregnancy, I had never worn it, but with my long underwear wet, there was nothing else in the house to cover my legs. I particularly abhorred the print of the dress, black and orange and dark violet, in a chaotic mosh of squares, circles, and triangles. Snapping it from hem to neck, I stood at the window, watching Tansy run in eager circles, her face up and tongue out, catching snowflakes. The mountains and fields were masked by snow. Even the barn was dimmed by the steadiness of falling snow. Wearied, I sank on the foot of the bed, watching up through the windows where snow tumbled out of the sky.

Lucien came in and sat beside me. "It's coming down steady. Tansy's all right out there?"

So near to him in the daylight, with my enormous printed belly obliterating my body, I noticed how pared down to the bone his own had become, wrists, thighs, waist, chest.

"Why wouldn't she be fine?"

"Fern, I didn't know. I didn't know about . . . How could I not have been thinking?"

I arched my sore back, shifting that baby, garnering what shallow breath I could. "To Tolstoy," I said. "Let me add this. Every act of creation is first an act of destruction."

His eyes narrowed intently. "Who's that from? Picasso?"

"Me." My hands arrowed at my breast. "Look at me. I've had to destroy myself, twice over now, to bear these two children. To have Tansy, the rest of my life was destroyed. Is there any bit of that left? Nothing. I am no longer a daughter, even." Exhaustion sifted through my body. I imagined the very marrow of my bones was dirt, plain old dirt, not the loamy soil of my garden, but the dirt of ashes and dead skin and refuse I swept from our floors and chucked in the ash heap.

"Jesus," he said. "Family."

The house creaked in the wind.

We sat without speaking for a bit, as if we had run out of things to say, or maybe I was merely too tired to follow any trails of thought. Lucien sighed, bowed forward, and rubbed his knee. "What a miracle it would be if the snow buried the road in and he never came back."

"You think snow could stop him?"

"He'll be here soon. He'll be looking for me."

I stood and opened the window, unlatched the storm and pushed it out. Cold rushed over my hands and face, and the scent of wet snow, of growing snowflakes and spiking ice, filled my lungs. I had forgotten winter's exquisitely alive beauty. Tansy rolled snowballs, arranging them in some oblique way.

"It's freezing," he said.

I stuck my hand in the snow piled on the sill.

"Fern, he's going to come at me again. Tell me what to do."

I turned around. "Tell you what to do?" A cold draft from the open window blew the dress against my thighs. "Are you crazy? I can't tell anyone what to do. I can tell Tansy to put on a hat, be polite, and set the table, but I can't really tell her what to do."

"Fern." On his feet, he leaned toward me. "What do you want?"

I slammed the window shut. "Why do you ask me that? What kind of question is that? Is it not clear I've shot my quota of want for this life? Is it not clear?" My fists knotted over my chest, rising jaggedly for the breath that baby was squeezing from my body. "Is it not *obvious* that no decision is in my hands now? I need to bring this child into the world, first, before anything. There's no choice for me here, Lucien," I wheezed. "Then I'll raise these two children." My voice wound down to a whisper. "God help me to do what I need to. God help me and my children." Like a rapidly approaching storm, I could sense how near I was to walking into that lonely place of labor, the strange shadows about me and great fires of unearthly folk flickering in the distance. My arms crossed an X over my heaving chest, my heart rattling wildly.

*There is only one heart in my body, have mercy on me. Have mercy on me.*

Cradling my hands in both of his, Lucien kissed the back of my palms, my chapped knuckles and burred fingers, all ten digits, his lips lingering at a bloodied cuticle.

Then, one by one, he pulled apart the faux pearl snaps, sharp clicking breaks, and pushed aside that gaudy dress. My belly and breasts poured white into the dim morning. "Oh, Fern." He held me by the hips in his wide hands. My belly glistened, round and white, celestial. "My lovely full Lady Moon." Bending, he put his ear to the crest of my belly's orb.

His breath blew warm on my skin. Naked, I was not cold at all. Nor was I afraid any longer. It was as though a door had opened and I stood on its threshold, the season of winter growling behind my back, before me the sunlit radiance of spring, the urgency of fresh life sprouting up, songbirds twittering in the trees as they fluttered about, mudding their nests.

Looking down at the untended whorls of Lucien's curls, those deep piles of tangled hair, I said, "I want you."

He straightened, my face turned up to him like a blossom to the sun, between us my abundant belly. For the first time, I didn't see my lumpy abdomen as an ugly necessity, as fat and flesh scarred and ruined, but miraculous as the quickening itself, a gift beyond any merit in ourselves. His hands caressed me, from where the baby kicked at my ribs, down and around to where I could no longer see, in that damp thatch between my legs. "Love," he whispered, "oh, my love. Oh, my lovely, lovely Fern. How much I want you."

His arms stretched around me, around all of me, folding me close to his bony body. We stood there for the longest time, arms around each other, holding tight in that small space of stillness.

## CHAPTER 37

TANSY SLAMMED the front door so hard the floor beneath us trembled. "Did you see my snow mamas?" she shouted. "I made babies and cakes and blackberry bushes."

I held Lucien's hand. As we went downstairs, he slipped free, saying, "Watch the stairs now. Hold the railing. The steps are narrower than you might think."

"Lucien? I've been walking up and down these stairs for how many years?"

He didn't answer.

My girth sailed like the moon, unbound from gravity, streaming light.

I emptied a basket of baby clothes to sort and fold on the couch. Tansy whined for a snack. Lucien toasted her little cheese sammies, and she sat beside me, licking her greasy fingers. "Snow White was under the lilacs. Did you know that? The bush closest to the house that always scratches at the window? The one with the creepy fingers that scares me? She's there but she's awake now, looking for the prince. Where the heck is he anyway? Isn't he supposed to come in on a white horse or something?"

I laughed. "I thought it was a mule." I looked to Lucien. He stood at the window, distracted. "Did you hear?"

"He's always the same prince," he said. "Same cardboard figure. Notice that? He's supposed to rescue the princess from her suffering and rags."

Tansy said, "My princesses rescue themselves. They always find their way out of dungeons and never get lost in the woods."

Lucien winced a little, at the center of his lips. "Those clever princesses."

My hands held a onesie. "Are you all right?"

"Oh sure."

Baby things spread over the couch, blankets and tiny shirts and a jumble of rag dolls. He stood beside me, looking down at these miniature clothes, patterned with chubby teddy bears, golden ducks, red stars.

Tansy zipped up her snowsuit. "I'm going to make a carriage for my snow lady!" The door banged behind her.

Mesmerized by the clothes, Lucien asked, "Was Tansy really that little?"

"This one might be bigger. If I'm any indication."

I piled the baby clothes in the basket, reached up for his hands, and tugged him down beside me. Sighing, Lucien leaned back into the couch. The house's cheerful chatter had absconded with Tansy. Except for our hands together on the couch cushion between us, the house exuded cold and damp.

"Fern, you want to know why I came back this time? It was entirely selfish. Jorgensen's sister was a nice enough old lady, in this fancy B&B with a flower garden all around. You would have liked that garden so much. Rows of peonies. She had me doing stuff here and there, painting and a little carpentry. It was fine, and then I started feeling low again. I got worn down, I guess. I wanted to come back here and see you and Tansy again. Then one night I was feeling so blue I got in the car and started driving. I thought I'd just stay a little, just visit a little with you and Tansy. And then I walked in and saw you. What a selfish jerk. Jesus."

We sat together, snow drifting down soundlessly outside. I leaned against him, breathing lemon and camphor, the muskiness of sweat and wood smoke. He spread an arm around my shoulders and held me tight. I was so tired and we were so still, the house so quiet, that I was drifting toward sleep when Lucien's stomach grumbled near my ear. "Hungry?" I murmured. "I don't know what there is. Oatmeal. Wouldn't a bowl of cherry tomatoes from the garden be nice now? Those little sungolds?"

"Is that my brother driving in?" He stiffened and jerked away.

"That's the town plow on the road. Lucien? What is it?"

Shrugging, he bent over his folded arms. "I don't know. My gut's not doing me any favors." He squeezed his eyes tight.

I pushed myself up. In the kitchen, I strained some tea I had brewed that morning into a pan to warm and, at the window, watched Tansy, crouched on her knees, busy with snow. I couldn't figure out what she was building, a house or a garden or menagerie. Through the small rooms, I heard Lucien sick, sick. When the tea steamed, I poured it into a cup and wrapped my hands around it.

Tansy scurried from one mound of her snow creations to another.

Lucien was draped over the wing chair, face drained pale.

"You'd be more comfortable lying down."

"I'm all right now. It's nothing, really."

I leaned over my huge middle and stroked his stubble-rough cheek, his skin cool beneath my fingers. "Lucien, I'm not your brother." My hand cupped the back of his neck, his knobby bones, the tenderness of body there.

A crooked arm hid his eyes. "I'm not asking for pity."

"It's not pity I'm offering."

"Is that my brother? I'll get up."

"Sh. It's not him." I smoothed my hand over his shoulder and stood up.

I cast around the room, at the tipping pile of baby clothes, Tansy's wet tights inside out on the couch, ashes spilled over the floor, Hal's emptied coffee cup upside down on a chair beside the door, Lucien's fists clenched over his troubled stomach. The chaos of the house this morning didn't drag at me. Like the moon, I had risen a little from these cloistered rooms, certain all would fall into place as it should. Inside me, the baby moved, nestling, readying to exchange its hidden world for ours. Lucien's eyes closed.

In the kitchen, I poured myself more tea and stood at the window, facing the garden. Tansy was still mightily working with her red mittened hands, sculpting forms of snow. Curls had wound free from her hat and swirled over her cheeks. In a flash I realized what she labored at: out of those frozen flakes she was crafting a shimmery world of what she loved, mamas and babies, blackberry bushes and nursery rhymes, omitting cooked mushy carrots, charred sammies, the inevitability of bedtime.

Through the doorway, I eyed what I could see of Lucien, his legs sprawled, and I knew he faced the front door. To one side was the window where Hal would suddenly appear, leaping from that pock-marked truck, hurrying with that grim-set jaw and narrowed eyes, determined to right us. Through the window on the door's other side diapers rose and flapped silently on the line, whitening up.

I was imbued with the same pure light, this new snow freshening the frozen earth, buoyant and joyous. Like the princess's frog, Lucien's kiss had shed my ash-stained exterior. My body was flooded with a brilliant light, suffusing me so greatly I imagined that ugly housedress transformed into an iridescent gown of silk. I shimmered in the perfect end of the fairy tale.

Lucien's legs shifted restlessly. I dragged the ottoman beside him and sat down.

His eyes, watery, near to tears, sought mine.

I freed a strand of curl caught in his eyelash. "You're skin and bone, Lucien, so thin. Couldn't you find any sustenance out there at all? You need some of my roundness."

He smiled wanly. "Oh, you're lovely, Lady Moon. Every bit of you." His fingers caressed the sleeve of my dress. Then his gaze swept across those two windows. Blinking the tears in his eyes, he passed a hand over his face and said, "He's going to come jabber at me. Any minute now."

His eyes, cracked through with red, lay on the door. He had come through that door just yesterday morning,

Lucien, who I had determined would never return. "We'll get all this figured out, Lucien, we'll put our heads to it, and I'll have you feeling so much better. Steady meals, none of this craziness of staying up all night. You've been on the move for too long. No wonder you're turned upside down."

He touched his fingers to his forehead, half-hiding his face.

I went on. "With the money you have from the twenty acres, that'll give us a start. We have that to begin with. We'll untangle all this. Maybe we'll find a warm, sunny kitchen. Wouldn't that be lovely? We could get Tansy a goldfish. She's been wanting a goldfish. She says she'd name the goldfish Miranda. Miranda! And then we'll have the baby coming." He closed his eyes, tears slipping from the edges. With my fingertips, I whisked the tears away, then patted his skin dry with my sleeve. "I'd love to lie down with you. All day. The whole long day. Wouldn't that be nice? Tansy would find us. She'd snuggle in with Margy Cream Cheese and all the rabbits."

I lightly laid my hand over his middle. Even through his shirt, I could feel his insides churning, wrestling. His hand spread over mine, holding me tight and warm. "Fern," he sighed. "Pitiful is what I am. Pitiful."

"You didn't sleep at all last night, did you? And the night before? No rest, and all this going on, no wonder your belly's soured. I'll give you some chamomile tea in a bit. The Peter Rabbit remedy."

He sighed again, from deep down in his chest, his torso shaking a bit all over. "I used to get stomachaches as a kid, even before the accident, and those two would tease me. Make fun of me. They were always coming at me, looking for weakness. You know what it was like, living with the two of them? My dad was such a falling down drunk. Hal's not much, compared to him. I've had a lot of time to think about them. About Hidden View." His fingers wound through mine. "When I came back from the hospital, Mary used to come, every day. I was on that couch, lying there, not sure I'd ever get up again. She'd bring me nice things, butterscotch pudding and stewed chicken, and clean up. She was so kind to me. But they hated her, Hal and my dad. I couldn't ever remember a woman in the house, and she drove them crazy. What time is it? The morning's getting along."

"I'm listening for him."

"It's hard to hear outside, with the snow." His eyes flickered across the two windows, one filled with those billowing white diapers, the other that blank rectangle of tree and driveway where Hal would shortly materialize, with his fury of determination to set us on his course.

"I know. I'll hear him." The baby knocked my ribs. "Oh," I said, stretching back, away from Lucien, to turn the baby. I pressed my hand on that stitch.

"Fern?" His hand reached for my knee, then slid off. "I should have told you about Hal and the money and Jorgensen's sister. I should have."

"Don't torment yourself."

"It's not all right."

"Lucien, the world is chock full of hidden things, right or not."

"The goddamn world," he muttered.

His eyes darted at the windows, then back to me. "Fern? Here's something else. I keep thinking about your sweater. That green one? When he made me leave that last time, I wanted to take it even though it wasn't mine to take." He blinked again, staving back tears. "You'd left it over a chair. Hal and I were arguing about something, and I put my hands on it. I couldn't take it with me when he was standing there, watching me."

"That sweater hasn't fit me in months. You know where I got the yarn? Sh, that's not him. Lie back. I'll tell you about it. I found this old sweater kicking around in the library's lost and found and washed it. Then I unraveled it, the whole thing. It was worn over the elbows, and I had to knot the yarn. The inside of that sweater is a mess of knots."

"How do you do things like that? How can you take something the rest of the world considers trash—trash—and make something so fine?"

"I wanted the sweater. I didn't have any other yarn."

"Fern, it's you that's so fine. This house, the garden, everything, is the complete opposite of when I was a kid. I didn't want to leave at all." His eyes darted across those two windows, back and forth, back and forth. "That's it. He'll be here any moment. I've got to pull myself together." He gripped the chair arms and forced himself upright, his jaw set.

"I'll heat that tea now, see if a little will comfort you any."

With his wrist, he wiped tears from the edge of one eye. "What does it matter? It's one thing or another with me. It will *always* be that way. Why would you ever think to trade him for me? For *me*? His strength for my weakness? You'd be crazy to."

I clasped his hands. "Lucien Hartshorn. Is that what you're thinking? Is that what's troubling you? That?"

His eyes bore on me. Limp his hands were, limp.

"Listen. Listen, when I came here, I was just a young girl, a silly thing who had never done anything—who had always been *done to*, including making that first baby. But then I was carrying that baby, and I was all alone here, and it was very clear to me I would have to carry my baby in so many ways." I wove my fingers through his. "Where's my strength? It's here, in my hands. That was all I could do, put my hands to the house and the garden and the child. Order is our salvation. To not give in to chaos. Don't look to him, Lucien. There's no need for that."

"Hal's my big brother. I've been afraid of him, always. He's coming back. I don't want him to see me down like this. Hal! He's always done whatever he wants."

"He's never going to get what he really wants."

"What do you think he wants, Fern? The farm, that's all. He has it. He'll never let it go."

"*Us*," I said. "He wants to be like us."

Tansy stomped in from the snow, her cheeks and eyes slick with snow joy. "What's wrong?" she asked, looking at the two of us.

Startled, Lucien yanked his hands from mine and straightened crookedly. "Nothing's wrong."

Tansy scampered over the chair's arm and sat beside him.

"Lucien's belly isn't feeling well, sweetie. Be gentle, now."

Tansy laid her cheek against his arm. "That's not nice for my nice uncle."

He let us cosset him, our little morsels of rubbing and kissing.

Tansy asked, "The billy goats gruff? We never figured this out. Do they escape the troll? Do they make it to the pasture? Do they ever reach the daisies? This is important."

A burnt log fell against the grate in the stove.

Quietly, Lucien said, "I don't know. I guess we're not quite there yet."

In a bit, he stood up and went for his coat and boots.

"Where are you going?"

He lifted his face, pale against the dark curls around his eyes. "I was going to look at that woodshed again, then the cows. Get some air."

Tansy sat beside me and stowed her hands under my thigh, her face turning from me to Lucien: a flickering goldfinch, wild and radiantly beautiful, flashing yellow and russet, poised between us.

His eyes steadied on us, then swept around the room. He went out.

## CHAPTER 38

IN SILENCE, I folded the pile of clothes.

Hal came back and stomped snow on the floor. "You're going to Chesterfield, girl."

I set the baby clothes neatly folded in the box.

"The Sundowner ordered pork. I put the cooler in the back of the truck. I don't care how far along you are. I can't do everything. Make sure you get a check."

"Tansy, go put on jeans over your tights. And extra socks. Go on now." I went upstairs and took off that dress. I folded it and set it in a drawer, then put on the safety-pinned long underwear and the damp shirt of Lucien's. Coming downstairs, I glimpsed Hal in the kitchen, an opened bottle on the table. I knelt before Tansy and tightened the buttons on her coat, wrapped a scarf over her hat and around her neck. "Go on out. I'll just get my things on. Don't get wet. We'll be in the truck for a bit." She shut the door behind her and walked away, disappearing at the turn in the porch, where the lilacs covered it at the south end.

He stood in the kitchen doorway, drinking and staring at me. "With the window behind you, you're big."

I struggled my arms into his old coat. My back to him, I spread our receipt book on the counter and wrote The Sundowner's invoice. He was behind me, the reek of bourbon wafting over my shoulder. His hands came around me and pulled that coat apart, then stepped back and studied me, smiling in a strange glinting way that alarmed me, rubbing his heavy hands together, fingers over palms, maybe merely because he was cold, or perhaps in glee. "You've packed on some lard with this one, girl. This is a boy, I'm betting. I'm in a betting mood today. You're looking good and fat, girl. Fat." His hands stretched toward me. "Fat and sassy."

Nausea wound up like a snake in my chest. "Don't, Hal."

Very slowly I stepped away from his moving hands. But he followed me, and as I stood at the door, clumsy with the knob, he pushed me back against the door so I couldn't open it. So awkward with my width, I was afraid of falling, and I simply stood there and waited. His hand pressed hard over me. "Just the way I want my farm to be. Fat and producing."

"Miserable."

He laughed and stepped away, toward his glass. "Where is he, that brother of mine?"

"Around, somewhere." I pulled on my hat, my eyes at the window, looking for Tansy. "Cooler in the back of the truck. The Sundowner."

"That's right, girl." His hand came at me once more, grabbing my shirt where the coat didn't meet. Then his palm slapped me, a jolly tap, that sent my flesh rippling.

"You got a hell of a belly on you now. You're almost there. Bet this one's a boy."

I opened the door and went out into the blowing snow.

Tansy and I didn't see Lucien. I buckled us in and drove off, snow coming at the windshield in great clouds. At the bottom of the road, before I turned out onto the snow-splattered highway, I stopped the truck and held my hands to my heaving middle.

"Mama, mama, you okay?"

"Yes," I said. "Yes." I waited there until I had stilled myself, calmed that fluttering child and my knocking heart with my hands, and then I drove on.

## CHAPTER 39

WE DIDN'T return until nightfall. The snow had diminished, the sky cleared off, and a steely cold settled in. On the way back from Chesterfield, Tansy fell asleep in the carseat, her head lolled back, little hands open on her lap. At a gas station, I bought two Milky Way bars and unwrapped them as I drove, determinedly eating. I thought of my mother and her grief over that gnawed leather purse. As I neared the time of my second labor, I wanted her in a way that was keen and powerful, as raw and biting as late autumn rain. Yet—*yet*—I didn't alter my course and seek her. Driving, I pressed a hand over my sternum, the tips of my fingers sweetly scented with chocolate. Deep in my chest, in some odd mixture of flesh and spirit, I ached for her and that box of my childhood to fortress around me. Yet I did not turn. Perhaps it was nothing more than shame over the tatters of my grownup life, or the faith I could mend those tatters. Make my life, and my children's lives, whole.

Outside town, I followed the highway north, deserted under the moonless sky, the river flowing stealthily, not yet frozen, dark mountains rising steeply on both sides of the road. My hands held the large steering wheel at its top, and as we left the few lights of Graniteville behind and headed into that stretch of empty darkness, I imagined my hands possessed a brass goblet borrowed from Tansy's fairy tales, filigreed but darkly tarnished with use, held vigilantly upright. My unborn baby was quiet, sleeping, readying its little self for the nearing journey. Tansy muttered, one hand stirring in her lap. That goblet's elixir I pictured as wine-dark, neither saccharine nor bitter, but earthy, brewed by humming bees, seasoned with myriad sparkles from butterfly wings, fermented from a plethora of wild berries and roots. I held onto that image as I drove, perhaps to stave off exhaustion or maybe to still the trembling that had begun, somewhere deep within me.

The night was so dark the few lit windows I passed shone as portals in the night, evenly arranged, lacking even the outline of their houses. What was it I wanted? To have the door to my own house open wide, streaming light and warmth into this thick night, a savory dinner bubbling on the stove, arms reaching happily for my little one and me. Or then, I might be satisfied with far less, with the fire burned down to ash-covered coals and Lucien sleeping easily. I would lift that warmed quilt and tuck my slumbering daughter against him. I turned off and over the river and went up, up, up Still Hill. The truck's heater was poor, and I lifted my hands to my mouth in turns, breathing to warm my cold bones, holding that chalice before me, hoping in the darkness whatever it held would not spill. I turned on VPR, and an incantatory music filled the cab, an archipelago singing, voices rising and coming together, falling apart, joining back. The words were in a language I did not recognize, and I kept thinking *Gaelic*, *Gaelic*, a beautiful word, although for all I knew they might have been the voices of woodland sprites, or maybe a buried cache of pebbles improbably enlivened in song. Against the freezing night, I held the memory of the warmth of his body against my hands, his lips to mine.

When I pulled into the driveway, the house was dark. I parked and left the truck running. One headlight was out, reflecting back to me in the vacant windows, a crazy one-eyed wink. Lucien was gone. Although I knew that, although I could see his car absent, although I could see the house untended and cold, the fire no doubt gone out, I didn't believe it.

"Mama," Tansy cried restlessly in her sleep. "Geese."

But the fowl I thought of wasn't a flock flapping and honking its clamorous clan way south, the gorgeous and awe-inspiring great Vs winging along their ancient pathways. In the moonless night, lit only by that broken half of a headlight pair, the blue heron on that rainy Common day appeared before me, slategray dull, standing in a muddy puddle of water, inscrutable, twistedly ugly, utterly graceful. Where was this winged creature's home and sustenance? How had it come to wait so patiently—and for what—*what*?—in the driving rain?

I turned off the truck and sat beside my sleeping daughter.

As the heat drained out, cold crept in through the metal cab. Hal opened the door, and night scraped my face. He set his work-gloved fist on the rise of my belly. The scent of manure and booze rushed at me. "I'll take the keys."

I pulled them from the ignition and handed them over. Hal pocketed the keys.

Something fell out of the truck with a clank. I looked down, expecting to see that goblet, upside down, but only a greasy vise-grip had clattered against the running board. Its screw had been broken and mended with a sheered off bolt.

"My brother," Hal said, "had to leave abruptly. You know how he is. He hasn't the guts for this farm." His hand spread over my jerking belly. "Or the will."

# Part Five

## CHAPTER 40

I WAS NOT BRAVE in that labor. I made it through, the child arrived, I survived, but I was not brave. I cried piteously for my own mother, believing myself the youngest of children again, but three or four, scarcely Tansy's age, abandoned in a night wood. "Mommy, Mommy," I wept. The pains clawed at me with a primeval darkness, gnawing flesh and tendon and sinew from my bones.

I had gone nearly a month longer after Lucien left. Those northern days were short then, night closing in tightly by the afternoon's end, and the mornings slow to lighten up. By the end of my term, I struggled to walk under the weight, pausing twice on my journeys upstairs, sleeping in ragged bits on the wing chair, my swollen legs dead weight on the ottoman. The contractions that had intimated to me the pregnancy's culmination continued for that month, waking me from scant and fitful sleep or halting me as I crept along the driveway to the mailbox. I was so tired then that Hal's presence only ebbed into me: his feeding the stove, boiling oatmeal and noodles for Tansy. "Good lord, girl," he said, his hand exploring my lower belly where clothes no longer even haphazardly stretched. "What have you got in here? A calf?"

That baby worked steadily at what I imagined must be a suppurating wound under my ribs.

Somewhere along that exhausted haze, the back left burner of the range gave up its ghost, too, and my cooking was reduced to a single burner. By then, I was beyond caring. Stew or chops or fried eggs would suffice.

Consistent pains began in the night. I rose, went downstairs, and walked through them, welcoming their onset at first, joyful at the winking light in the distance, promising an end for this. By mid-morning, the pains were far greater, sharp metal bands screwing into my abdomen. I stood at the window, my hands on the frost-blind glass, willing myself not to panic. Even then, early in the labor, the pains were so keen I fought against weeping.

Hal appeared from the milking and sat in the kitchen, watching me pace and then pause, panting, holding the sides of my great belly. Dripping sweat, I yanked off my shirt and labored in my underwear, the contractions rippling across my belly. A wind appeared to be rising and tunneling sand into my ears. Through that dirt, I heard Hal laughing. "What have you got in that barrel of a belly, girl? An elephant?" In a gap between contractions, he laid his scratchy face against my navel.

"Jesus," I said, "get out of here!" I bent over into the contraction. Metal spikes drove into my back.

"Take it easy, chill out. These things don't happen in a moment."

When I emerged from the contraction, my husband and Tansy seemed to have disappeared. Again, the pains gripped me double, then released. Gripped, released. I paced through the living room, naked. Outside, snow began falling, thick loose flakes drifting down. When Hal and Tansy returned, I had traveled a far distance in a land wholly exotic to me. I had planted the kitchen stool as near to the woodstove as I could, and dragged a chair before me. When the pains tightened, I rose from the stool and leaned all my weight forward on that chair back. I had been riding a camel through a wide and empty desert, rising as its hump bore up through my spine, as its angry teeth turned and gnawed into my back. My eyes followed a meager swab of sunlight slowly trekking across the sand, or was it merely the floor, before me.

The light trailed from my landscape. We were in the truck then, in the cold and dark, and I could not stand in the stirrups of my camel's saddle. That hump smashed my bone and nerve. I rode into the hospital on my camel, who was drooling considerably down my legs. With the dark, the desert heat had fled, and I shivered against the scratchy hairs of the camel's coat. Somehow, I was no longer able to know if I wore clothes or not.

The nurses' words were lost in the blowing wind. I closed my eyes and held tightly to the bridle, urging my beast to ferry me through this wasteland of a desert. When I opened my eyes, I was surrounded by strangers. My eyes sought a window and, seeing it was black, wondered at how terribly lost I was in this godforsaken desert. I longed to lean forward on the beast's neck and sleep but the animal was jerking and thrashing, convulsing, its hoof snagged in a rocky enclave. I wanted out.

Somehow, the odd notion that my belly contained an elephant reared up in me, and I felt that elephant stampeding, desperate to get out, but stuck, trapped, confined in my thin flesh. I was thrown off that camel and the delicate bones in my back shattered on the rocky ground. Unknown hands were on my arms and between my legs, and someone urged me, "Come on, little mother, keep at it. Keep at it!"

At the end, the pains were unbearable and I gave in to them. Wild animals devoured me with their spiny teeth and nasty claws.

What remained of me lay unmoving, and then old Mary Atkins' voice came down to me, drifting like a maple seed pod on a warm breeze with the scent of spring and muddy life. "Fern, Fern." A comforting warmth covered my sore body, like goose down, and I closed my eyes to sleep. "Fern, Fern." The baby was laid beside my cheek, its skin fragrant as budding lilacs. So I had come through. The child's eyes were near to mine, slate blue, the oval shape of Tansy's. Alive.

I gradually became aware of a woman washing my legs, then covering me, turning on a small lamp in the corner of the room. I looked around for the window, and saw pink streaks across a black sky. I might have asked the time. Mary sat in a rocker beside me. "A little past four," she said. I was so confused I wasn't certain if that was morning or afternoon, and if the season was winter, or had summer with its early dawn turned round again. She told me it was afternoon, and the baby had come so suddenly they had difficulty helping me.

The other woman stood looking down at the baby and me. "This one just tore out of you. They don't usually come so quickly."

"Quickly? I had expected this baby weeks ago."

With a fingertip, Mary touched the baby's brow. "When she was ready to come, she didn't drag her little heels at all."

She.

## CHAPTER 41

Bill and Mary brought me and the baby back to Hidden View the next afternoon. With great glee, Tansy admired her tiny sister. For lunch, she told me, Bill had taken her to the diner and ordered French fries, crunchy chicken, and a chocolate milkshake. He did not come in the house, but took Tansy by the hand and walked down to the barn. I leaned against his pickup, watching them go. Tansy wore a dress she must have chosen herself, as I had put it in the top drawer of her high bureau, where I kept outgrown favorite clothes for the next child. Over jeans, the dress was more shirt than dress, so high on her thighs and tight around her waist. The skirt had three tiers of taffeta ruffles, the edges sparkling with a rainbow of sequins whose stitching was loosening so fallen sequins trailed her as random bits of glitter. Watching her walk down the snow-trampled path holding Bill's hand, I thought how like coltsfoot she was, vibrant gold pushing up through winter, improbably strong. A flower that wilted if picked.

I limped into the house. The old woman settled me on the couch with the baby and a pillow and the red quilt. I had torn terribly when the baby crowned, and I tried not to cry, sitting down. The baby gnawed on my nipples until they split and bled.

Mary wrung her hands in her lap. "I won't be able to help you, much. I'll send some meals with Bill."

She must have sent meals. I don't know what we ate in that time, any of us, except the baby, who nursed and nursed. Despite my size and the long pregnancy, the baby was small, at not six pounds, and she hungrily tried to make up for whatever she hadn't gotten.

That was a terrible time for me. I could not care for the baby and Tansy and the house. I could not do it, and there was no one to help me. I shriveled into myself, no longer wanting food, only sleep and quiet.

I remember Hal drinking in the kitchen one night, muttering to himself, Tansy curled against my legs under the quilt.

I remember giving Tansy a bowl of cold oatmeal because I was too tired to heat it, and she looked at me with reproach.

I remember the tangles in my hair were so thick I couldn't wield a brush through the mess, even if I had had the strength to do so.

Very slowly, impossibly slowly, I gathered strength again, a few handfuls at a time. The fat dwindled off my bones. I snipped the knots from my hair, set to work on Tansy's curls. The baby's belly and cheeks rounded with milk. She began to smile at us. The days lengthened. Hal set a quart jar of golden syrup on the table one morning. From the porch, I saw the sparking glow of the sugarhouse. I opened a kitchen window one afternoon and breathed the damp scent of thaw, the ineluctable promise of spring. I inhaled deeply, sucking the almost rotten scent into my lungs, desperate for that wild gush to sweep away the stale tatters that lingered of my withered, broken heart.

"Mama! Baby's awake! Baby's awake!"

"Coming, girls."

☾

That year was the lushest of sugaring seasons. Still marooned in the house, I paid little attention to what Hal said, until VPR carried news of a banner syrup season into the kitchen. By April, in the kitchen before boiling one afternoon, Hal figured this year's syrup would carry us further away from the bank. I stirred batter for cornbread with one hand, the baby nestled in my other arm. "Good," I said.

He didn't lift his eyes but kept on figuring.

When he left, I stood on the porch and watched him go. The snow was gone, opening the fields in great running streams of mud and runoff. Miniature suns of coltsfoot sprinkled the edges where the path was worn ragged. In his black mudboots and sweatshirt, Hal strode quickly down the path, already focused on the evening's work ahead. Without turning, he disappeared down the hill. I had not once that season walked down to the sugarhouse, and the distance now seemed unbreachable.

Tansy squatted at the edge of the porch, her chin in her hands. "Mama, when are those robins coming back?"

"Any day. I've been watching." The baby in my arms, I sat on the top step and leaned against the porch post.

In a few hours, more out of exhaustion than any sense of cleanliness, I had Tansy play in a sudsy tub while I cleaned the kitchen with my one hand, the baby sleeping over my shoulder, her breath coming in tiny sips. In the bathroom, Tansy sang in her pure little bird voice, "Winken, Blinken, and Nod one night sailed off in a wooden ship, sailed into a river of crystal light, into a sea of dew." Twilight gathered around the house. I thought of lying on the couch in its grayness, letting the dark pull around me like a downy nest. I had only the one light on over the kitchen sink, and I stepped through the house, picking up a sweater, wooden blocks, one stained sock.

A car pulled into the driveway with no headlights.

"Where are you going, and where have you been? the fisherman asked the three," her clear voice bubbled.

The baby on my shoulder, I stepped out on the porch. He stood on the top step. I shut the door behind me, firmly twisted the knob, and hissed between my teeth, "Get out."

"Fern." I couldn't see his face distinctly in the dusk.

"Get out. Get back in that car and get out."

"Fern."

"Get. Out. Now." Spitting between my teeth, I snaked my head forward, the baby's face hidden under my hand.

"Fern."

"I don't want any of your useless words. Turn around and get out of here."

He bent his face down and sunk his hands in his pockets. I glanced over my shoulder, desperate Tansy not see him. With the door closed, her little voice dampened.

How I longed to lean back against this old farmhouse and let her hard-used beauty and strength cradle me. Behind my waist, I placed my hand flat against the door, beneath the knob where the paint was worn away entirely, down to the exposed bone of weathered wood. The ball of my middle finger rubbed there.

"Fern," his words came at me. "Fern."

My fingers and thumb flexed and spread wide, as if in one hand I could cup this entire farmhouse, this decrepit beauty at once my captor and my haven. Behind me, the shabbiness of our lives lay in those close rooms: the peanut butter baited mouse traps, crumb-smeared picture books, Hal's whiskey bottle uncapped on the pantry counter beside bread dough rising yeastily and a wadded cloth diaper caked with baby spew. Last summer's fat garlic cloves, withering at their ends, lay on the kitchen table, beside sooty cinder bits fallen from candle wicks, a gleaming shard of quartz Tansy had plucked from the roadside, thumbnail-sized. That afternoon Tansy had performed a puppetshow with birchbark curls, narrating the three billy goats gruff, with bridge and troll. Laying her cheek on the table, she tenderly exhaled on the littlest billy goat, easing that scrappy curl of bark over the turquoise yarn snippet of river, toward imagined greener pastures. Remembering this now, I realized I had been distracted by chores, and, rushing, I hadn't bothered to watch her ending. Just how had she worked out this story?

I looked up into the twilight-lit sky, deepest blue before dark, Lady Moon so unfathomably far, lopsided, either waxing or waning; I was so jumbled I didn't know. The scent of camphor and lemons folded around me suddenly, as familiar as the dust-sprinkled scent of Tansy's hair in sunlight when I buried my nose in her scalp. The scent of Lucien. Far down the fields with their patches of snow, I heard the rumble of the sugarhouse generator, the keen grind of machinery cutting across the night fields.

"Fern, I found us a little house, with a patch for a garden. An apple tree for swings. A job with enough coming in to keep you and the children in milk and syrup. It's not much, but I thought we might try."

I shook my head, no, no, even as the camphor scent and Tansy hollering from inside, "Mama! Who is it? Mama?" set jangling in me a thin cord strung between the small washing girl, the nestling infant, myself, and Lucien in his lumpy coat with the torn hem: a slender cord of tiny twinkling lights between the four of us. As if we were a constellation.

"Fern?"

Hadn't I done that before? Hadn't I stepped into a life for a kiss and a promise, a mirage spun before me of a life that might become if I put hands and back to it? But now I was no light-footed girl myself; I had my own two girls with me. How could I exchange one kind of hardship for another? One I didn't know? My hand cupped over baby's warm downy head.

I pressed against the kitchen door, my head hitting glass. I knew I should turn away from Lucien's shadowy presence. I should go into the house and latch the door behind me, secure myself and my daughters in that farmhouse and farm life: this life and this marriage I had chosen, and not fling us into more tempestuous seas. Baby shifted under my hand, her tender bones and body. Glancing down, I saw my t-shirt crusted with dried bits of oatmeal where Tansy had wiped a messy hand that morning, my front wet and souring from leaking breast milk. Soiled vessel of a mother I was. Between us, in that open stretch of porch, Lucien's hand spread wide in that white light, palm and fingers pale as moonlight, lined and creased like a plowed field. I couldn't help myself: I bent toward his hand's camphory scent, the astringent medicinal warmth of it, laced with lemons that whispered to me of sunlight and a wild kind of joyous abandon, as far from this patch of bitten-up earth as I could imagine: a sour infused with iridescent golden beauty.

I cupped my restless baby's head and tiny shoulders.

He waited.

In the dimness, from the edge of my eye, I saw something I had completely forgotten. At the crest of Lucien's high forehead, a black curl circled, just the smallest bit of round that fit into the tip of my little finger. In our lovemaking, I had pressed my fingertip there with no remarking, no words, merely laid my hand there. Improbably, the name Hilda Mayberry sprang into my mind, Mary Atkins' long-silent companion with her black slate stone. In that moment, with my daughter murmuring her singsong, my littler daughter rooting on my shoulder bone for her milky nipple, Lucien's hand wide open and wanting me, and those sparks overhead from the sugarhouse firing across the sky, I saw my own inevitable death before me, the place where my soul would part from this mortal life and greet my maker, or not. How would I be mourned? Would any bereaving hand etch a clenched fist pointed heavenward? In a great howl of accusation? A screaming fury of rage? Or acknowledgment, that, yes, *this is*? In great sorrow borne of great love? How far would that tendril of hair carry me? Would it suffice as succor for myself, and my girls?

In that bit of distance between Lucien and me, close enough that I could reach out and clutch his shoulders, tendrils of his own cluttered living, camphor and coffee, wafted against my face. Around us, the night carried in cold, as the day's thaw began to freeze, skimming over puddles and crusting lumps of melting snow while night settled in.

Far down the steep field, sparks burst from the sugar-house stack, an unchecked tear of fire streaming through the night. The heavy arch door smashed shut, a rattle and clang, metal beating on metal I heard all the way up past the barn, over the fields with their snow patches: a clangor and pummeling of flesh and bone wielding brute strength to metal. I didn't need to see a single stroke of movement of what went on in those flimsy walls. I had been there, over and over. I had lived that poem in my heart: *repeating* and *repeating* and *repeating*. I had no need to be lifted above this farm, no need to witness again the broken circle of our paths, garden and barn and sugarhouse, the hub of strife this old farmhouse. I knew, in that ash and dust and steam-filled shack, with the fire roaring and machinery screaming and the chugging boil of sap, Hal would be standing beside the cherry-hot arch door slammed with a shovel, shoulders thrown back, shaking a shower of bark and cinder, eyes clouded by toil and anger and something else I had no name for. In his gloved fist, he would clench my abandoned garden shovel, handle jaggedly broken.

"Fern?"

I didn't need any name for what was going on down there.

I knew as I knew the unpainted wood beneath my hand, where the sweep of fingers had worn a groove through all these decades of opening the door, the lightest act repeated over and over.

Lucien tugged the zipper on his coat pocket, then stepped to one side, so the porch light shone on those stuck teeth. I was distracted for a moment, mesmerized as his slender fingers struggled with that broken metal. The cuticle on his middle finger was torn red, jagged and sore-looking. His stepping aside had widened my view of the sugarhouse. The one window glowed, and the stack emitted a frenzied jetstream of orange-red sparks. Uneasily, I sensed the door would fling wide, light would erupt, and Hal would appear, chest thrown out, arms spread-eagled over his head in the doorway, his fury cast at me like an immense fishhook hurled through the night, its grapple lodging in my breastbone, tethering me to this house, this land, to him.

But he did not appear—although my eyes searched, suspicious. The machinery clattered on, unceasing, reverberating in my chest, as though Hal and his machinery and his unyielding ambition inhabited even my throbbing breath and beating blood.

Then, down at a distant reach of the field, an animal shadow trekking out of the gloaming caught my eye as it hurried up the hill. I blinked, thinking the blur an illusion, but that dog-sized shadow proceeded persistently on a path of its own making, lesser dark out of deeper dark with some scrap of white. Instinctively, I knew it was not a roaming dog, although its four legs scissoring back and forth emerged from the night, and as it came steadily closer, strength undulating through its shoulders and chest, I saw it was a coyote with a rabbit hanging limply from its long muzzle. Without pause, the creature passed so near the house I saw its eyes flickering around, keenly watchful, its gaze passing over me appraisingly, without alarm or even apparent interest. The rabbit, in twisted death throes, hung jaggedly and limply upside down, its eyes rolled back into its skull, so near I saw the sapphire-tinged white of its eyeballs. Not hesitating a moment, or tripping a beat in its quickly moving legs, the coyote abruptly cut off the path and was swallowed up in nothingness. The night seamed over again, complete, whole, unbroken.

I glanced at Lucien, but he had not seen the coyote, his face turned down to his zipper. Predator and prey had moved through the night like a silent arrow, for just one moment our territories conjoined. Distantly overhead, the Milky Way sprawled in its infinite greatness, pure white, a bridge far above, a great spanning arch of light in the dark cosmos. So far down below in this night world, beneath the heavenly stars, my baby's lips dug at my shoulder, murmuring *raw-raw*, and again that skinny cord between the four of us—child and child and woman and man—tugged at me, unseen but pulsing with my hammering heart, through all of me.

With my fingers, I tore at one eye, digging it free of tears.

From his unzipped pocket, Lucien took a small apple and a pocket knife. He cut the apple in two and handed me half.

"An apple? All that? And you give me half an apple?"

He waited for me to take the fruit.

In the cool air, the baby stirred over my shoulder, mewling. In fury, I took the apple half and crunched it between my teeth, devouring the savory flesh, the cut of core, even the poison in its bitter seeds. I chewed it up and swallowed until nothing remained, not even the stem. "How could you?" I cried. "How could you, how could you, how could you?"

He stepped toward me, looking at the baby.

I pressed back against the house, shrank into the cold unyielding glass and wood, the baby beginning to cry in earnest against my shoulder. "I should hate you, I should hate you over and over and over, all of you. The whole damn world."

All the pieces of everything I loved, my little girl and my baby, Lady Moon and the stars, the multitudes of garden green, and all those bluets, everywhere around, everywhere, *everywhere*, had been trampled under our rude soles: all this, the whole world as I knew it, had fallen into gray and despairing chaos.

I was crying then, my sobs drowning the weaker ones of my daughter. My chest ached, and my sight was worthless, and my breasts stung with rising milk. His mouth was near to mine, carrying the scent of coffee and something unfamiliar, the world out there. "I'm sorry," he said. "I am so sorry, Fern."

I would not relinquish the baby to his outstretched hands. "How I wish I could hate you. Hate the world."

"Mama! Where are you? Who's here? Mama!"

"Get out. Get out, Lucien, get out."

To his outstretched hands, I raised one of my own to shove this man away, to quell his radiant dreams of love and lust, to thrust from me what I longed for so fiercely I was quaking on this shabby porch, a sodden motherless child abandoned in an autumn downpour. How I feared! My fear soared before me, swept up by the moon. Lovely Lady Moon, my faithful companion sailing through my years of nights. I had poured my misery and uncertainty into her streaming pearly presence, her shine ever ebbing and waxing, varying from a thin arctic trickle to a bounty of light vanquishing the rural dark. Her Ladyship's moonshine glowed as a force beyond wild, so iridescently luminous that in her presence the universe chorused an ethereal rainshower of light-gems, her unbounded and untamed light so cosmically alive the molecules of my coursing blood aligned toward her grace. From unmarked time, she had traversed her mysteriously silent journey across the sky, a heavenly globe of unfathomable beauty, and to her again, sweet Lady Moon, I revealed my abject fear and trembling, the ugliness of my muckled mouth and tear-runnelled face, my vision rapidly deteriorating into wavering smears of distortion. Through that mess of tears, beyond Lucien's flickering eyes, his breath's eager draw rasping between us, I saw a coarse rope swinging from the maple's lowest branch, fat knot at its end, a makeshift version of a child's swing I had cobbled one lonely afternoon, stirring now in some rogue breeze I could see but not feel on my wet face. What would happen to this place I loved? The garden I had salvaged from rampaging weeds? Tansy's cherished hideaway in the lilacs, where her round knees had unevenly dimpled the mud that very morning? These rooms where mice roamed and I had baked an endless litany of maple cakes? My weeping face turned up to Lady Moon—peerless nomad—and through those silvery moonbeams of ineffable radiance I witnessed my own intractable and mellifluous desire singing mightily for dear life, profound as spring, urgent and single-minded as flowers burgeoning in bloom.

"Come with," he said. "You come with."

☾

I was so young then, so ripely full of blood and milk and desire and work. I was so young I believed my heart might freeze and thaw and blossom. How little I knew that cycle would repeat over and over and over, that our life, while brief and mortal, is also long and tedious and bound to the constraints of our weak flesh.

As we left that evening, I searched through the bag on my lap, checking diapers, baby clothes, Tansy's doll Margy Cream Cheese, a ball of green yarn with my needles stuck through.

Tansy said, "I so *so* want a vanilla ice cream cone. With rainbow sprinkles on top."

Lucien was laughing, baby Juniper was cooing, and I jerked around suddenly. Hidden View was already gone, swallowed up in the night about us.

"Rainbow sprinkles all over. I've seen these, I know, they are really real, I'm not making this up at all. And the billy goats feast on daisies in the meadow and get faaaat and happy."

Snip snap snout, this tale's told out.

☾

I OWE IMMENSE THANKS to many people along this book's way, but particularly to the generous encouragement of David Budbill, who, with his poet's eye, insisted the novel retain its Vermont grit. Buried back in the past, I owe an upayable debt to the late Omar S. Castañeda; this novel can only be a meager acknowledgment. How I wish I could lay this book in your hands. Ernie Hebert's lunchtime lesson in rewriting gave me a rare epiphany. To Diane, my coffee colleague, I hope to savor many more years of books and laughter. Tanya Stanciu and Sheila Post gave abundantly of their time, keen reading skills, and bountiful cheer. Always, my first and dearest champions have been my parents and siblings. To my beloved daughters, with their steadfast grace and humor, my love and gratitude will forever be unmatched. You are the true lucky gems in my life. And then one cold January day, I opened my email in the co-op, and Dede Cummings said *yes*. For that one word—and much more—I can't thank you enough.

CPSIA information can be obtained at www.ICGtesting.com
Printed in the USA
LVOW08s2335191015

458962LV00002B/2/P

9 780996 135702